PRINCE OF MONKEYS

Prince of Monkeys

A Novel

Nnamdi Ehirim

Counterpoint
Berkeley, California

Library of Congress Cataloging-in-Publication Data
Names: Ehirim, Nnamdi, author.
Title: Prince of monkeys : a novel / Nnamdi Ehirim.
Description: Berkeley : Counterpoint, 2019.
Identifiers: LCCN 2018044345 | ISBN 9781640091672
Classification: LCC PR9387.9.E3222 P75 2019 | DDC 823.92—dc23
LC record available at https://lccn.loc.gov/2018044345

Jacket design by Linda Huang
Book design by Wah-Ming Chang

COUNTERPOINT
2560 Ninth Street, Suite 318
Berkeley, CA 94710
www.counterpointpress.com

Printed in the United States of America
Distributed by Publishers Group West

10 9 8 7 6 5 4 3 2 1

To the memory of Rachael Adepeju Adebayo,
an original member of my mailing list and
one of my very first readers

Our fathers, though once belittled, were placed with responsibility to serve with heart and might, to defend our freedom and to chart our route back to paradise.

Our fathers, though once noble, were corrupted by power. They took to power ad hoc, shed blood ad nauseam and plundered our coffers ad infinitum.

Our fathers, though once our hope became our fear. Fear, necessary to fuel their power over the zoo, once their jail, now their kingdom.

Our fathers, though once the jailed died as jailers. And we, once heirs of paradise, live as monkeys in a zoo.

The only difference between our kind and the kind on the other side of the fence is resolve. Resolve necessary for a few to find a route, which often trod will become a footpath for all, to paradise.

We, once victims of circumstance, should become protagonists of our own fate. So the labors of our heroes past shall not be in vain. And we, once princes of monkeys, shall die kings among men in paradise.

Prologue

1992

Nigeria, in its entirety, is a wonder of this world. Like all other wonders, it stands as a testament to the ambition of humanity: how one man can dare and indeed succeed at imposing a personal dream on an entire populace, leaving a polarized legacy of successes and failures for future generations to gawk at in awe. Everyone has seen or heard something about this wonder and so naturally assumes that in certain genres, or in general, they know about Nigeria. They seem to forget that wonders are so called because it is their nature to characteristically surpass anything our minds could previously imagine, regardless of whatever they might have seen or heard. But, excluding individuals with firsthand experience, most people have no clue or insight into the wonder of Nigeria, its beauty and grotesquery.

Of all the troubled misadventures of my Nigerian existence, the affair I reflect upon with most enthusiasm is my going to a prison cell. Not my first venture, which was at the age of eight, when I followed the prison-support team of my friend's church to evangelize to inmates back in 1983. That particular venture was quite uneventful. On the other hand, my second venture, about nine years later, was all sorts of incredible. I always find it difficult sharing the details because I believe the past, like stale water, should be left unstirred lest the petrifying odor of our mistakes rises to distort our perception of the present. Regardless, I will proceed, because I have an even greater conviction that the past, still and unmoving, reflects our selves in our clearest forms.

The night was young and promising, and my friends and I had escaped the supervision of our parents to witness the gospel of our youth preached live at the Afrika Shrine. The message was simple: Indulge in a vice today, but be guided by virtues every day. At least that was the message I had deduced from the statement. After all, the morality of any gospel, though founded on an unwavering statement, is subject to every person's own interpretation. This was the interpretation my friend Mendaus had passed on to me the very first day he brought me to the Shrine. The same very message I had confirmed to myself when I'd visited the Shrine time and time again to witness the King of Afrobeat, Oracle of the Shrine. And the same message we were trying to share with our friend, Pastor's son, who was still a nonbeliever.

As the four of us walked closer to the Shrine, I could hear the message blaring loudly over the fence of its premises, guiding me through the darkness into its gates. Then this young man, a total stranger, called out to us from his shame, which appeared to be arrant boldness under the cloak of the night, and asked if we had any spare change. He did not plead for mercy like the beggars at the bus station. He did not attempt to coerce us with God's infallible promises to reward cheerful givers. He asked for it with sheer audacity, almost as a scorned woman exchanges her dignity for reckless spite and then demands retribution from God. And I gave to him, not out of pity or any desire to reap divine dividends but out of understanding. An understanding of how much a man must have suffered, his natural pride withered away by the attrition of desperation, before he is able to approach another of his kind and demand to be fed.

I saw more men and women like this as I drew nearer to the Shrine. They seemed able to exist only in the darkness, like bats and cockroaches, filth in the eyes of the world, and I would be a liar to claim it was easy to see them differently. Closer to the Shrine, their population, though not necessarily diminished, was diluted by a crowd of brighter spirits. It was just about eight o'clock, but a multitude was already gathering on the street in front of the Shrine: beautiful women, some in turtlenecks and street-sweeping bubbas, while others were in almost nothing at all; competent men, some connoisseurs of accomplished trades, while others were diligent slaves of ambition behind the curtains of society's approval; all, united by a common gospel.

We struggled through the crowd, eventually fitting our way through the narrow gates of the Shrine under the probing eyes of the plainclothed security men. Despite the multitudes outside the gate, there was not as much activity inside. We got a table by the wall, not too far from the entrance, where we could observe—the continents of the world shaped in colorful murals on the wall, the portraits of civil rights activists, Rastafarian icons and negritude priests, all rebels of their time, none accepted by their popular society. At this point, it was not so difficult to see why all believers of the message were deemed misguided.

My ears adjusted to the music blaring from the speakers as my gaze hovered around. By the pool table, a group of three laughed over cigarettes and maybe something else; they didn't seem too focused on their game. A white man moved in the open, afflicted by a severe gyration as his fists pumped in the air and his legs wiggled like noodles being spun around a fork. I assumed he was dancing to the music. Then the little boy I had almost missed, without any legs, on a skateboard paddling himself to and fro with his thick arms. Occasionally, he would stop and spin in circles to the music. They all appeared like they had no cares, lost to the fantasies of their own worlds, however crude, however refined.

"The naked women or the music," Pastor's son asked, "which one of the two keeps you guys coming back?"

"The naked women and the music are part of the same package, along with the drinks," I replied. "You have to take everything together to enjoy it."

"Exactly!" It was evident from Mendaus's tone that he was already in high spirits. "Like bread, butter, and tea. Or garri, milk, and sugar. One alone is trash. Two together is the bare minimum. But if you combine all three, you know you're working miracles."

"You mean magic. Magic, not miracles," Pastor's son added.

"What's the difference?" Zeenat asked rather indifferently.

"Miracles are divine, ordained by God," he explained. "And magic—"

"Magic is of the devil?" I interjected.

"Well, if that's your theory, then this is indeed the heart of darkness," Mendaus said.

"To hell with you," I thought I heard. I sat up and adjusted my glasses as if that had anything to do with my hearing. Everyone at the table appeared quite taken aback as well. "I said to hell with you," I heard more definitively, "and to hell with Joseph Conrad."

I turned toward this voice and saw a figure leaning by the wall in the darkness of the corner not too far from me. The figure was making an effort to stay concealed in the corner, and with good reason, as he looked reminiscent of some sort of highlife band leader. He stood bare-chested with his tight trousers hanging at the lower parts of his waist, which might have distracted a less critical eye from his rather short stature, and he had an obnoxiously large wooden pendant on his necklace. The stranger folded his arms across his chest, showing off what seemed like a trace of nicely fitted muscles gone terribly malnourished, as if replying to my quizzical look with a dare to say something out of hand.

I wasn't the kind to respond to physical challenges. "Excuse me, did you say something?" I replied instead.

"I should be asking your friend," he said. "He was borrowing ideas from Joseph Conrad." I could not remember Mendaus saying that loudly enough for him to hear from where he stood.

"Well, curse Joseph Conrad. He wasted his talent on a book of lies," the stranger continued, paying particular attention to Mendaus, "portraying the black man as a wild beast waiting for the white man's captivity, as if it were means to redemption from his very own savagery. Now you're here, my brother, looking down on these people because you're in a fancy shirt and expensive spectacles, just like Conrad."

He paused for a bit, as if expecting us to say something, but continued when our blank stares seemed like they would never end. "You know even though our brothers are suffering right at our feet, if we don't bring down our legs from the footstool and pay attention to what's going on around us, we can never really be aware of what they suffer. You know a wise man once said that we have to place ourselves in our brother's situation and become in some measure the same person with him, and then form some idea of his sensations, and even feel something which, though weaker in degree, is not altogether unlike what he feels. I hope that's not too many big words." The stranger gave a coy smile.

"It's not," Zeenat replied, still indifferent. "But it's also beside the point."

"Adam . . . Smith?" Mendaus asked in awe. Then he moved closer to me and whispered into my ear, "This bloody riffraff just quoted a piece from the theory of moral sentiment." I nodded like I had a clue what was being discussed.

"Standing ovation!" acclaimed the stranger as he clapped his hands and made a mock bow. "I should have guessed from your fancy shirt, you're the fuck-fruit of a capitalist somebody. Well, then, with all due respect, to hell with capitalism and to hell with Adam Smith. That line was probably the only intelligent thing the man ever said."

At this point Zeenat was beginning to get visibly upset by the man's brazen rudeness and was about to get up to change her seat when he offered to pour out palm wine for all of us from a bottle that I had not realized he was holding. Then he paused and put the bottle down on a nearby table and picked up a bottle of whiskey, poured it into a clean glass, and handed it to me. He did the same for all of us.

"You're a smart young fellow," the stranger said, facing Mendaus. "Let's see if you recognize these words—'Africans had never aspired to wealth and status just for the sake of dominating his brothers. He had never had laborers to do his work for him till the foreign capitalists rowed up to the shore in their fancy boats. They were wealthy. They were powerful. And the

African naturally started wanting to be wealthy too, which led to exploitation. There is now a need for Africans to re-educate themselves and regain their former sense of community. And so in rejecting the capitalist attitude of mind which colonialism brought into Africa, we must reject also the capitalist methods which go with it.'"

Mendaus brooded over the words for a while. Pastor's son remained unvoiced in all of this—I did not know whether it was out of ignorance or disinterest—but I figured I should keep my lack of knowledge hidden beneath the cloak of silence.

"If I could recognize those words, *abi*?" Zeenat asked, twirling her fingers in the air. "Frantz Fanon? Marcus Garvey?" She was making lucky guesses.

"Never in my life!" exclaimed Mendaus all of a sudden. "Never in my life have I come across those words."

"Julius Nyerere, father of Tanzania," said the stranger, finally relieving us of our ignorance. "You see! Even Africans can be intelligent."

I pulled out a pack of cigarettes from my trouser pockets and offered him one, but he declined my offer, which was weird because he had a lighter in his hand. I shrugged it off and asked him for a light. He handed it to me and told me to keep it.

"I hate lighting other people's cigarettes," he said bluntly. "I mean, if you're the one who wants to smoke, then light it yourself, my brother. Don't bother me. You know, I'm a straightforward guy, even though most people assume I'm some type of bloody riffraff."

He paused, and suddenly the air got colder, or maybe it was just my mind. Then he continued as I bent to sip out of my glass of whiskey: "I'm not like those bureaucratic lunatics, like those bastards from up there in the government house, who travel on a few diplomatic assignments and come back trying to copy the whites, showing off that they've been abroad, offering each other lights. But when they see an ordinary man on the road, they'll just throw matchsticks at him." He sounded a bit angry, but when I looked up I saw him speaking with an unconcerned smile. "But enough of all this. Let us enjoy the underground spiritual game that is Afrobeat music, okay?"

As he spoke, a troupe of tall, slim women ran up the stage on their toes, while a few of them diverted into different cagelike contraptions at various ends of the hall. They all had a noisy collection of wrist and ankle bracelets and would have been naked save for the light clothing and beaded mesh wrapped around their waists and bosoms. Then the musicians took the stage one by one, and eventually the music began, drawing in person after person from the multitude outside. The saxophones at each end of the stage blared passionately at the command of their masters. Two men positioned around the middle of the stage caressed bass guitars. The lone drummer and keyboardist were almost hidden away behind the talking drummers and backup singers who crowded the back of the stage. After instrumental jams and solos, a hoarse voice of pidgin incantations personified in a tall, strong man clad in a tie-dyed bubba took to the center of the stage. He was probably an opening performer, whetting us before the King took the stage. But it was indeed Afrobeat, the religion of the Shrine, and his message was live in action.

"What do you do, my brother?" the stranger said, speaking in the direction of Pastor's son, as I filled up my glass with more whiskey.

"I'm a student. I just finished school at—"

"That's who you are, my brother, my question was what do you do?"

"Oh, okay, well," Pastor's son stammered for a bit, "it's very complicated, and there's really no way I can tell you what I do without saying what I am."

"No, my brother, I think that's bullshit. Let me help you out. I, for example, am a retired man. But a few years ago, I was a musician, public speaker, newspaper columnist, and general loudmouth, to be honest. And even though they all sound a bit far apart, they made up a core part of what I did. I try to liberate the black man from the oppression, and that's so difficult because most of them don't want to remove the veil of ignorance from their eyes and accept that they are being exploited. And all of what people say I am, the musician, writer, public speaker, and so on, is just a medium for me to do what I do. That's why it's easy for me to do one thing today and do another tomorrow with as much passion and happiness—because I'm doing what destiny called me to. You feel me, my brother?"

"Yeah, I guess," Pastor's son replied, slightly defeated.

"Nah, I don't think that life is for everyone," I said, "and truth be told, I've tried to get on that 'save the world' boat you're on, but all I'm good at is punching calculators and reading graphs. Not every shoulder was built to carry the weight of the world."

"Don't get it wrong, my brother," the stranger replied. "I'm not trying to judge you. In fact, I'm not one to judge. I've had over a hundred criminal charges in the last ten years, and I've had over twenty divorces. And none of my court charges were divorce cases, so I'm not exactly above mistakes. Let me try and make this a bit clearer for you. Tell me what you know about this Shrine?"

Mendaus took the baton. "I guess the same thing everybody knows about it—it's a nightclub, recording studio, concert venue, residence . . ."

"Yes, it's all of that, but do you know the history behind it? That it was an abode of those who resisted the oppressive military government and declared independence from it? That it was burned down and had its followers beaten to bloody pulp and thrown to their death from its windows? And despite all of that persecution, it was rebuilt at this new location with the same undaunted resistance to oppression of all forms. And I know it looks like a lot of the people who come here are bloody riffraff and write-offs."

By this time I was a bit distracted by one of the dancers on the stage, and he tapped me on the shoulder to regain my attention. "But they come here because they share in the solidarity of this movement that resists all forms of oppression in their lives. And when they toil for their freedom by day, and are put down and frustrated, they come by here at night to hear the message that would spur them on by sunrise and keep that fire alive. Now to come home to my point, my brother, I'm not expecting or suggesting that you should know all of who you are and what you do today. Most people die without ever answering those questions. All I'm saying is you should never give up trying to answer those questions, because by the blood of my mother, I swear that there is a superhero, as you call it, in each and every one of us."

"So now that you're retired from being a superhero," Mendaus said, laughing, "who are you?"

"I am Anikulapo—he who emanates greatness, carries death in his pocket, and cannot die," he said in a hoarse tone as he stepped out of the darkness. I laughed out loud, slightly embarrassed by my drunkenness but way more humored by his reply. I lost my balance and fell off the chair. When I regained myself and tried to sit up, I could see the flush on Mendaus's and Zeenat's faces.

"I knew this whiskey was much stronger than I was used to," said Mendaus, and he, Zeenat, and Pastor's son burst out laughing. The stranger, the king of Afrobeat, laughed as well. He then withdrew some folded-up naira notes from his tight pockets and threw them in the middle of our table.

"I guess I carry more than just death in my pocket," he said with a smile that exposed browning teeth. "Use that to have yourselves some fun tonight. Get another drink or something. As for me, I have a show to perform." Then he walked away, as slow as he was assured.

Mendaus obliged and called the waiter. I tried to pull myself together, to no avail, so I allowed myself to collapse slowly back to the ground and sit there till blackness covered my eyes.

I'm not sure what exactly I felt first, the bucket of water that was thrown at me or the migraine. My neck and back felt a bit sore, and it wasn't hard for me to realize why when I saw myself lying on the floor of a dark, musty room. Mendaus, Zeenat, and Pastor's son were standing beside me. A man in a police uniform, holding an empty bucket, was on the other side of the steel bars of a prison cell. I tried to recall the events of the night before and how I could have gotten there. "The inspector has resumed, oh," the policeman shouted at us, "very soon he will call you to his office and ask you to tell him your side of the story. Just make sure you tell him the truth in black and white."

Mendaus waited for the police officer to go away before

speaking—in a lighthearted tone, given the situation. "You know why you should never trust anyone who asks for a witness to tell a story in 'black and white' whenever he claims to want to hear nothing but the truth?" I paid predatory attention, like a seagull would attend to a trawler at the marina when expecting sardines to be thrown into the sea.

"It's because words, sounds, and actions are too loud to conceal the secret of this world, and so hush-toned messages are best conveyed in colors. A black-and-white picture of a sickly child with skinny limbs and a swollen belly, wrapped in nothing but a knitted scarf bearing a design of the rising sun, tells well-known facts of starvation in Africa. But a colored picture showing a sickly child embracing the red, black, and yellow of the Biafran flag, even at the point of starvation, tells the less-known secrets of the oppressed African child's resilience and defiant hope. Always pay attention to the secrets in colors that are too terrible to be mentioned out loud."

Part 1

1985

In Omole, where I grew up, the colors of childhood were white and blue. I never got out of bed until the white and blue shades of misty morning diluted and ultimately wiped the darkness from the sky. After I got out of bed and tasted the fresh morning in jaw-breaking yawns, my mother cleaned me up and dressed me in the white short-sleeve shirt and blue shorts of Oasis Primary School. Then with my schoolbag strapped across my chest, as if to anchor me to the earth and save me from the treacherous morning breeze, I would march the two lonesome streets to school, wary of strangers, each step knee-high, as instructed by my mother to keep my white socks and navy blue Cortinas unsullied.

In school I would smudge and stain the white spaces and blue lines of my notebooks with the incoherent pencil marks that my teacher demanded of me until she was pleased. During free periods, these white spaces and blue lines were torn out and reshaped into paper goalposts, and the button of someone's white shirt was donated as a ball, so my friends and I could play kanta-ball on our classroom tables. And after school, we returned home and had our lunches and all came out to partake of the elixir of life itself: the white and blue football.

As expected, he who was the best at football ruled the

world, so Boniface was king. And as king, he was called Maradona. After school, Maradona always wore an oversize purple hoodie with LOUGHBOROUGH UNIVERSITY across the chest. The hoodie had been given to him by his father, an alumnus of the British university, and for this and other reasons, Maradona always talked about his father, whom none of us had ever seen. One time when we had trouble with some older boys who tried to bully us out of playing football, he threatened to call his father, who was in the army and therefore stronger than all their civilian fathers. One of the older boys called Maradona's bluff and struck him across the cheek, leaving a whisker of blood. Maradona cried and ranted. His father never showed up, but at least we kept our ball. The whisker of blood on his cheek turned into a permanent scar to join the hundreds of dark bruises on his body. The first and last time he took off his purple hoodie when we played football, Pastor's son kept calling him a leopard till Maradona threatened to have his father arrest Pastor's son and their entire family just because. Pastor's son pissed on himself that day.

Pastor's son's actual name was Enoch. His father headed a rather new Pentecostal church in Omole, so all our parents called his father Pastor and him, Pastor's son. Pastor's son was a beautiful boy. He always wore the smile of a tickled baby and was blessed with neatly laid hair and brows. He would always try to sabotage all of this with ugly oversize shirts advertising his father's prayer crusades tucked into undersize trousers, but it always proved futile. Personally, I didn't know anyone who attended Pastor's church; the drinks mart in front of their house seemed to attract larger crowds. Another thing about Pastor's son was that he pissed on himself whenever he was scared; the day Maradona threatened to have him arrested was neither the first nor last time. He pissed on himself whenever he was among the homework defaulters in school and the teacher made to flog them with her cane. He even cried when we played too long, forgetting the progression of time, and his elder sister came around to announce that his father had arrived home from work and was asking about him. But Pastor's son was also really good at football, so nobody cared too much about these things.

In our little group, I was the only one whom everybody called by his actual name—Ihechiluru. Maybe except Mendaus. He was much smaller than the rest of us, and he didn't even play football. He walked with us to and from school, but no one knew his house because it was much farther down the street than the rest of ours. And when we came out to play in the afternoon, he came out with a book and would stick it to his thick glasses as if to get a focused perspective of the world; he raised his head only when an argument broke out.

Honestly, the only reason we allowed him to stay was that he cheered when we scored and laughed the hardest when Maradona dribbled with skills that had the boys sprawled like banana peels in his dusty wake, even though most times Mendaus never saw what actually happened because his face was buried in his book, and he reacted only after other boys had begun howling.

If Mendaus had no other lasting purpose, we could always depend on him for the occasional bright idea. One afternoon we all came out to play football after school to find a little fence being built around our field. We all stood firmly at the boring side of the fence, staring more out of a lack of understanding of what was going on than a show of resolve. Then a man in blue jeans,

T-shirt, and helmet walked over to us to tell us that we could no longer play football on our field; the landlord had decided to develop his property, and we would have new neighbors in about a year or so.

That was the way Omole was at the time, a land of potential. It was not a forest of tall concrete structures with a mass of beautiful Negro petals adorning the ground below, like the pictures on the Lagos postage stamps. From a story above the ground, the windowsill view had the lush green appeal of virgin land. It was still barren of the overcrowding and overhustling of the city center, and so pregnant with the possibility of a postcolonial utopia. It was a settlement of small intermittent houses along dust paths of imaginary road networks that spewed forth construction engineers and estate developers of all sorts each day. When all hope was being buried with the foundation blocks of the fence and we were retreating home, Mendaus came up with the idea of simply carrying the tires we used as goalposts, and the old kegs and other things people sat on while waiting their turn to play, to a new field.

This new field was a field out of our desire, not necessarily by its nature. Its grass was still strong and sharp, unlike that of our old field, which had turned barren under constant trudging, and it sloped awkwardly toward the road. We set up regardless and settled at our new field, and all was rosy till we discovered Professor Nebuchadnezzar, the university professor–cum–lunatic scoundrel who plagued this area of Omole. Nobody knew exactly how long he had been in the area, or who had christened him, not even the boys who lived nearby and joined us in football. But we were all cautious of the legend that described the short, frail figure with grayed Afro and beard who walked around in slow, calculated steps while rambling all dialects of gibberish. Some boys said that he carried a collection of pens and pencils and chased down the occasional stranger who came a bit too close, but we acted like we did not care as long as we had a field for football.

Eventually, what we feared the most did come upon us. On that day, the goalkeeper at one of the posts wandered away from his position. An opposing player had suddenly picked up possession of the ball and had tried to catch him off guard with an audacious lob from the other end of the field. He had been slightly too eager and overhit the football, sending it flying all the way across the field, over the goalpost, the bordering fence, and into the bush of the adjoining property. None of us assumed the extent of the danger at first, so we all jeered and laughed until we saw Professor round the corner of the fence at terrifying speed, arms akimbo, wielding an office pen in each hand.

Everybody scampered in a different direction. I could not attempt running in the direction of home simply because that was the direction the Professor had been headed, so I bounded up the dirt road with every morsel of strength I could muster till I heard my name called from behind me. I turned around without stopping and saw Mendaus trying to catch up with me. I slowed to a stop as he lumbered toward me in tiny, uncoordinated leaps. He collapsed to the ground, his body spread out, after he finally reached me. I stared at him for a while, then burst out laughing. He began laughing, too.

"Okay, get up, juh," I said after a while, stretching out my arm to help him up. "I don't even know where we are."

"Are you serious? My house is right there," he said, pointing forward and farther away from my house. He got up and started walking; I stood still, caught in both directions. "C'mon, Ihechi, you can't even be thinking of going back now. Professor would be running around there till evening." The thought of that shook me, but I contained my fear and followed him. We walked side by side in silence.

"Why don't you play football?" I asked.

"Because Marcus said so . . . Marcus Aurelius."

I scratched my head and nodded very slowly.

"He's my friend," Mendaus continued. "I want to be like him when I grow up."

I tried to figure if I knew any Marcus who went to our school or lived in Omole, to no avail. "What school does he go to?"

"He's not in school anymore," he replied with a giggle. "He was the emperor of Rome, that's somewhere far away, sha."

"What's an emperor?"

"Like a king. Their ruler."

"So you want to be a king?"

"No. Not really. But I want to know something about everything. Like Marcus."

I stared at Mendaus for a minute as we continued walking through the valley of thicket and bushes, too confused to even nod.

"What do you want to be?" he asked.

"A footballer," I said. I puffed my chest and raised my shoulders with pride. "I want to travel and play for Abroad or Argentina, like Maradona. I mean the real Maradona, not Boniface."

We got to a boulevard of taller houses, much bigger than the types around my house. I swirled to take in everything, and by the time I came to a stop, I saw Mendaus standing in the open gateway of the very first house. It was beautiful. You could see the verdant garden and tall white walls of the house through the circular patterns cut in the fence.

"C'mon, Ihechi," he said, waving me in, "are you waiting for Prof to get here?"

I walked toward him cautiously, half-expecting a security man afflicted with Professor Nebu's disease to rip open the gate at any moment and pursue us for trespassing unto sacred ground. Mendaus, with his tacky, uncombed hair and his thick glasses, did not look like he belonged to this kind of place. Neither did his ever dry skin, which was a pale shade of black, nor his scrawny arms and legs, which dangled from his undersize clothes. I would have been less surprised if he'd brought me to a collection of trees bound by a wire gauze fence that bore an indiscreet sign:

Welcome!
This is the home of the mysterious Mendaus.
Do not cross over!
Do not feed!

Eventually, I walked with him through the gateway. We were in the compound hardly a second when the huge door embedded in the tall white walls cracked open with an obnoxious creak that prepared me just in time for the girl, or woman, or female, who came running from them. I'm still not sure what Zeenat was on that first day I saw her. She definitely had the small frame of a girl, even though she was much taller than Mendaus and I. But she moved with more surety of step than any of the girls at my school, briefly swaying her hip to one side when she walked and flinging her arms in a way that allowed them to dangle from her elbows. Her skin was a darker black than Mendaus's when she stood beside him in the light, away from the leaning shadow of the house, with a glossy sheen like my mother's sculpted image of Ọṣun that lay among many others in her room.

"Lester! Lester!" she shouted, walking toward Mendaus in brisk but calculated steps, and for the first time I heard her feline voice.

"Urrgh, Zee, you've been watching Mami's videos again, *abi?*"

"Watching Mami's videos? I don't know what you're talking about," she replied, fiddling with her lips as she spoke. "And I'm Jackie now, so don't call me Zee anymore. I'm Jackie Shawn. And you'll be my boyfriend, Lester."

"You see! You have been watching Mami's videos. She's going to get you one day or I'll report you to her myself."

"What else should I do when all of you forget me in this stupid house every day?"

"Why don't you just watch the videos Mami bought for you, like that *Aristocats* one? I'm sure they kiss in those videos."

My mouth dropped. I had heard about *Aristocats*—my seat partner from school had told us about it after he had returned from his holiday in Abroad last year, and I had imagined the scenes he'd described for days and nights—but Mendaus had never mentioned that he had the video. He had never even mentioned that he had a video player at home.

"I've seen *Aristocats* too many times. It's boring. And is that why you're afraid of being my Lester?" she asked, placing her long arms around his neck and making a pout with her lips. "You're afraid of a little kissing, Lester?"

"No, urrgh, leave me alone, Zee." He pushed her away and walked toward the front door. I followed.

"Then your friend could be my Lester," she said as she caught up with us. I didn't turn to look at her but hoped she'd try to put her hands around my neck like she had with Mendaus. I wasn't afraid of kissing. I had imagined it plenty of nights before going to bed. "Have you seen the movie *Shampoo?*" she asked, placing a hand on my shoulder. That was good enough for me.

"No," I replied after a second's hesitation. My voice came out a bit soft, so I cleared my throat before I continued. "I haven't seen any movies."

We were inside the house now. We had taken our slippers off at the door; now the warmth of the colorful carpet that spread across every inch of floor ushered us in. The walls were hidden behind heavy wooden shelves with glass panes that reflected a skewed image, but when you peered through closely enough, you would see shiny white ceramic plates standing upright and side by side, like the proper officers of the air force on the posters in school. After we were past the officers, there was a gentleman in white laying dishes on the table.

"Good afternoon, Mr. Thomas," Mendaus and Zeenat said. He acknowledged them both with a smile and continued with his doings before I could say anything. They marched up the steps, and I followed until we got under a large arch that opened into a larger room. On the other side of the room, directly opposite where we stood, was a television, bigger than the one at my house, with a small box I assumed was a video player settled above it, and more shelves on either side. I attempted moving toward the shelves, but the floor between us was an uncoordinated soiree of books spread open and videos half-tucked into their flaps, with names and titles I could barely recognize or even pronounce.

"Now let's show you a video," Zeenat said quietly to no one in particular. "We could start with *Aristocats* before somebody reports us." She picked up a video from the floor without paying attention to the title, rubbed it on her shirt roughly, and then forced it into the video player. Mendaus had picked up a book and relaxed into the couch in a pose that backed the television; I sat on the same couch in the opposite direction, which faced the television. The book was small and red, and the cover read:

MEDITATIONS
BY MARCUS AURELIUS

"What's your real name, Lester?" Zeenat asked as lights flickered on the television.

"Ihechiluru. Or just Ihechi."

"Well, it's okay if you don't get the words at first. Just follow the pictures and it'll make sense. After a while you'll get used to everything, the way they sound and what they're saying."

We sat quietly, enjoying Marie, Berlioz, Toulouse, and of course Thomas O'Malley, the alley cat. With time, I learned this was how it was for them. Mendaus spent most of his time reading volume after volume of his father's books, very abstract titles that really should not have concerned him for any reason. And Zeenat, much more alive, would always lie entranced by sample VHS videotapes that had not been released to the public, which Mendaus's father procured for his mother by means we never knew, even though his mother spent more time traveling than lazing at home in front of the screen. Mendaus was a scrawny ten-year-old who lumbered a dictionary from one chair in the room to another as he tried to wrap his sense around the vocabulary of Emerson and Goethe; while Zeenat, at twelve, had her attention irretrievably indulged by explicit scenes of adult romance with the same entranced interest as with animated films more suitable for her age.

It was the very setup in the room that day that defined the colors of our childhood in Omole, the unison of white and blue, and not all of those other things I mentioned earlier. White because we were still pure, unmarred by the dangers of trying and the fear of failure. At that time of our lives, we were masters of our dreams, our very own kingdoms, without the bordering walls society would later place around us. A pearly slate tinted with a little blue, just enough so the brightness of our futures did not overwhelm our spirits, merging to form an umbrella of protective tranquility as we led our unassuming lives, just like the morning sky.

My childhood was not only pretty colors that described fancy, albeit infrequent, bits and pieces of the popular media of those days, or I would have ended up in art galleries and not prison cells, yes? To an extent, the idle presence of my parents at home impressed certain patterns on the person I turned out to be, with an influence that rivaled anything football, literature, or film could ever conjure.

My father, despite spending barely three waking hours with me every day, was ever present in spirit. To appease whatever regard you may have for facts, he was unforgettable in the flesh, which made it difficult to let go of any of his instructions. Most prominently, the man was a severely hairy somebody; patches of thick black curls flourished on his head when not curtailed on Saturday morning, but he usually kept it to a well-groomed turf of even blackness worn like a cap, with his beard joining at the jaw like a knotted scarf. His gait was almost as remarkable; he was a huge black mammoth of a man, though more pudgy than firmly built, who moved about with the same destructive tendencies of an ancient beast in spite of a limping right leg.

In speech he was a man of few words, not always sensible in logic but always with such confidence in tone, which possessed the occasional pause of the thoughtful and husky-voiced slur of the powerful. Deep down in all of our hearts, I think we knew that destiny had meant for him to be a soldier or something of that order; he probably would have been richer if he had not missed his step somewhere along the line and ended up a banker.

My mother was somewhat easier on the eye and the mind. She was like a palm tree, tall and thin enough to be frail but strong and beautiful enough to be adored. Unlike most others, she was not a deity weaned on praise. She barely left her home, preferring to be isolated from everything in her studio, which nobody else ever entered. In fact, she was the only one I had seen move in or out of the room for years, and when she was in, nobody bothered to get her till she was out of her volition. Once upon a curious day, she had managed to explain after many attempts that she needed to be alone to get her work done. I lost interest eventually; the fleet-footed memories I had of the studio portrayed a shabby room breeding clutter and hoarding air. The only area with any semblance of order was her working table, which had neatly arranged stacks of letters and blank papers and the carved statuettes of the *òrisà*, sacred spirits, which she prayed to.

She did leave the house on Fridays, to submit the articles to her editor for her weekend column in *The Daily News*, but she usually preferred to meander from one chore to another in a single ankara wrapper tied along the valley of her back, adding a shirt only when people visited and my father insisted. If you asked me, I would say it created a little more appeal than the ordinary that she had fair skin. Not as fair as Jackie Shawn from the *Shampoo* movie I watched with Zeenat, but more like that Bianca Ojukwu lady whose picture, anywhere, at any time, would choke my father's thoughts until he vomited at least a smile. My mother's fair skin was with a long nose and bold cheekbones, just like mine, which was in stark contrast to her full spread of darkened lips, which were also just like mine. She always wore her long clumpy hair packed into a full bun above her head like a wool crown, which was rather unlike mine, because I was male and expected to wear my hair trimmed.

Despite our differences, whenever we did spend time together, the contrasting shapes of our persons dovetailed into a seamlessly woven embroidery of an ideal family. No matter how many football matches I played in a day, I always managed to get home before dark: This was one of my father's many instructions. So by the time he had returned from work, not too long after it was dark, I would have washed myself, changed into cleaner clothes, and set out my parents' dinner on the center table in the parlor.

My father instructed that I have my own meals on the dining table, but I did not mind, because it was in the corner of the same room. From that vantage point, I could enjoy the heated arguments between my father and the man telling the news on the television from a distance, without becoming collateral damage. My mother was the only acknowledged mediator between the two suited men at either side of the room, even though my father occasionally took off his suit and folded up his sleeves if the nature of his dinner required it. So each night when the clock struck nine o'clock, over a sonic salad of traditional instruments blaring from the television, it went pretty much thus or some variation of this sort:

Good evening, I am whichever unlucky reporter the station fielded against my father that night, reporting live from Lagos, the federal capital territory, and this is NTA nine o'clock network news. Today, the head of state hosted government officials from India . . .

"You see! You have come again. Your *oga* is dipping his hands into our pockets again," my father would begin in midswallow.

. . . in the first of what would be a three-day parley discussing matters central to convening a memorandum of understanding that would have the Asian powerhouse invest in the revival of Nigeria's health system . . .

"But deep down in his heart, you know if your *oga* wanted to do something about the health system, he would go to America or Germany. *Abi*, that is where everybody travels for operation. Nobody ever travels to India for operation."

. . . in a reception held for his guests at the Lagos Airport Hotel, the head of state declared that . . .

"You see! What does the health system have to do with parties at hotels? The house we built for him, is it not for hosting guests?"

"Cletus, eat your food before it gets cold, you know spaghetti doesn't taste nice when it's cold," my mother would say,

always interrupting a few sentences into the dialogue with a total anathema to the matter at hand.

"It is as if these army people breed their recruits at the
devil's feast, the devil's feast of Ilmorog," my father would reply,
more often than not oblivious to the statement my mother had
directed at him, "all of them, their motto is: 'Reap where you
never planted, eat what you never shed a drop of sweat for, and
drink what has been fetched by others, shelter from the rain in
huts you never carried a single thatching grass for, and dress in
clothes made by others,'" getting increasingly agitated with each
declaration.

"And make sure you eat that cow leg. I'm tired of throwing
away money in this house. If you don't eat it, I'll warm it again
tomorrow and put it back on your plate," my mother would continue. And then, when she noticed my father quiet a little, she
would cool his flames with a warm reminder that *Esu* would
only act on our behalf: "Don't worry, Cletus, *Elekun n sunkun,
Esu n sun eje, Esu* is shedding blood when the owner of the problem is shedding tears."

Esu was one of the *òrisà* my mother prayed to. "*Esu* is the
gateman to the land of the *òrisà*; the bearer of sacrifices to the
òrisà; bringer of blessings from the *òrisà*; and messenger of
Orunmila, the godhead of all *òrisà*" were some of the first words
my mother had me memorize when she started teaching me the
ways of Ifá about two years earlier, when I turned eight. The
very first words were "Ifá is our way of life; through Ifá we commune with *Esu*, and through *Esu* we commune with Orunmila."
Traditional religions had never been part of my school curricu-
lum, and my mother was bent on remedying the situation. So on
weekends when there was neither school nor football to arrest

my concern, she taught me the practices of Ifá: the songs and stories and the prayers of divination. She told me how some people would eat sweet potatoes so they could be nourished with good fortune, and how people made different sacrifice offerings, from pounded yam to rats, to appeal for blessings from the òrisà. She shared the order of ranks of Ifá, from the ògbèri—people like me, who were untrained—to the Awo and Iyanifa, the male and female priestesses who could recite the over two hundred verses of divination from memory. My mother was an Iyanifa, and a passionate one at that. When she spoke about Ifá, she was not brash and reactionary like my father. All of her words seemed to originate from a personal agenda so cleverly concealed that sometimes it left an aura of the sinister, like when she told me about the place of the Yoruba king in Ifá.

"The kings are Olóri Awon iwòrò, head of priests, and they are next in power to the òrisà; their political position is a secondary duty. Just like passing in school is your primary duty, and questioning me and your father, as you always do, is your secondary." I was never sure if her references to me were cues for me to comment, so more often than not, I kept on silently. "But the kings we have now in Yorubaland, they have things mixed up. They haven't taught their children what they learned from their parents, and that is why things are falling apart. Some of them have even left Ifá for Christianity. So now our faith is in our own hands, and we have to be our own priests. And if we are our priests, we might as well be our own kings, too."

Her most frequent words when she spoke to me about these things were "Never forget you're a king, and you answer to no man, only to the òrisà." But that whole king business sounded like much more responsibility than I was ready for. At the time my circle of interests contained football, school, the wonders within Mendaus's house, and listening to the curious tales of the man on the television when night fell. There was room for nothing else.

Awkwardly enough, things were much cozier on nights when we suffered the double tragedy of power outage and having no fuel for the generator. It was an infrequent occurrence, and we would all sit around and play ludo under the flickering bright orange canopy of the kerosene lamp after dinner. The winner—usually me—would be in charge of sharing portions of whatever biscuit or chocolate my father brought out of his special suitcase on such nights.

After dinner and the things that came along with it, I would sleep and then dream about school and football, the cloak of strength in my father's demeanor that eagerly awaited me at the end of my childhood, and the comforting feel of creation that cushioned my palms when I oiled my mother's hair before she herself went to bed; about Mendaus's shelves of books and the view of the world through his thick glasses; about Zeenat's films and her view of me.

And it was not long before I had a proper chance to understand what that view was like, dreams aside. Not too long after my first visit to Mendaus's place, Zeenat started coming along with him to the football field in the afternoons. She would play around the borders of the field, allowing herself to be distracted by the street vendors on the other side of the road or the occasional food hawker, hardly ever paying any actual attention to the football. Mendaus did not seem to mind her presence at all; he always appeared passive about most issues until his opinion was demanded.

Maradona would bicker about my lack of focus, which affected my performance as soon as she started coming around. His claim that I often stood staring toward her whereabouts, instead of marking the opposition whenever we lost possession of the ball, was not entirely false, but it never became a big deal because Pastor's son counterclaimed that Maradona was just jealous, since every time he looked toward Zeenat with hope of catching her gaze, it was already fixed on me. I never seconded his claim, but before his mention of it, I believed the images of her fleeting gaze were just tricks of my imagination.

When we lost a game or were on any kind of break, I would casually drift in her direction and we would cram as much of a conversation as we could into the few minutes we were stringently afforded. She would brush the dust off my elbows and shins, and I would poke at her belly button till she squeezed my finger and refused to let go. It was during these few minutes she told me about her origins: about Kano, the city of her birth, and her devout Muslim upbringing that permitted nothing more than domestic chores and fidelity to the faith; her father, who had mysteriously slumped to his death while involved in land disputes with his stepbrothers; her submissive mother, who had become slightly unstable after her father's death. She was taken in by one of her father's stepbrothers, and her three older sisters were married off in an annual sequence before their teenage years were over. She told me of the year she was expected to be married off, how her mother managed to persuade one of her father's oldest friends to kidnap her littlest daughter and promise to provide for her the closest semblance to a normal childhood and fair life that he could manage. And how, as a result of that ordeal, she was misplaced in Kano and later found hidden in the home of one of her father's oldest friends in Lagos.

This new man was unlike all the others she was used to, especially her father, to whom he was apparently very close. He was the first man in her life who did not care at all about Allah or anything at all pertaining to being a Muslim. He had loosened his grasp on faith when he lost his first two wives and five children in a car accident. And though he did marry another wife, he barely had time for family. He allowed his business interests to lead him around the world in pursuit of solace while providing enough for his wife in Lagos to furnish a lifestyle of whatever nature she pleased. His young wife, bored with lonely married life, adopted an orphan from her village named Mendaus to busy herself, but she soon got bored of him, too, leaving him in the care of the house steward, Mr. Thomas.

All this history of Zeenat's new family transpired before her arrival. She and Mendaus became cousins by their own definition. They were to each other as bread was to butter despite their difference in personalities: He enjoyed going to school and loved to read; she did not believe in school because her parents did not believe in it; and she was sold to anything in a VHS videotape.

Some days she would convince me to forfeit football for whole afternoons so she could show me a new movie she had fallen in love with. When I finally yielded to her unending troubling, we sped off like chickens relieved of their heads at the abattoir down the long dirt road, through the large gates, and in deliberate aversion of Mr. Thomas, barely stopping for a moment till we held the black screen of the television in our sights. I watched her fiddle with the player for a while and then take a seat beside me on the floor. And just before it felt awkward, the television flickered alive. I remember the first of such afternoons, lost in the darkness till the consecutive images of script scrolled down the television:

> *. . . LITTLE CIGARS are hazardous to your*
> *health . . .*
> *. . . American International Pictures Presents . . .*
> *. . . The LITTLE CIGARS mob, starring*
> *ANGEL TOMPKINS . . .*

It did not take me any reasonable time to figure out who Angel Tompkins was. Her face had that brilliance of the sun which could not be indulged for more than a moment, with golden rays of effervescence gracing her from the top of her head to just beyond her shoulders. The fact that she spent most of the movie running around with a faithful clique of grown men the size of children, the Little Cigars mob, in all kinds of criminal adventures, did not quench my interest for a bit. Nothing at all quenched my interest until I noticed Zeenat staring at me as I stared at Angel Tompkins in a close-up scene. And just as the raging tides of panic and guilt made a confluence in the rivers of my soul, Zeenat leaned in and whispered into my ear: "You don't have to be my Lester anymore. If you like, you can be my little cigar."

1986

Meanwhile, of all the colors in the world, green soon became the theme of my family. If there was a particular day I could single out as the start of it all, it would probably be the night the man on the television had shut my father up. Everything leading up to the incident was as usual; nothing had happened to warrant any suspicion of my father's humbling.

Good evening, I am whichever shepherd-boy reporter the station had fielded to fell the huff-and-puff Goliath, reporting live from Lagos, the Federal Capital Territory, and this is NTA nine o'clock network news. Today the inspector general of police announced the arrest of Africa Independent Bank chief executive Marcel Asikhia at the bank's Lagos headquarters over a five-charge case centered on advanced fee fraud . . .

I already had my eyes on my father when I noticed his jaw drop. The reporter had gone a fair extent into the headline, and a retort from my father was overdue. But for the first time, I watched him sit in icy silence.

. . . the arrest was the end result of a discreet yearlong investigation carried out by the Nigerian Police Force in conjunction with the United States Secret Service. But rather than celebrate this accomplishment as a milestone victory in the fight against corruption, the inspector general stated that this was just the beginning of a sweep of arrests that would implicate other crooked members of not just Africa Independent Bank but the entire banking sector, emphasizing as he brought his statement to an end that Nigeria had enough to provide for every man's needs but not every man's greed . . .

"Cletus, what's this all about?" my mother asked in a tone lacking the usual warmth. She picked up the remote control from my father's side and powered off the television. "Cletus! What is it that man is saying?"

"Puh-puh-puh-put on that rubbish let us hear word," he thundered with boiling immediacy. "How else will I know, *abi*, I am a witch now?"

He snatched the remote control from her and restored the man on the television as the sole breaker of silence, but now he was giving statistics on the success rates of high school students in the recently released O-levels examination. My parents began talking, but only in whispers. I remained in my chair, tracing my fingers through the thick threading at the hem to disguise my eavesdropping, but still I could barely make out complete sentences, just disjointed phrases when my mother screeched at high-pitched junctures.

"Didn't you say you people had a man in the house of as-sembly . . . But you were not directly involved in that part of the deal . . . *Esu onigbowa aye, Esu* is the one in control of this world . . . If it is the same Marcel that I met the other night, I know he won't say *pim* . . . We don't have to go anywhere, *abi*, you did not change your address in your file when we moved . . . But I told you that Adeniran did not look trustworthy, *Efifi uwa e i, da ka da ugba apee bo a ru jade*—character is smoke, even if it is covered with two hundred baskets, it will ooze out."

My father went into his room and came out with black polythene bags and empty suitcases. I fell asleep on the chair in the parlor, watching him and my mother neatly arrange green dollar notes, like cutlery in a cupboard, from the black bags into the suitcases. But not the lush green that signified hope, growth, a lush utopia, or maybe even life itself. Rather, a tattered shade of green that seemed to camouflage a world of treachery behind the darkness of its frayed edges, a green that embodied in its appearance, as much as in its quantity, the sickening nature of excess.

Any color, whichever, on its own can only be selfish. But in harmonious or disruptive union with others, colors possess and excite the mind, heart, and all feelings. Color is most similar to the unison of souls in romance. The whites and blues and greens of my life thus far, and the myriad of tints and shades of the rainbow that had adorned the fabric of Zeenat's past, soon came together in an ever emerging beauty describable only by itself yet visible to the curious eye.

Mendaus and the other boys knew it was out there, but they only teased me about it and did not bother sniffing out its evidence, except Maradona. When Pastor's son teased, Maradona laughed louder than everybody else and then said something that always implied that Zeenat was beyond me. Whenever she did come to the side of the field during our matches, he dwelled on the ball longer than he usually would, trying tricks he usually would not, even though he pulled them off most of the time. I did not mind, because she cheered only when I was on the ball. Zeenat had lynched both our hearts; I seemed to be moving on to an eternal paradise with her, while Maradona drifted toward damnation.

With hope fleeting, Maradona desperately began playing it off like she was barely an issue on his mind, paying less attention when she spoke. But I knew from the way he looked at her when he did look, and the way he spoke to her when he did speak, she remained an issue. It was the same way I looked at and spoke to her, which portrayed without reservations all of my feelings toward her.

To be honest, I really never minded the boys teasing about Zeenat and me. But it did get to me whenever Maradona became a third character in the joke; his name was like a serpentine presence lurking around the Garden of Eden Zeenat and I had created for ourselves, a presence that had to be expelled. So I began trying to get the boys to stop, first cautiously and then curtly via daily crescendo, until the day I snapped. The boys were laughing over something Pastor's son had said about making up a trophy called "Zeenat" because all the boys seemed to play for her. I tried to interrupt with a loud "Shut up!" But nobody seemed to notice, so I shouted again, an extended effort that was even more livid than the first.

"Somebody is burned, because if we really had to play for her, he knows he'd never win," Maradona said, and everyone laughed louder. A few other boys had started coming closer to find out if we were sharing chicken or something.

"Shut up! You're just . . . stupid," I replied.

He retorted, "If I'm stupid, your mother is stupid."

The crowd was growing. Whispers were getting louder. I had to reply, but my lips were heavy, my eyes heavier. The boys in the crowd noticed and started offering sticks and stones:

"Call his mother *ashawo*" and "Call him a bastard." I was not sure what either of the words meant, so I cowered.

"Take it back! Take it back!" I forced out of my quivering lips.

"Take what back?" We all looked to Zeenat, who was oblivious to the tension she fueled. Before somebody could think up a lie, Pastor's son offered her the truth. Apparently, he was oblivious to the tension, too. Maradona shoved him off his feet before he could continue.

"What about 'my little cigar'?"

"Little cigar? You people already have stupid names for each other, just like husband and wife," Maradona quickly added.

All the boys erupted in laughter, and perhaps a tear rolled down my face. I meant only to punch Maradona on his cheek, like they did in the movies I watched with Zeenat, but Pastor's son had stood up and reciprocated the shove he had received with even more vigor. Maradona staggered off balance; my punch to the cheek was miscalculated, and I felt my bony fist squish his eye. On days when I think about the moment, I can still taste the vomit that filled my mouth that day as Maradona cried bloody tears until the street vendor had to come and hurry him to a hospital.

I was not allowed to go to the field for a week. During the time I would usually be playing football, I would stare out the window toward the dirt road that led to Mendaus's house. But my mind barely wandered toward him or Zeenat. It was my way of steeling myself for the barrage of slaps my father would dispense at the slightest irritation when he came home. It was also during this time that I tried to understand the news about Maradona. After a week of no results, I decided to talk about it with the boys in school, so I brought it up during our break time.

"What does a bastard mean?" I asked. Mendaus and Pastor's son were both present in the huddle we formed close to the swings, far away from where the other boys were. Maradona had still not returned to school. Our teacher had announced after assembly the day before that we should all take time out to pray for our classmate Maradona, who was recovering from eye surgery. There was silence for a while.

"It means when someone is really stupid?" Pastor's son suggested.

"It's something different from that," I said.

"No, it's not. My mummy always says our driver is really stupid, or she calls him a bastard. So they can't be too different."

"A bastard is someone who does not know his father," Mendaus said firmly.

"It's something different from that, too," I replied as firmly.

"How would you know?" Pastor's son inquired.

"Because Maradona's mother came to my house the day after he got injured. She said that Maradona needed surgery. That she did not have any money and Maradona was a bastard, so my father would have to pay for it. So Mendaus can't be right, because Maradona's father is a soldier. Everybody knows that. Maybe he would have paid for the surgery if he was around."

Mendaus said, "Maybe? Well, have any of you 'maybe' seen Maradona's soldier father, ever?"

"I haven't," Pastor's son said.

There was silence for a while. "A bastard is someone who does not know his father. So Maradona 'probably' lied," Mendaus said with an air of finality, and he walked away.

After the night my parents packed money into the suitcases, unexplainable changes started happening. Unexplainable because neither of my parents thought it necessary to bring me into an understanding of things. On my first attempt at tapping the palm wine, I asked my mother, "Why were you and Daddy packing suitcases the other night?"

"Because the first thing people do if they want to go on holiday is to pack."

I got excited. "When are we traveling? Are we going abroad? Can we go to Argentina?"

"I don't know when, I don't know where," she said, laughing. "We'll know when the time is right."

"So why pack if we don't even know when we're going and where we're going?"

"Good question! But I have a better question for you." Her laughter quieted, and she squatted down to be face-to-face with me. "Do you know the particular time the airplanes in the sky fly past, or do you know exactly where each one is going?"

"No. Nobody does."

"Exactly! And that's why our suitcases have to be ready. So whenever any airplane lands near here, we can be ready to jump on it. And if we're lucky enough, it'll take us somewhere beautiful. Maybe it will even take us to Argentina. But we'll never know if we're not packed and ready."

I fell for the bait, and after a few minutes of daydreaming

about playing football in Argentina, I ran off to inquire more about our holiday plans of my father.

"Mummy said we would be traveling for holidays. Is it possible for us to go to Argentina?" He coughed out loud echoes of laughter, and I felt comfortable, so I foolishly pressed on. "Is that why you stopped going to work?"

"What rubbish is this?" I did not predict his mood swing. Neither did I predict the smack on the back of my head that his hand immediately dealt. "Your business in this house is not whether I go to work as long as I put food on the table for you to eat. When I was your age, my father used to leave the house from morning to night every day but never put food on our table. Your only business is to go to school and pass your books." My mother came in just in time, ignoring the tension, as usual, and changing the topic without the littlest bother in the world.

If I'd had any wisdom those years, I probably would have curtailed my questions to my mother as well. She lured me with her answers to ask even more. So I kept asking. She would answer me in her own words at first, and then with old proverbs in Yoruba, until she progressed to drawing from the *Odu* of Ifá, ultimately declaring that I was of sufficient age and curiosity to witness the divinations and direct my concerns to the *òrìsà*. I could have objected, but to sit in the presence of the initiated and commune with the high powers that guided my fate from my birth and ordered my haves and have nots, all while managing to stay enshrouded in a cloak of invisibility, was alluring to me.

I was not ready. My first divination occurred almost two weeks after she first mentioned it. I realized it was upon me only when I heard her summon me from her studio that Saturday morning. My feet shuffled with hesitation the moment my hands felt the knob of the studio door; although unknowns often yield to the wooing of fear, they are romantically enslaved to the voice of curiosity. I twisted the knob and pushed the door forward in a single motion. The room was emptier than I had ever seen it, the tables and shelves hidden away behind yards of scarlet cloth, and the curtains were lifted over the window. My mother knelt on the floor, wrapped at the breast and all the way below in more scarlet, and had her yellow arms flickering above her head from one side to another like the fiery flames of burning sacrifice that I would live to see in hundreds of later divinations. Her face was marked with white circles that diminished along her neck and across her arms into little spots.

She began chanting as I knelt opposite her, tucking in my legs from below my knees beneath my lap, as she had. She turned around to face the statues on the table behind her, a tall carving from black wood of a man standing with an exaggerated chest and legs spread. Just beside it was a smaller and browner clay mold of a figure that was woman from the waist above but fish from the waist below. The wooden image was *Esu* and the other *Yemoja*, the mother *òrisà* and mother to all mothers. My mother whistled three times to the right of the statues and three times to their left.

"*Esu Alare na ode orun. Esu* the middle man between heaven and earth, I am calling on you, answer your child." Then she balled up her left fist and smashed it against her open right palm.

"*O lo daindain mookun oro*, one who has the anointed rope to success, wealth, and all the good things. *Onen yi a se oiye ko de dupe, bi si gi l'osa gbe eun iaye lo e i.* He who does not show appreciation for a good deed done to him is like a thief who has made away with one's goods. We have come to you with gifts."

45

She lifted the cover of the wooden bowl between us. I had never seen a fish so finely dressed in leaves and pepper as the one inside the bowl. She took the fish and broke off a morsel with a bite, handed it over to me, and I did the same, albeit hesitantly, and then she lifted the rest of it upward.

"Your son has come to begin his journey with you. Show him the path to follow." I remember wondering how my interest in our travel plans to Argentina had brought this about.

We did not see Maradona for a while after the accident. He could not make it back in time for the term's end, so we could not see him at school. He did not come to the field to play football anymore, so we could not see him there, either. And when we summoned the occasional courage to go knocking at the gate of his house, it never opened up for us. Somehow, we knew he knew we had discovered the situation about his father, even though none of us ever mentioned it. I think we avoided the issue because we were not sure if it was going to be like one of the many awkward incidents we laughed over, or if this particular case would have dire implications on our friendship with Maradona.

Our trimmed-down group slowly took a new direction. We stopped playing football as much, maybe because we'd stopped winning as much since Maradona left. But it was not altogether removed from our lives: 1986 was a World Cup year, and we had waited four years for this. We had saved money all year and added it up to buy a radio we could use to listen to the games, straining to hear the British commentary over static. We would gather in the television room of Mendaus's house because it was the quietest place and everything would be as still as a lover's gaze when we listened. All our minds would focus on the football as it was passed around. It was a fixed star at the center of our universe, and all the players, great and celestial as we imagined them, revolved around and oscillated from it according to the quality of their skill. Even though we all wanted Argentina to come forth victorious, there were mixed feelings when the commentator announced after the final game that the Argentine cultlike leader, Diego Armando Maradona, was leading his team in a victory parade.

After the World Cup, our radio was relieved of all its football commentary duties and became our karaoke machine. We would gather by four o'clock for the MusikAfrika show, which basically repeated the same songs every day, so it was not difficult to get the hang of the lyrics. The show would start with Sunny Okosun's "Now or Never," which would merge into Onyeka Onwenu's "Ekwe." It would then pinball between tracks from Chief Osita Osadebe, Oliver De Coque, and Fela Anikulapo Kuti, and when it was a few minutes to five o'clock, as the show was winding down, we would all clear our throats and chorus Nico Mbarga's "Sweet Mother" when it came on to close the show. For the rest of my life, I would relive those moments in the dark living room when, with reckless abandon of any care in this world, we chanted:

> Sweet mother I no go forget you
> for the suffer wey you suffer for me.
> When I dey cry, my mother go carry me, she go say,
> "My Pikin' wetin you dey cry ye, ye,
> stop stop, stop stop make you cry again oh no."

Mendaus still read as much, maybe even more. Sometimes he rocked back and forth from between the pages of his books and reality, peering at the words for short periods and then jumping into conversation with the rest of us. Other times he would snarl at Pastor's son and me when we spoke too loudly or tried to barter his attention for gist. Zeenat, on the other hand, was more used to his moods, knowing when and when not to speak. Her presence in our group had become more accepted. She followed us everywhere, talking and laughing much louder than any of us boys did. Her being two years older than the rest of our scrawny lot was much more evident, as she was a clear head taller than Mendaus, Pastor's son, and me.

I never brought up the matter of Ifá and the òrìsà. There was no oath of secrecy that confined me, and sometimes I even admired the way Pastor's son spoke about the Holy Spirit, Jesus, and the "power of the resurrection." My primary school was a Christian mission school, and everybody had to pray in the name of Jesus, and at home all of the street vendors and most of the security men punctuated their sentences with *Insha Allah*, but my house was the only place I had heard any talk about Ifá.

On one occasion, we were watching a movie at Mendaus's house, and there was this scene where an old woman with gray frizzy hair was making incantations in a dark room with little dolls. It was the first time I had ever seen anything remotely close to what my mother did at home in her studio. I was just about to bring up the Ifá issue when Pastor's son started preaching about the horrors of the devil's black magic. Zeenat looked relieved that the film had distressed someone else and quickly changed the tape even as Mendaus teased them for acting like little children.

A few weeks after the black-magic incident, I followed my mother to the market. Our return journey was silent; whenever we made such trips, she hated to see silent moments go unspoken. Normally, she would start pointing at places we passed, showing me buildings and roads I already knew, or begin telling me how different things were when she was my age, but that day her words were a little less casual.

"Why don't you play football with your friends anymore?" she asked without looking at me or making any gesture.

"We never win anymore"—I was still unaware of her intentions—"and losing every day is boring."

"Oh! Well, is playing with girls more interesting?"

"I don't know." My dark cheeks managed a blush.

"You don't know? Alhaja thinks you would know." Alhaja was one of the street vendors. "In fact, Alhaja says you've started chasing girls up and down the streets of Omole."

"It's a lie!" I exclaimed. It was a weak defense, but it was all I could muster in my moment of shame.

"So who is the liar, me or Alhaja?" She allowed the silence to dwell for a while. "I don't know where you got this one from—your father never used to chase girls, and even though I don't have any brothers, I know your grandfather never used to chase girls, either. Maybe Esu would help us find out from Orunmila why these small girls are trying to put your destiny inside their brassieres." I usually would swoon at any thoughts of Zeenat's brassiere, but instead my body cringed at the thought of my mother making divinations over her. "A woman is like fire, Ihechi; if you must take some, take a little."

"Yes, Ma." I cherished every silent second for the rest of the journey home.

I did not have to worry too long about further discussions of Zeenat with my mother, or about my mother's Ifá teachings with Zeenat and the rest, because that was the summer I finished primary school and began secondary school at a boardinghouse in Ofada, a few hundred kilometers and a state border away from my parents, Mendaus, Pastor's son, and Zeenat.

1992

There can never really be a sovereign definition of the secondary school experience. The only stable concept is a group of teenage students being taught basic science, commerce, and art in large and largely ineffective bundles, and every experience outside this pretty well depends on the particular school. To illustrate: My school was a boarding school that accepted both boys and girls; Mendaus's boarding school, on the other hand, registered only boys. We had constant contact with the girls, developed likes and crushes, some people fell in love, and we shared this overall Romeo-et-Juliet-esque relationship. In Mendaus's school, they saw girls only on weekends, when they scaled the school fence and sneaked into their sister school down the road. Each expedition was treated as a hunt in every form of the word—a survey, interested predators took shots at the prey, and then the conquest ended successfully with the pleasure of a new kill and bragging rights, or unsuccessfully with amassed ridicule. Pastor's son's school was a Christian mission school that had no boarding facilities and endeavored to pray and anoint the lust of the flesh out of all its wards.

The one thing that brought us all together was trends: From the rounded Afro to the Afro-punk, and from highlife to reggae, all transitions of popular culture were en masse. During and after our six years of secondary school, it was these trends that kept our friendship alive. At this point we had outgrown Omole and drew our thrill from the city of Lagos in its entirety. The population of Lagos was growing exponentially. Millions of people had been blessed by birthright to constitute the life that was the city, and thousands more immigrated each year through every available aperture, hoping to fit in to the dynamism of the metropolitan organism, for indeed, this was a city that had life. The adrenaline-infused thumping of the city's heartbeat amid the blistering heat and quick tempo of the daytime emphasized the spirited life of the city and its inhabitants' pursuits of happiness. Yet after the exasperations of each day, the night emerged proudly as a testament to the divinity of the human spirit which contained the capacity to face daunting challenges head-on and, regardless of the eventual success or failure, still laugh, love, and live. Fibs forsaken, so vibrant was the city at night that it was once spoken to me, by someone who was told by another, that whoever controlled the nightlife of the city wielded the most influence in the corridors of power during the day. And even as the sun set each day to the dreams and fantasies of the satisfied, it rose each morning to the hopes and aspirations of the desperate. Ultimately, nothing captured the essence of this city of life like the break of dawn, each new day blind to its own destiny, yet coming alive nonetheless like the accentuating cry of a baby.

We knew too well that it was always better to get going with the city as it came alive at the beginning of the day, or else risk a psychological disconnection from the flow of events as the day continued, so when we set out in the city on weekends, we set out early. Our muster point was the street vendors' kiosk, and from there, we would make our way to the bus stop. The cold air of the morning would burn my nostrils as I drew every breath. But I was ever unfeeling toward it, much too overwhelmed by the climax of grandiose that remained after I exhaled the smoke from the smoldering roll of lint and grass (smoking marijuana was another trend that had spread around our schools).

I was alive, not in the ordinary sense of merely living but in complete exhilaration. I kissed the edge of the roll and sucked in more smoke, holding my breath to make sure my head was airtight, and letting it out only when I began smiling helplessly like a victim of ancestral witchcraft. My eyes would remain focused on the particles of smoke as they diffused under the headlights that throttled down the road toward us. Mendaus and Zeenat would share drags of smoke in no particular order, poking fun at Pastor's son, who never smoked with us.

The bus would begin from the stop at Berger, hurtling on to the main expressway at Ojota, where almost all of the state capital's rubbish was dumped and its cattle egrets nested. And it was always somewhere between these two points that the circus would begin. Lagosians, above all other things, were exclaimers. Their spoken sentences began with exclamations as their written sentences began with capital letters. An exclamation would be sounded if the bus was moving too slowly, because there was always someone who had to be at a destination quite urgently. Another would sound if the bus moved too fast, because there would always be someone else who figured that arriving at a destination with stable blood pressure was more important than arriving at all. There were those who exclaimed because they felt they knew shorter routes than the driver's choice, and there were those who exclaimed simply because they did not want to feel left out of the circus.

When people on the bus were not exclaiming, they were preaching gospels that Pastor's son derided as homemade versions of Christianity: praying down holy fire from heaven to consume enemies, wearing the ring of King David for good fortune, and other rubbishes of that sort. Pastor's son never spoke out to contradict any of these bus bishops; he just grumbled and mumbled and whispered his complaints every now and then, to my amusement.

If we could count on anybody speaking out, it would be Mendaus, and he never failed us on the bus. Occasionally, when the bus had quieted, he would rise to begin his own sermon of what Pastor's son tagged "The Gospel of Mendaus." His gospel was mostly excerpts from all of the "Save Nigeria, Save Africa, Save the World" books he had been reading, and though most of his audience jeered and cursed, he was relentless. There was always the odd commuter or two who would see reason with him and exclaim in delight; this always startled Mendaus. He would have to peek into the bible of his gospel, Frantz Fanon's *The Wretched of the Earth,* to remember the rest of his lines. And then he would conclude always with the same words: "These rich people divide us up. They think they're different. They call themselves the upper class, and us the lower class. Now, this upper class paints the lower class as a society lacking in all forms of values and ethics. They starve us slowly and then blame us for stealing, they leave us in the worst living conditions—no light, barely any water—and then they blame us for acting like mad people. And still we grasp at these rich people whenever we cross their paths; we seek handouts, a helping hand, and a way out of the asylum they created for us. But the upper class's view of the lower class is always too genuine to be masked, because disregard can't be hidden, just as love can't be hidden. And we the lower class have noticed. We have to realize we're never going to be offered a helping hand or a way out, so we have to sharpen the methods of our madness, which are the only tools life ever gave us, and then go on to take our freedom by force. We're all going to have to take sides; be merry now and be damned later with the upper class, or be damned now and be merry later with the lower class."

"You need to calm down with all this world-liberation talk, man," Pastor's son said.

"So we should just relax and allow the truth to shine its shoes while the lies are sprinting all over the place?" Mendaus retorted.

"Oh, please," Pastor's son replied. "What they don't know can't kill them. It's safe for you to talk like this in a bus, but what happens when any of these people echo your words in the wrong place or in front of a soldier? They're in the Garden of Eden, and you're giving them the apple of knowledge that could destroy them."

"Destroy them? These people are dead already. I'm trying to get their hearts pumping again."

"All he's trying to say is that not every truth needs to be spoken," Zeenat butted in with a calmer approach. "That kind of talk could get you killed in a Mafia film. And let me give you a tip—the real world outside the safety of this bus *is* a Mafia film."

I was not entirely certain the Mafia films Zeenat had watched bore any relation to real life, but I understood her point. As children in Omole—which was safely concealed on the outskirts of Lagos—we had never been cognizant of the strict and often brutal manner with which the military regime regarded public opinion. The kind of statements Mendaus made could be considered in the best interest of the public until they traversed the domain of a military man.

There was barely any traffic early on weekends, and so after about thirty minutes, we would be across the Third Mainland Bridge and onto the island, where most commuters got off, bringing the circus to a close. A stark contrast existed between the parts of Lagos at either end of the bridge, and as always, the colors told the stories. The mainland was teeming with urban savages, their haphazard streets and houses donned in the brightest paints and decorations, which betrayed their ineptitude in the finer things of life. The more refined people on the island, experts in luxury and vanities, avoided such things in preference for a strict, hypocritical code of self-effacing colors: Roads were black, sidewalks and walls gray, and most houses white. The mainland was probably so because savages never lived by rules. Rules are instruments of maintenance: maintenance of order, wealth, or whatever. But savages have nothing to maintain, so they risk nothing for everything with every moment of their lives.

We would sometimes travail in the market just opposite the marina. Other times, when more money was available than usual, we would scavenge Victoria Island, where the air tasted sweeter and the buildings resembled those in Zeenat's videos. Our first day on Victoria Island, Pastor's son asked, "So when God destroys the world at the end of time, would he really destroy something as beautiful as Victoria Island?" Most times we would go to Bar Beach. It was not as clean and proper as Lekki Beach, but it was much more populated, so it was easier for us to run into people we knew from school or wherever else.

Everybody ranged from dwarves masquerading around little children as òrìsà in raffia-made costumes to the devout members of the Celestial Church of God ringing bells, dancing barefoot, and chanting the incomprehensible in their white angelic robes. If we were lucky enough, we would stumble upon a rave party or reggae concert; we had seen Majek Fashek perform "Send Down the Rain" in his dreadlock-twirling rage, and Mike Okri croon "Time Na Money" as the palm trees by the waters mimicked the sway of the enchanted girls.

It was Bar Beach where we saw Boniface for the first time in six years. Pastor's son sighted him, Pastor's son alerted the rest of us, Pastor's son reached out to him from within the crowd, and Pastor's son doubted it was Boniface long after we had left. The doubts were initially raised by the earring in his left ear and the gold front tooth in his smile; all chances of acquittal were relinquished to the abyss when Mendaus called him by the name we were all used to—Maradona.

"Ol' boy, no shit for church. Bee Money isn't called Maradona anymore," Maradona said.

"Who is Bee Money?" Pastor's son asked through a stutter, as if Maradona's reappearance had suddenly reinvigorated the condemnation to confusion that he had suffered all through our childhood.

"Bee Money is the G who used to be known as Maradona back in the day," Maradona continued. "Bee Money doesn't play with football anymore, Bee Money plays with money." He spoke with a half-baked American accent that was obviously mixed and rolled in the shoddy kitchens of Lagos backstreets, the type that made him say, "Bee Money never experred to see you here" and "Bee Money will be flying ourra the country in a marra of

57

weeks." After about an hour of listening to "Bee Money" relate the stories of his life and business in third person, we were all convinced that none of us had missed seeing him around as much as we claimed to, and that he was a profiteer of advanced fee fraud—an affair the poor described as "business" but the rich stigmatized as "larceny." In the most private part of my mind, just before I went to sleep that night, I wondered if he would have turned out another person if events had played out differently on that football field many years ago.

Mendaus, a predator of all things feminine by virtue of his secondary school training, always met new girls at the beach. There was the one he met on the bus to the beach, who we agreed had a pungent odor. There was another who flirted with him despite coming with a male friend she denounced being involved with at every possible juncture. And then there was the one he had sorted out through a crowd of bodies splattering in the advancing and receding tide, the one who stuck around. Her name was one of those long but common names shared with supernumeraries of males and females of her two-million-strong Ijaw tribe, and when he inquired of it, she told him. *Ayeebaato-nyeseigha* meant "what God has planned to do" in English; she told him this after they began exchanging opinions on trivialities at the suya spot. They had been waiting for the butcher, who had run off to a nearby mosque to say his midday prayers.

Atonye had that innocent but clearly evident physical appeal, but I think what attracted Mendaus to her the most was that she believed in his gospel. She agreed that Léopold Sédar Senghor was a coward who had more faith in the French than he had in his own people, and not the righteous hero of African liberation, as was taught to us all in secondary school. She believed that tribalism was the new imperialism, though none of us except Mendaus knew what imperialism stood for. And she was unshakably convinced that Nigeria was a child kidnapped by military dictatorship that needed rescuing.

Atonye had no responsibility to anyone and took instructions from her curious will alone, like a palm-wine drunkard leading the adventures of her life in the bush of ghosts. I think Zeenat's issue with her was more a result of Zeenat being used to having neither female friends nor gawking at bare-chested white men and the other ultra-feminine things Atonye was inclined to do from time to time. Pastor's son's concern was definitely her brazen disregard for the things he held dear. It was bad enough that she smoked and drank as much as we did. It was worse that she furnished the same sentence with swear words and the name of Jesus.

The final straw was her suggesting our visit to Afrika Shrine, the home and performing theater of Fela Anikulapo Kuti. Mendaus and Zeenat had visited it a couple of times but had never been able to overcome the skepticism shown by Pastor's son and me. Atonye gave their argument the numerical advantage. When we eventually did go, Pastor's son refused to follow us. There was no live performance, as we had desperately anticipated—Fela had fallen ill, reminding us that he was human after all—and so Mendaus, Zeenat, Atonye, and I just had drinks as we bobbed our head to tapes blasting from the speakers. With time, subsequent visits became a Saturday habit after the beach. The first time Pastor's son did come with us was the first time Atonye did not. That was the night we met Fela, the legend, the same night our consciousness got knocked out by alcohol, which led us to picking a fight with patrolling policemen well after midnight, the same night we spent our first night in prison.

By the time I had left secondary school, my family portrait was a debased representation of its expected order, depicting fluctuating hardships instead of increasing prosperity, and strife in place of accord. My father had not held a proper job since leaving the bank six years ago, just in time to avoid being held for corruption charges, as most of his colleagues were. Not a lot of them had gone to jail, but all of those who had were still behind bars. Since then, he had peddled secondhand vehicles and transported shipped containers across the Seme Border. And so, all through my secondary school, when I was asked about my father's profession, my reply was a nondescript "businessman."

My mother, on the other hand, had managed to transform our blatant portrayal of dysfunction into an exhibit of melancholic splendor that ignited curiosity in our gossiping neighbors, something akin to Nicolas Poussin's representation of the great flood and Noah's Ark in *The Four Seasons*. She still wrote her weekly column for the newspaper, but she had also begun putting her doctorate to use by lecturing at the University of Lagos. My mother had quickly become the go-to person for my needs. But she made sure I had my father's endorsement for anything at all, and she would give him the money to pay for any expense before we left the house. So as in Poussin's *Deluge*, the tragedy of the portrait was held at the fore while the scene's ark of salvation was modestly concealed in the background.

However, the day I was released from prison, the leviathan in my father, which had been subdued as I grew out of childhood, reared its head again. Pastor's church had matured into a large congregation over the last few years, and the inspector in charge of our case was a devout member. He had contacted certain members of the church as soon as he became aware of Pastor's son's involvement in the altercation, and by midday Pastor had bailed us all out. But Pastor could not prevent the gist from floating from the mouth of one church member to another, and then one church member to a non–church member, until my father had heard of it before sunset of the same day! He had stepped out of the house for an hour to read newspapers at the junction, and when he returned, he was a transformed man. The pulsing veins on his balding head did little to tone down his menace, and his oversize shirts extending over his belt and cuffs by a few inches did justice to his hooligan tendencies of the moment. When he spoke, his voice thundered off the four corners of the house.

"*Araruola!* Abomination!" he shouted, clapping to each word he spoke. "Is this how your mother trained you? To sniff hard drugs, *okwia*? Is this why I paid for you to go to expensive schools? So you can become a prisoner, *okwia*? The son of a dog is a dog, and the son of a cow is a cow; your mother and I are not hoodlums, so Ihechi, whose son are you? I will kill you in this house, oh, you cannot set a trap with a chicken and expect a goat to show up."

He barked rhetorical questions, the pitch of his voice fluctuating as his insults became an incomprehensible psychobabble amid drops of spit jetting out of his mouth. My heartbeat set off mimicking the percussions of a talking drum and my vision spun around like a white-draped masquerade at the *Eyo* festival. A firm conviction had arrested my heart that the end of the world, as taught to me by the good Christian teachers of my primary school, was upon my deviant soul and my father, the Antichrist sent by the devil himself, was the apocalypse made flesh to dole out retribution. The one-man army of the apocalypse laid siege on my body, raining down blows, kicks, and his metal belt buckle.

My mother came in just as I began tasting the blood between my teeth and scurried me off to the embrace of my bed. The loud voices, his and hers, that spurted through the crevices in the door kept me awake all night. By the time I woke the next morning, my father had already left the house, so I prepared bathwater and breakfast for just my mother. My father did not return home, not that day and not ever again. Every night as she waited for him, my mother locked herself up in her studio and made divinations to the òrisà.

I never really talked about the happenings of my house with Mendaus and Zeenat, but doing so was inevitable after the bruises my father had left on me.

"You know, if this was in America, you could report him to the police. He would have to pay you or the government would give you new parents. This country is so backward," Zeenat said.

"I'm not sure you'd get money or new parents in America," Mendaus added. "But I'm sure if you tried reporting in Nigeria, the police would lock you up in prison."

"Which is why you got beaten in the first place, abi?" said Zeenat as she passed on the joint she was smoking to Mendaus.

But I was not in the mood for either the buzz or the banter. "It's really not funny," I said, trying to conceal the sobs that made my voice croak. "I saw him in my sleep the other night. It was nothing terrible, but seeing him in my sleep is creepy."

"Well, you're one lucky bastard," Mendaus replied. "My father has been dead for about seventeen years and hasn't bothered to show up once in my dreams. And look at you—your ol' man isn't even dead, and he's showing up in your dreams already."

"It's not funny."

"Not funny? So it's not okay for us to throw jabs at you, but it's okay when your ol' man knocks you out?" Zeenat retorted between giggles.

"Forget about my father. The issue is that I messed up. We messed up. And it rubs off on our families. If you're so smart, why is that so difficult for you to understand? Some of us have parents who hold us responsible for what we do!" I regretted the words as soon as they'd left my mouth. Zeenat stared at me, jaw ajar. I stared at Mendaus, and he stared into space.

"I am not a child of a happy family," he said finally, smiling and appearing to have little or no consideration for my outburst. "I was brought up by books and stories, not hugs and kisses. I might not be able to offer you candor, but my friend, I can offer you truth: Your free will is not an entitlement; it's the spoils of war. Just as you suck out the buzz from these blunts, you have to force out your free will from the hands you were born into. And if you take too long, the flames of your aspirations will crumble into ashes of regret." He stood up, buttoning his shirt, and on his way out of the room, he added, "Ponder upon that for a minute. I have an appointment with Atonye, and it will be really shitty if my buzz wears off before I get over to her place."

The room was dim and silent after he left. Zeenat came close and tried to put her arm around me, but her elbow brushed a bruise. I winced, and she withdrew immediately.

63

"I'm really sorry about your father," she said.

"It's not your fault. We were all in jail together."

"You've never kissed me before, Ihechi," she observed. My muscles stiffened, and the rate of my heartbeat quickened. "Why not?" she asked.

"What movies have you been watching lately, Zee?"

"That's not the point. Ihechi, do you still like me?"

"Why are you even asking all these questions?"

"Why? Because Mendaus and Atonye like each other, and they do these things all the time. And they just met a few weeks ago. I know you did all these things with a few girls in secondary school. I hear you and Mendaus whisper. I just want to know why you've never tried it with me."

I could not tell her that all of the things I had told Mendaus were either lies or exaggerations, I could not tell her how shy I was despite how long we had known each other, and most of all I could not bring myself to tell her how much I wanted it.

I replied, "I still like you very much, Zeenat." I looked away. I did not see the reaction on her face, but I heard her get up to turn on the television. She slipped a video into the system and returned to the couch, where we sat a bit closer, with her leaning slightly in to me. In a few seconds, the television announced in black and white:

A Mercury Production by Orson Welles
CITIZEN KANE

The pictures translated from a wire fence to a lofty steel gate and then a magnificent mammoth of a building with several towers starting at different heights but all desperately stretching to bridge earth and heaven. My eyes were just as unstable, oscillating between the television screen and Zeenat.

I remembered Mendaus's final urging before he left the room: "Your free will is not an entitlement; it's the spoils of war." I shifted my arm to rest just along her shoulder, and in that instant, she slouched in the chair and nestled closer to me. The narrator in the movie had begun telling a tale of irrelevancies as I slouched into the cradle of the chair. Her face was right beside mine. She turned toward me and I could feel her breath on my skin. Testosterone flooded my veins and my groin bulged at the zipper of my trousers.

The rest of Mendaus's urging echoed in my head: "And if you take too long, the flames of your aspirations will crumble into ashes of regret." I closed my eyes and plunged toward her lips. She relaxed deeper into the cradle of the couch and pulled me in, guiding my hands into her blouse. As we kissed, touched, and writhed, an obstinate legion of spirits tugged at the cornerstone of my sanity, blowing aggressive trumpet tunes and banging on drums in declaration of war on my peace of mind. The lyrics of these war songs resembled the very words of Ludwig van Beethoven to his estranged spouse in his collection of letters, *Think of Me Kindly*. The steps of the war dances mimicked the vain motions of Paris in the battle for the hand of Helen in the film *Troy*. The fast-paced drumbeats took after the accelerated heartbeat of a virgin bride on her wedding night. The aggressive trumpet blasts were like the cries of Jesus Christ as he died for the world on Cavalry's cross.

Love is a force of passion, and like all other forces, it is neither created nor destroyed; it only changes from one form to another. The overloaded passion that Zeenat and I shared that day must have been sourced from my house, because over the following days, the force of passion that held my family together appeared to dissipate completely. My father's presence was sparse, and whenever he did manage to come around, he reeked of alcohol; in the manner of King Midas, all he touched was re-born as a symbol of filth. He brought a brutal silence with him. Brutal in the way it isolated each member of the family, as if daring and goading any one of us to make any ridiculous state-ment and risk being smitten. My father was the only one who spoke at ease, and when he did, everyone shuddered. Not at his words, because he was barely ever audible, but at the ferocious pulsation of his hands and the undulating tone of his voice when he spoke. Sometimes he would break away during meals into conversations with thin air.

"*Nno nwoke m!*" he would always begin, welcoming his imaginary friend and proceeding to offer him a portion of his meal, "*bia n'anu nri.*" His voice would trail off and then, from the ignominy of the brutal silence, burst out harshly: "*O di egwu!* You are a fool! *I nugo!* Did I not warn you? How many times did I—" Then my mother would reach out to him to calm him down. Other times, while going about his business in the house, he would suddenly start singing, in a recklessly hoarse tone, songs that little boys always sing: "*Nzogbu nzogbu enyimba, enyi . . . enyimba, enyi.*" Eventually, he would burst out again, "Fool! *Lekwa!* Look at what you've done. Didn't I warn you?"

I had never seen my father experience such severe loss of composure. But his problem was now our problem. We were one family, each of us a different color that together formed a single portrait. As in all portraits, each individual color affected the perception of the others. Taking a lighthearted tone might have reinforced his doubts that we were not taking him seriously enough, while a darker shade of behavior probably would have intensified his frustrations. We helped him bear his cross with the only tool we had: the gray of silence.

"You know your father. All he was ever good at was expressing disappointment," she told me when we were alone at home during one of those days. "It's not so bad to see him mumble about other things nowadays." Her gaze darted around the room just like mine would whenever I was struggling to keep my emotions in check. I moved closer to her and gave her a half embrace, just as she would whenever she noticed I was struggling to keep my emotions in check.

"It's okay," I whispered. But then I corrected myself after a few seconds: "It'll be okay."

"You know your father loves you, *abi?*" she continued.

"Mummy, saying all these things out loud wouldn't make them true."

"Don't ever think like that, Ihechi." Her eyes had regained focus and now they were fixed on me. "Dark clouds come into our lives. We do our best, but they don't go away. At times like that, we should remind ourselves, no matter how dark and heavy the clouds are, no matter how they cover the sun and prevent us from seeing it, the sun is still there, shining as brightly as if there were no cloud there."

We spent the next afternoon in the studio, our skin marked in white spots, our bodies robed in scarlet and bent toward our little altar, making pleas to the *òrisà*. She began reciting verses from the *Odu* of Ifá; they were words she had taught me many years ago, just after my initiation. It told of how Ifá said the faithful would receive blessings of joy, joy springing forth from provision and provision in excess. It told of how the faithful's recent experiences had been a labyrinth of intersecting paths of fortune and misfortune causing the faithful to lose hope and now question opening the door of his life to anything new, even though it was now joy and not despair knocking. I spoke the words with my mother, but I could not generate the same conviction that resonated through her every word. To me the words were religious, but to her, they were spiritual.

I understood my mother's convictions, but with each divination we made, it became clearer to me that it was her conviction alone and not mine. I understood Ifá was the way of her fathers and those before them, that the traditional religions were very much bullied by Christianity and Islam. I understood that other people now had no regard for the gods of their fathers. But these people had no obligation to worship certain gods because their fathers did, just as they had no obligation to wear bubba and *sokoto* instead of shirts and jeans, and neither did I. I had every obligation to conform to whatever allayed the distempers of my soul, because ultimately, it is people who define culture and not the other way around. But I could not bring myself to express my convictions aloud and unashamedly, as my mother did.

She began making the sacrifices, by far the largest I had ever seen. Pigeons and hens, a catfish, and a rat were laid on the altar, all doused in palm oil. I did finally remember one of my mother's convictions that I shared: "In the end all a man has is his god and his dreams." I looked at the way her life was set up and knew that if her words were right, then there was a problem with either the dreams she pursued or the god she chose. I was determined to make better choices.

—

Mendaus's parents were in town for a while, and both my parents were out for most of the day, so we shifted the location of our afternoon loafing to my house. It was the first time we'd all been under the same roof since the police prison cell sheltered us for a night. Even Atonye was around. She demanded we give her the gist of that night, since Mendaus had been hoarding the tale from her, hoping to barter it for an under-the-sheets favor.

"What about Fela Anikulapo Kuti?" she asked, sitting up from her slouched position beside Mendaus on the chair my parents usually occupied.

"I just always assumed that guy was a basket full of booze and smoke," Pastor's son replied from the other side of the room, at the table where I had dinner and observed my parents from.

"I thought he'd be much taller and built . . ." Zeenat said.

". . . just like me, *abi?*" I added. She made some sort of sarcastic exclamation and leaned in to me before withdrawing herself again.

"That guy knows his stuff," Mendaus said, finally agreeing to open up. "He quoted Adam Smith like it was his wife's birthday wish list."

"Well, if I had all the dancers on that stage, having a wife would be the last thing on my wish list," said Pastor's son. Everybody paused to stare at him, and then we all burst out in laughter.

"You know, we could do it all over again," Mendaus started again. "Atonye says Fela performs live every Thursday, but this week is even going to be bigger because they're celebrating the release of his brother Beko and those other guys, Fawehinmi and Falana and the rest, from military detention."

"The old pastor hasn't even recovered from that other night," replied Pastor's son. "My mum said he was saying his morning prayers when the news got to him. When he heard I was in prison, he choked on his Holy Communion."

"It's just my father I have to worry about," I added. "We really have to pray he makes it home drunker than I do that night, if he makes it home at all."

"Atonye, what about you?" Zeenat inquired. "Your parents won't mind your being gone with the wind till after midnight?"

Mendaus tried to mumble out an answer on her behalf, but his thoughts staggered and fell too many times till she eventually rescued her rescuer. "My mum used to dance for Fela around the time he first started. The last time I let her know I was going to be chilling there, she had me handing out notes to her old friends like a postman around the whole bloody place."

Zeenat stood up and asked for the bathroom, breaking the awkward silence, and I pointed her in the direction of the corridors and doorways she would have to navigate. Our eyes stayed fixed on each other as she walked away, and even when she left the room, my thoughts escorted her. I could hear Atonye say something in the background, something about garden eggs and gin, and the other boys started laughing again. I looked around and saw Atonye trying to stifle her giggles and maintain her composure as she prepared to say something else. Mendaus was already teary in the corners of his glasses, while Pastor's son had cackled his breath away and was now wheezing animatedly. For that brief portion of time, I knew we were victorious over all of life's tribulations. For that moment in my living room, we had paid no regard to rolling the dice of fate; instead, we had tossed the game board into the air and sent the little totems hurtling into the face of our fears. For that while, no spirit from our torrid pasts, reckless presents, or uncertain futures could stand unbowed before us, because we had found happiness in each other.

A loud, guttural scream echoed around the house. We all fled in the direction I had pointed Zeenat. But even before we got to the bathroom, I saw her standing in the corridor, in front of the wrong door, and I understood. The same fear that had possessed her a few seconds ago arrested my will and brought me to a standstill as the others ran past me to meet up with Zeenat. They, too, on getting to the door, stood in shock as they looked through the doorway of my mother's studio: the scarlet drapes and the decorated altar, the craven images of the òrìsà, and the sacrifices my mother and I had offered to them the day before. As if still being orchestrated by that same screaming fear, they all turned to stare at me inquisitively at the same time, except Zeenat, who started throwing up.

If the Afrika Shrine was truly the temple where the Afrobeat faithful gathered, then Thursdays were the acknowledged days of worship. By sunset that Thursday, Fela had already begun dispersing his tunes through speakers mounted at the corners of the auditorium, which pulled people of all ages from blocks beyond. With our elbows, we paddled through the sea of the devout that had filled up every crevice between the banks of concrete buildings lining the path to the Afrika Shrine. And just as the legend of *Akara-Ogun* preached, beyond the forest of a thousand daemons lay gifts of peace and fortune, both of which the Afrika Shrine espoused in abundance.

My friends were still trying to come to terms with all I had revealed to them the last time we were gathered at my house. After the others had cleaned up Zeenat's vomit and calmed my fidgeting, I had begun an hourlong soliloquy without any further urging, telling the story of my initiation and all else I knew from the very beginning, except, of course, the parts that were to be always kept secret from the uninitiated. I had hoped deeply for some sort of reaction, any at all. The fact that I had kept so much from them for so long was a cold betrayal of trust, but somehow, I had expected that the precarious nature of my secret would make its discovery more palatable. The silence they all replied with, which resonated on their forlorn faces, hacked fiercely at my serenity. But at the Shrine, all the opinions found their misplaced voices.

Pastor's son bombarded me with questions. "So, your family has been practicing some coded kind of witchcraft since forever? If it's not witchcraft, then what's the difference?"

"Calm down, church boy," Atonye replied on my behalf. "It's pseudo-witchcraft, something less terrible. They never sucked blood by day or flew the sky by night, at least according to his version of the story. Besides, if our ancestors were as uptight as you are, they never would have given Christianity and Islam the chance to defeat our traditional religions."

"You can't even compare Christianity with these folks," said Pastor's son. "We're peaceful; they're always shedding blood for one reason or another. The Islam folks call it jihad, and the pseudo-witchcraft folks call it sacrifices."

"Nah, there's no such thing as religious tolerance. You

Christians are pseudo-peaceful," Atonye said. "Every religion openly desires dominance. They're all just very diplomatic in their approach."

"But that's not a bad thing," added Mendaus. Before then, he'd seemed less concerned with the conversation and more engrossed in watching Atonye spar with Pastor's son. "Ambition is necessary for progress, and there really isn't any point in demanding followers if you don't have a progressive cause. Hating other religions because they aren't tolerant is just mis-yarns."

Pastor's son realized he was outnumbered and so surrendered to defeat for the time being, living to fight another day. He was never the sharpest blade on the farm, but he was the type that would keep chopping at a tree once a day until he brought the whole forest crashing down.

Zeenat had not said a word all night. Her emotions were like pigments on a palette, and it did not help that I was an inexperienced painter. I was learning the hard way that the behavior of pigments existed not in absolutes but in relativity. Zeenat's behavior had no set rules; she could appear as an iroko trunk in the wind in certain circumstances, and as fickle as ixora petals in others. It was impossible to determine from her silence if she was brewing contempt or breaking into pieces.

The argument diffused soon enough into loud melodies from the speakers that reverberated from my head to all parts of my body, which was triggered into a lethargic version of disco frenzy. Fela crooned, "Look how they slap our face for Africa."

And his singing dancers chanted "Dem go gbam-gbam" while clapping to imitate the slapping sound.

"Balewa carry right side dey beat them," Fela continued. "Gowon and Obasanjo carry left side dey beat them. Shagari beat us for our heads. Buhari and Idiagbon beat us for yansh. Babaginda beat us for our necks."

The crowd cheered as he continued naming past leaders whom Mendaus constantly badgered for their alleged barter of Nigeria's future to the capitalist forces of the Western world, reincarnations of our tribal chiefs from the slave-trade era who sold out in the same manner centuries ago. Of course, Mendaus's voice was the loudest around me, the veins of his neck pulsating as he screamed along with the lyrics amid intermittent puffs of smoke.

I noticed Zeenat heading for the exit, which was also the entrance, and I pursued her. She noticed me trying to catch my breath in her trail just a few paces outside the auditorium.

"Why didn't you ever mention it?" she asked after I had gone speechless for about a minute while staring at her feet, her crossed arms, everywhere but her eyes. "Was it fear that held you back? Or shame?"

"What difference does it make? Whichever it was, you still wouldn't trust me," I replied.

"No fault in your assumptions. But if it's shame, it means you didn't believe in us—Mendaus, Pastor's son, and me. And if it's fear, it means you didn't believe in yourself. I want to know which it is."

I lied: "I was never ashamed or afraid of talking about it." Then I spiked the sweet lie with a little of the bitter truth. "I never spoke about it because somehow I wished there would be nothing to speak about. I wished I could ignore it away, and talking about it to anyone else would have spoiled all of that." She still looked terribly unconvinced. "Kind of like those children at the beach who close their eyes and stand still instead of running when a masquerade chases after them, as if in failing to recognize its presence, they can be somehow unaffected by it."

"You're a fool, Ihechi, and you say a lot of rubbish. How can I pray so much for a Rick Blaine or a Jay Gatsby and end up with your numbskull?"

"Rick Blaine was ugly! But what do I know? You said it right, I'm a numbskull."

"You're not a numbskull for thinking Rick Blaine is ugly; you're a numbskull because you don't understand that I pray for Rick Blaine and Jay Gatsby because what I really want is for someone to love me without shame or fear." She started giggling, but I was unsure whether to join in. I tried to kiss her forehead, but she tiptoed backward, and when I tried to hold her hand, she retreated farther. "But it's all right. I'm also a fool for being so wishful with my prayers. We're just birds of the same foolish feather flocking together."

"Well, for what it's worth, I think your feathers are beautiful."

"Because I said we're birds of the same feather? Never mind, I came out so I could go piss. Go and get some more smoke and be back here to take me inside, like the gentleman Gatsby would." I knew Rick Blaine from *Casablanca*, one of her favorite films, but I still had not figured out the Jay Gatsby character she was referring to, and I was not ready to ruffle her feathers, however foolish and beautiful we agreed they were.

I watched her walk away before I embarked on my errand. There was still a crowd on the street. People in clusters, standing and smoking, seated and playing draught, idle and out of place. Within a minute I had sighted and approached a vanity vendor. A few heads turned as we bickered over prices but were quickly recaptured by the previous jailer of their attention. I had already paid for and collected the smoke but was waiting on my change when I noticed two men in an altercation farther down the road. One man's trousers were jacked up by the belt by the other, who was half-wrestling and half-bargaining his way out of a public embarrassment. It looked very similar to the incidents of military men manhandling civilians that we'd all witnessed from the safety of bus windows while returning from our escapades. A few more men gathered, and the altercation escalated into a stick-and-fist melee. I had just turned to the realization that my smoke vendor had run off with my change when I heard the first gunshots. Torches of fire began lighting up the far end of the street, pushing the entire crowd in a stampede toward the Afrika Shrine, and anybody not already intoxicated by smoke or alcohol was fueled by fear. Then I felt a sudden jab to my left side. Instinctively, I spun on the balls of my feet and held on to the weapon before it could be withdrawn. It had neither the solid mass nor the sharpness necessary to cause any serious damage, and it was not until I saw the pitiful face attached to it that I realized the error of my judgment and let go of the stranger's straying arm. I wiped off the beads of sweat that had gathered on my eyebrow with my forefinger and continued moving forward.

I tried returning to the rendezvous point Zeenat had set with me. I turned the corner, away from the crowded street, and onto the dark dirt road. I slowed my pace. There were five men in uniform about a dozen paces away from me. I fluttered my eyelids in disbelief. The sight was as familiar as it was unwanted; these uniforms meant military men, and military men meant trouble.

I tried to remain calm and slowly retraced my steps; fretting never saved a life. But unfortunately, no one else shared my opinion; the entrance to the auditorium was already crammed with people fleeing the sounds of gunfire, creating a confluence of terror on the streets. More torches lit up, not just flaming sticks but cars and vanity vendors' wooden marts. More gunshots sounded, and the only audible word amid the screaming was "*Soldiers!*" I searched the crowd for Zeenat, Mendaus, Pastor's son, Atonye, or any familiar face. Alone in the crowd, I surged through the riot, pillars of smoke towering overhead and bloodied soil underfoot, thrusting forward to evade the desperate grasp of death reaching out for me.

It was possible that my mother had not noticed that Atonye had fiddled with her òrìsà statuettes and replaced them in different spots. It was also very possible that she'd never noticed the darkened patch on the rug in front of the studio where Zeenat had vomited. And even if she had noticed, she never whispered a word. But when I had stumbled into the house just before midnight, sweaty and out of breath, she hooted and tooted for an explanation.

"Ihechi, these people you're running around with, do they share the same values you do? Do they believe in Ifá?"

"Mummy, this has nothing to do with Ifá. These are the same friends I've had for years, and I haven't changed since."

"What rubbish, change? Listen to yourself. You've started talking back at me when I'm talking to you, *abi*? They are the ones who will change you. It's already happening, and you're too stupid to see it. Your father was right, how wouldn't you come home smelling of smoke every day? You're listening to Bob Marley and going for Fela concerts, *abi?*" She had started out yelling, but her voice was now whittling into a teary tone.

"Fela and Bob Marley are not the reasons why the world burns, they are the reasons it doesn't burn to the ground."

"Well, go ahead, fools meet fools at the burial of a fool," she said with an air of finality, then walked out of the room.

The next morning, from my bedroom window, I saw Pastor's son trek past my house to the street vendors, and the tensed knot that had lodged in my throat through the night dissolved. He was safe. The newspapers had carried news of the military's siege on an anti-government gathering at the Afrika Shrine the previous night. Soldiers had contained the situation peacefully, despite the riot triggered by the anti-government anarchists on their arrival. The article had reported about a dozen injured victims but no casualties. My mother spat anonymous curses in the name of *Esu* as she read the headlines and declared my house arrest.

I did not move from my bedroom window for the rest of the day, hoping to see Zeenat or Mendaus and quell the last of my fears. And about midday, Mendaus's lonesome figure appeared on the dirt road's horizon. He was still wearing his clothes from the previous day. He did not grin, as he usually did when he approached my house and sighted me by the window. And when I gestured to him that I could not make it out, his features showed no reaction. He scribbled a note with a pencil and paper he withdrew from his pocket and lodged it in the narrow space at the side of my gate. I was on my way before he was finished writing, but by the time I got to the gate, he was gone. I opened the note. My eyes widened, my knees buckled, and my heart jerked in my chest as the words dissolved into the blackness of my mind.

> ... Mr. Thomas found her body this morning in
> the gutter. Don't come over. I won't be home. I'll
> be here same time tomorrow ...

I sat in the living room all day, on the very same chair where Zeenat and I had cuddled the last time she was at my house. I did not cry. I refused to believe. I just stayed still, with my eyes shut, like the children at the beach whenever the masquerades came chasing. But the masquerades refused to go away. They taunted me with masks that bore different faces of Zeenat: her laugh, her pitiful eyes when she teased me into kissing her for the first time, the way she looked at me just before we separated in front of the auditorium the day before. Once again, my mother hooted and tooted without any reward, so she left me alone in the living room and didn't return until nine o'clock, when she put on the television for the NTA news.

"Today a series of reprisal riots occurred around Lagos, protesting what the rioters referred to as the massacre of innocent and peaceful civilians at the Afrika Shrine yesterday."

I looked up at the television. The reporter's face bore no emotion. During my life, I'd heard very little of death: He had moved around me often enough, but in quiet and subtle motions, so I never really knew till he was gone. This time he had stared me in the face, spared my life, and killed me in another way—and, as he had always done, left it to others to testify of his exploits.

"Civil rights groups and activists have spoken out against the siege and have pledged to make investigations to ascertain the severity of the allegations. Our efforts to contact the Lagos state government were futile. NTA news has live footage from the protest in front of the Afrika Shrine."

The video took a few minutes to start playing. A mob of men and women, adults and children, suited up and bare-chested, screaming obscenities and carrying placards, filled the entire screen. At the mountain of madness were chants of "We no go 'gree oh! We no go 'gree! Give us democracy, we no go 'gree!"

The next scene showed a gawky young man ahead of the crowd, his back to the camera to incite the mob.

"Our fathers, though once belittled, were given the responsibility to serve with heart and might, to defend our freedom, and to chart our route back to paradise. Our fathers, though once noble, were corrupted by power. They took to power ad hoc, shed blood ad nauseam, and plundered our coffers ad infinitum. Our fathers, though once our hope, became our fear. Fear, necessary to fuel their power over the zoo, once their jail, now their kingdom. Our fathers, though once the jailed, died as jailers. We, once heirs of paradise, live by choice as monkeys in a zoo. Monkeys, so described to signify inferiority and zoos, so described to signify poverty, war, and corruption. However, the only difference between our kind and the kind on the other side of the fence is resolve. Resolve necessary for a few to find a route, which, often trod, will become a footpath for all, to paradise. We, once victims of circumstance, should become protagonists of our own fate. So the labors of our heroes past shall not be in vain. And we, once princes of monkeys, shall die kings among men in paradise."

The mob broke into raucous noise, and it took a while for order to return. It was then that the gawky young man turned to face the camera, and I realized it had been Mendaus on the television all along. I looked at my mother from the corners of my eyes and watched for any reaction, shifting closer and closer to the edge of my seat. Mendaus continued in his insidious rage.

"Misplaced patriotism and the lies of our fathers, military and civilian, should not dissuade us from our purpose. If our fathers have no belief in liberty or value for integrity, can they tell us how to live honest and free? Take off your blindfolds and say to those doctors and professors, major generals and comrades— thank you for independence! Thank you for the ports of the coast and the crude oil of the Niger Delta! But a new kingdom has been born, and we shall rule for ourselves, not as princes of monkeys but as kings among men. And no puppet master in Paris or Moscow, in London or Washington, will sway our resolve. We shall beat our chests like gallant warriors and chant, 'The crown is our birthright, and the whole world could never wrestle it away.'"

"You're not going to be any part of this madness," my mother said with an outburst. I turned toward her and noticed the tears streaming down her cheeks. "Nigeria does not need heroes. Nigeria needs Ifá. Those who think Nigeria needs heroes should bring up their children to be heroes. They shouldn't steal my child."

I tried to think of an argument, something thoughtful and intelligent and perfectly suited for the moment, as Mendaus would, but before I could speak, she had smothered me in an embrace.

"Pack your things, Ihechi," she said. "You're leaving Lagos first thing tomorrow."

Part 2

1992

The season of rains was at its peak. Consequently, my journey to Enugu from Lagos was scheduled to be a tedious ten-hour foray across seven states. We set out just before daybreak. The transition of scenery in my window kept me aware of the journey's progression; more than anything else, it cured the banality of the trip, from the loud bus radio to the other passengers' nonstop chatter. Once we left the bus terminal, all I could see was high-rising sport utility vehicles and the high-rising buildings of Ikorodu Road. A few minutes later, the high-rise vehicles were substituted with sedans and motorcycles, and the high-rise buildings became duplexes and the occasional bungalow. I knew we had left the city center and were on its outskirts when the bungalows became a more permanent sighting and possessed prominent aesthetic differences from the others. The emulsion-coated cement walls of the city center were now mud or redbrick walls. Eventually, my windowpane was a continuous yarn of rich forestry knitted to the sky at the horizon by undulating green hills, cradling me to sleep.

Phantasmagoric scenes of Zeenat being trampled into a roadside gutter, Mendaus and Pastor's son scurrying among the human avalanche to escape the burning Shrine, and my mother's manic threats played through my head as I slept. Their voices echoed in my conscience, growing louder as I moved farther away, and their surreal arms strangled the air from my lungs as I tried to escape the torture of the dream, writhing in the dirt and sweat of the sweltering bus.

Not often enough, I was awakened by a barrage of knocks and backhanded jabs that would have been nothing short of bloody murder save for the glass windowpane between my assailants and me. My would-be assailants were children, of an age more suitable for classrooms than interstate highways, hawking cassava sleeves with coconut, banana bunches with groundnuts, oranges, and bread of all colors and sizes.

By sunset, the transition of scenery at the start of the journey had begun to reverse, till we eventually arrived in Enugu. My uncle Adolphus was already waiting at the bus station; he seemed to recognize me as soon as I dropped down from the stairs of the vehicle. He had my father's face, which, in a way, was my face. But his was neither as clear and calm as mine nor as bruised and bitter as my father's; his was wrinkled and worn, yet it brimmed with life. And, of course, you couldn't help noticing his big, round belly. On that day, he was profoundly immersed in a short-sleeve suit, looking set to occupy my just vacated seat on its return journey and take Lagos by storm.

"Ihechi, yes?" he asked, placing a heavy right hand on my shoulder.

"Yes, sir. Good evening, Uncle Adolphus."

"*Hian!* That's not me," he sneered. "I am Adol, Uncle Adol. It is those who were born yesterday or those who are going to die tomorrow that you call by their full name."

"Yes, sir. Good evening, Uncle Adol," I corrected.

His frown somersaulted. "Your mother says there's nothing

but a sack of sawdust between those ears," he declared in a thick accent quite unfamiliar to me. "Is your mother a liar?"

"No, sir. No, Uncle Adol." I had found my huge box among the disembarked luggage and was now following his lead to his parked car.

He stopped and turned to me; his frown had returned. "No to your sawdust or no to your mother?"

It was a no-win question, so I chose the safer defeat. "No to my mother, sir, my mother is not a liar."

"Oh, you're a failure! I'm sure your mother is a liar. Trust me, I knew her before you. At least now I know you're a liar, too. A hen cannot lay guinea fowl eggs, after all." He was smiling once again; it was difficult for me to keep up. "Or should I blame your failure on your sawdust?"

From that moment, I decided the only safe choice for his no-win questions was no choice at all. Throughout the car ride to his place, he pointed at different buildings, speaking of them with a staunch surety that I had read about them in books or magazines in Lagos; Sunshine Guest House, the old government house, Polo Park.

As we drew closer to the house, he spoke more of its majesty. The house had originally belonged to my grandfather. It was my grandfather's prized possession partly because he was the first person from the Igbokwe clan to acquire a house in the then-blooming town of Enugu, but also partly because it was his only possession of any actual value. When my great-grandfather died, my grandfather sold off his inheritance, which was an enormous acreage of land, as soon as the burial rites were over, and married his teenage sweetheart before migrating from the rural life of Udi to partake in the urbanization of the state capital powered by the coal boom. But since his parameters for success were outlined by the shortsightedness of his rural upbringing, the pinnacle of his luxury was a nightly gourd of palm wine and a nose full of nicotine. My father, Cletus, was the second fruit of the newlywed couple's youthful exuberance, coming only eleven months after the first boy, Adolphus. It was shortly after Adolphus's birth that they moved into the great house.

But alas! My grandfather apparently shared his miserly parameters for success with his sons. I had observed that my father proffered many apologies and yet few solutions. He had definitely inherited that trait from his father, because my uncle had greatly exaggerated: The house was an apology of a shelter, the perfect illustration of my observation. Its mud brick walls were the physical manifestation of the fallen legacy of the British colonial era from whence it originated. Its cubic frame was fashionably misplaced in time, and it stuck out of the wide expanse of dusty ground like a lone piece of meat in a barren pot of soup.

My uncle circled the anthill in front of the house and managed to fit his Volvo in the little space between the anthill and the house. A woman came through the doorway and descended the stairs, which seemed a more recent part of the building and accommodated the devilish slope carved out by some form of erosion. She helped my uncle's door open and kissed him on his cheek: my aunt, I assumed. She was taller and heftier than he was, yet she eased into his arms as hot omelets would ease into a fresh loaf of bread. It would take me some time to get used to her toothy smile, but eventually, it would become my fondest memory of her. Two more people appeared at the doorway: One came closer, but not as close as my aunt, while the other stayed fastened to the doorpost like a hinge.

"Eh, Ihechi, this is your aunt Kosiso," my uncle announced as if her mere presence was a trophy being awarded to me, "and eh, these are your cousins, Thessalonians and Ephesians—that is, if your mother ever mentioned them to you."

My mother had actually spoken of my cousins quite often. She would always ask my father who had just finished which level of school, and who was writing which exam, and who was receiving which government scholarship, and then she would relay the information to me with the confidence of the newscasters on the network news, as if the òrìsà required her declaration to permit these events to come to pass. But she had always spoken of my cousins Tessy and Effy, never of Thessalonians and Ephesians.

"Nnọ, oh. Welcome," Aunt Kosiso said, "oya, Tessy, come and help your brother with his load."

Tessy was the one who had been standing at the summit of the steps. She waited for me to lug my box up the stairs before sharing the weight, while Effy was still role-playing the door hinge; her eyes remained fixed on me as I walked past. She looked a few years younger than Tessy, who was probably around my age.

The sun set after it confirmed we were all safely indoors. When I returned from a shower, Aunt Kosiso had served out a feast of *eba* and *ofe nsala*. Everyone was invited to eat in the parlor and even washed hands in the same bowl, unlike my house in Lagos. There was a television in the middle of a collage of framed family photographs on the wall, but we watched a foreign show that had English subtitles, not the network news, even when nine o'clock arrived. Uncle Adol would laugh till he choked and then beat his chest furiously. Aunt Kosiso would scurry across the room to lift his cup of water, which was right in front of him, to his lips. Tessy would laugh as loud as her father, though not as deep-toned. And Effy only smiled occasionally. They all had audaciously chiseled bodies and moved around the house half-naked, draped in loose ankara wrappers. And though I fell asleep for the first time in Enugu among mere men, I perceived, within my dreams, myself floating with higher powers. The Igbo language they spoke was familiar but indiscernible, their bold and everlasting laughter pulled at the seam of the four corners of the house, the majesty of their poise in action was seemingly rehearsed, and they constantly acknowledged the unquestionable superior among them all—the father, to whom homage was paid in all speech and deed.

My mother had not told me how long the dream was going to last—it could be a month, a year, or whenever I became old enough to be responsible for all of my choices. I just wanted the dream to fast-forward through its scenes and hurry me to the end, like the phases of a trance, so I could be woken up at the end, when I could return to Lagos and rummage around for Zeenat through the carnage of the riot, feel for her through the gyration of the Shrine faithful who would surely gather again when the mourning and protests were over, seek her among the faces of the millions of strangers in Lagos, taking solace in every unseen face as each upheld an extra probability of Zeenat being alive, to the very end, where I could share smoke and once-in-a-lifetime cocktails achieved by trial and error with Mendaus and hoist him up on my shoulders when he got fired up, so the whole room could watch him declare the injustices of a generation of Nigerian leaders, while Pastor's son echoed the final word of his every sentence in drunken passion. But that night I nestled into a comfy sleep because I knew that despite my desperation, there was no way the dream would end on the other side of midnight.

Every man had to love peppered snails. A little boy may be pardoned, but for a Nigerian man of full growth, justified by the drop of his pockets as much as the dropping of his testicles, an endearment to peppered snails is a scientific constant, just like the speed of light, and if I was expecting anything near to a tangible inheritance, I could have sworn by it all that my thought would soon be backed up by some kind of biological research. I had made brisk acquaintance of all pepper matters during my visits to the Shrine: Alcohol and pepper were hand in glove.

I hated the fact that there was a crowd around my table, and a hungry lot at that, so I stole away with my plate of peppered snails and watched from the corner of the hall as people danced to no music at all. The faces were blurry, and all but the location seemed vaguely familiar. No Mendaus and no Pastor's son in sight, but then again, I suspected it was the peppered snails playing tricks with my mind.

I clenched a fat piece of the rubbery flesh between the hinges of my jaw and tugged fiercely, all to no avail. The pepper remained rigid, chiseling away the caves of my molars instead of dissolving into the saliva, and the snail itself was throwing musty knockout jabs at my nose.

My eyelids bolted open, and I spat Effy's big toe out of my mouth, cursing through the viscous drool. I had spent five days in Enugu and had suffered one dream or another every single night. There was a power outage again, and the bedsheet was damp with sweat, which would add another layer of tint to the brownish-white color of the sheets by morning. I adjusted my sleeping position so our heads and feet aligned each with the other, and then my mind tried to clasp on the images of my dream before it diffused into obscurity.

I was not certain if it was because of the pepper from my dreams or some other machination of my past, but the very moment I caught up with fleeting sleep, I heard whispers by the window. My head bobbled around in the darkness, and that continued even as I opened my eyes and struggled for focus. Before I could pinch myself, Tessy had risen up from the bed we all shared and unlocked the window latch to let in what looked like a girl. I could not believe anyone had the boldness to climb through windows in the dead of the night. Such possibilities were confined to the crazy people in Zeenat's movies. I refused to believe windows existed without burglary-proof steel bars in the death trap that is the Nigerian night. But of all the possibilities I refused to believe, none compared to the ugliness of the girl Tessy had let into the room as I flicked on my torch in her direction. Bidding good morrow to lies and deception, she was by far the most unattractive girl I had seen in a while. Her disproportionate eyes bulged so much they were almost falling out of her head, which sat atop the broadest of torsos tapering down to the narrowest of hips. She seemed to have accepted the verdict of nature's condemnation, as she'd made only a haphazard attempt at looking presentable in her body-hugging red dress.

"*Idebe ya*, keep it," said Tessy in a hushed scold, "ọsọ ọsọ." I turned off the torch quickly and withdrew into the corner.

"Is that the Lagos *bobo*?" asked the stranger.

Tessy nodded, and they both giggled. Tessy untied her

wrapper and began replacing it with a black dress the stranger removed from her back.

"Don't you know better than to look at a girl's nakedness?" Tessy asked, her voice still hushed but not as harsh, more tease than scold. I flushed with shame and lay back on the bed.

"He's a Lagos *bobo*," added the stranger. "He's probably seen it all before."

I had not seen it all before. I had not seen it before or after Zeenat. And the thought of Zeenat had me wrought with collywobbles. The girls tugged and pinned their dresses into a perfect fit and then painted and patted at their faces as they giggled some more. Slowly but surely, Tessy transformed from *mgbeke* to *ọmalicha*, local girl to fair lady. No word seemed worth the effort; she was finer than my finest compliments. And without a word from anyone else in the room, Tessy opened the window again, and they both went out just as the stranger had come in.

As she had every day since I arrived, Aunt Kosiso came in to wake us up just before daybreak. My eyes were smoky, so I rubbed them with my hands. As things got clearer, I saw Tessy yawn and stretch in her night wrapper, and when Aunt Kosiso left the room, she brought out two fifty-naira notes from the fold of her wrapper and squeezed them into my palm. That was the first bribe I ever received in my life.

The old house, which still felt very much new to me even after I had been there almost a year, gave me new memories of old feelings I had not experienced in a long time—as far back as primary school, before my father lost his job and his spirit broke like a calabash, before my mother's fervent attempts to soak up his hopes and happiness lest the earth dry him out and he return to dust, before my mother became so fixated on lifting him up that she was unaware how much her tensed grip strangled me. I did not have to proofread my thoughts before replying to questions in this old house because they communicated with words, not silent grudges and sudden bursts of aggression. Uncle Adol adamantly corrected me into calling it my home whenever I referred to it as his house. Tessy, on the other hand, suggested that I call it my house, since the house was going to be passed down the Igbokwe bloodline somehow, and Uncle Adol had no sons. Aunt Kosi did not have opinions on such issues. She would rather pun on the idea that I preferred to use water to clean my buttocks instead of toilet paper and call me into the living room when her friends visited so she could have them ooh and aaah as I habitually pressed my forefinger to the ground to greet them in the Yoruba way.

The Yoruba greeting was the least obnoxious takeaway my mother had sent with me to Enugu—there were the òrìsà figurines she had sneaked into my travel bags. I had always despised the way she and my father carelessly shunned my opinion and casually forced their opinions on me. But I had taken after them, slowly growing into exactly what I always despised, in the manner by which I casually shunned my mother's figurines and her opinions on spirituality. And even though I had not formed a complete opinion on spirituality, I knew enough to know what I did not want, part of which was Ifá. Neither did I subscribe to bastardized versions of other foreign religions that exploited our diversity. Classism and tribalism were peddled with subliminal subtlety underneath the religious propaganda. And more than anything else, religion served as a hallucinogen for the poor and desperate who needed an excuse to live, hoping one day they would find solace in the realization of their dreams, and for the lazy who needed an excuse not to work hard, hoping some figment of their imagination fashioned of the supernatural sort would miraculously make an interrealm deposit into their purses. And for the dishonorable who had been caught in the act, hoping mercy would prevail against the thought of their bodies swinging loose and lifeless from the prison yard's mango tree. Religion was not for people like me, who were really just trying to find God.

I had witnessed people around me pursue different gods to different ends, and I had come to understand the kind of relationship I would want with my God, even though I had not found Him yet. I wanted to have the devotion of a Muslim: to awake with fervor by five every morning to whisper my loyalty to my God and at least four other times in the day without my spirit ever getting weary of it. I wanted to feel as inclusively as a Christian: to love those who agreed with me as much as those who disagreed, to love selflessly, which is to live above greed. To love enemies as mercifully as friends, never believing I was the hand of God to mete out judgment on His behalf, and even if the hand of God fell off by whatever incidence, I would not be a worthy replacement. I wanted to communicate as personally as an Ifá faithful: not strictly adhering to the black and white of religious diktats, but being aligned with the spirit of my God, hearing His whispers in the sway of trees, the colors of the sky, and the patterns of cowries, just as He heard the whispers in the groans of my heart, the worries of my mind, and the madness of my methods. There were more things I thought I wanted, more I thought I needed, and even more I was sure I could do without, of which the first was following a religion simply out of pity. I buried my mother's figurines at the bottom of my box. And when Effy came across them in an episode of mischief, I denied their original purpose with the calm shrug of a man who would deny having anything more than a platonic relationship with a woman who seemed underwhelming to his friends.

Still, I treaded carefully. Effy's episodes of mischief were never standalone incidents, always occurring in a series until she was thwarted by Aunt Kosi, who was as clever as a Baudelaire orphan. I had already heard of the infamous affair when Effy soaked the bottom of her school uniform in red palm oil, claiming she'd menstruated for the first time in class and was having cramps. Aunt Kosi allowed her to stay home from school for a whole week. The hoax was uncovered when she claimed to be menstruating barely two weeks later, and Aunt Kosi discovered she had learned about puberty in integrated science class and was exploiting the perks of her newfound knowledge. The week I arrived, Effy had stolen a few pieces of meat from the pot and insisted that she never would have done it if not for the voice of the Holy Spirit that had urged her on. Knowing that Uncle Adol would never tolerate any brutality on his children, Aunt Kosi had mastered the art of sneaking into her children's room in the dead of the night to enforce discipline, and the night Effy stole meat from the pot was not a shade different. Aunt Kosi huffed and puffed and slapped and knocked, and Effy cried quietly, mucus hanging from the cliff of her philtrum and threatening to skydive every time her body quaked in sorrow. Neither Tessy nor I dared to make a sound.

Soon enough Effy realized that the figurines were a bigger deal than I had initially admitted, and her awareness of them was more of a secret than common knowledge, a secret to be kept at a price. She demanded that I give her a token every month to buy her loyalty. I bluffed and told her I had long since changed their hiding place. She laughed a bit too huskily for her age, calling out the impossibility of it and demanding an increase in the value of her monthly token. I rebuffed her again and walked away, to the bedroom, specifically, to indeed change the hiding place of my figurines. But they were gone! I hurried back to Effy; there was not much left to be said. That was the first time I gave a bribe.

The nights Tessy disappeared through the window were usually on Fridays. On Saturdays, Uncle Adol dillydallied for an hour or two longer in bed while the rest of us swept and mopped and cleaned. Aunt Kosiso assigned chores to Tessy, Effy, and me as we filed out of our single bedroom, and in between our perambulation of house to abolish all speckles, she would point and scream more errands during errands.

When her orders were not dominating the entire house, we would be able to hear the music tapes she played from the radio in the living room. The music was different from anything I had heard before, and the cassette case was like nothing I had seen. On the case was a caricature of a woman, half black and half white, but beautiful, with her full hair and colorful makeup. On the top right of the case was the name Chaka Khan, and on the bottom left, *I Feel for You*. The music itself had a less frequent drum pattern than Afrobeat, and somewhere in between the soulful voice and jazzy instrumentals was a certain funk I was altogether unfamiliar with. I had to skim through *Crossroads* by Tracy Chapman and *Whitney* by Whitney Houston before I entered the familiar territory of Oliver De Coque and Osita Osadebe.

"Don't you have any Afrobeat?" I asked Tessy, and when her face contorted into a quizzical stare, I added, "Fela Kuti? Lagbaja?"

"Oh! Yoruba music," she said with the enthusiasm of a block of cement, and then she bent over and continued her sweeping.

Aunt Kosiso walked into the room and became livid. "Ihechi, is this why you're here? Igbo men are not usually lazy like this, oh, *abi*, you have spent so much time in Lagos that you have forgotten who you are?"

"He has spent too much time listening to Yoruba music, his brain is now soft," Tessy added.

"Ihechi!" Aunt Kosiso shouted, using her hand to pull her right ear open for emphasis, "the fact that a man swims in a river does not mean he should call the crocodile 'father.' A word is enough for the wise."

Every misplaced word or step I made for the rest of the day was attributed to Lagos or the Yoruba. They did not slander out of any feeling of spite or superiority, but as if their stereotypes were facts set in stone. They could not be dissuaded that they were in every way different from the Yorubas. The geographical divides set out by the imperial masters had been transferred from paper to ponds and parcels of land. These people had eaten up the paper and drunk the ink outlining our segregation, and now it had been absorbed into their blood, creating a slavery of the mind as real as the slavery of our forefathers.

After we all had our dinner, Aunt Kosiso called me outside to sit with her on the stairs in front of the house. She made small talk as she separated the chaff from the beans in the tray on her lap, about how much more expensive things were getting in the market, and how she had been trying to convince Uncle Adol to open a store for her at the market so she could earn some money of her own. When she laughed, I laughed, and when she complained, I looked on with all seriousness.

Then she hit the nail on the head: "Did your father ever tell you anything about the war?"

"My father did not tell me much about anything," I replied. "My father did not entertain chitchat except when it stood the chance of earning him money. Most times he talked about work with my mother because it earned him money, or he talked about school with me because it could earn him money in the future." I did not add that my relationship with him, save for these two topics, was a blend of bitter memories brewed from an eternity of unvoiced sentiments—and as with aging wine, the strength of the brew had increased with the passage of time.

"I cannot blame him. Parts of you die when you go through all that your father went through during the war and after it ended."

She started telling me from the very beginning what my father should have done a long time ago to allay the distempers of his soul, when the people of Enugu started gathering at marketplaces and schools and talk of a war was circulating with the wind. It was around the same time word started going around about some sort of rebellion. Comrade Odumegwu Ojukwu became a household name, not as the governor of the eastern region of Nigeria anymore, but as the head of state of a sovereign eastern region, and the Federal Republic of Biafra replaced the Federal Republic of Nigeria in conversational lingo. Then people started coming in from the north and the west, the north especially. There were stories of how the Igbos, our people, were being slaughtered like Ramadan cattle. Most of them brought along stories of destroyed towns and villages, each predicting the Nigerian military's certain arrival. Biafra was just purgatory until the Nigerian bullets came to convey them all to their afterlife destinations. All of them brought ghosts of dead friends and family. Children played with their friends' ghosts, wives reserved rations for their husbands' ghosts, and husbands recited love poems in whispers to the ghosts of their wives. Finally, as anticipated, the head of state of Nigeria, General Yakubu Gowon, declared war on the breakaway region of Biafra, and all hell, from demon to shoulder minion, broke loose.

Aunt Kosiso had dropped the tray of beans on the ground beside her and was now fiddling with the edges of her wrapper, poking the frayed cloth at her eye. Then she continued about how those of them in Enugu who were farther away from the borders of the region felt the hunger but not the violence of the war until after the first months. And when they eventually did, the Nigerian army still appeared as bloodthirsty as freshly weaned bloodhounds.

Then she told me of the afternoon in the market. She didn't remember the name of the market, but every other detail was crystalline—very awkward, given the fact that she wasn't even there. The sun hovered oppressively low over the stalls at the market, illuminating the colorful array of fruits and foodstuff arranged in the different stalls. "But since we are Biafrans, the sun only nourished and beautified our skins," she said, quoting my uncle Adol, the original teller of the story. My father, Cletus, had followed his mother to the market that day to collect rations that had been flown in over the weekend. The mishmash of dirt, which had become one with the landscape, and the stench, so dense it was almost visible, were not the most enticing of experiences, but nobody ever complained. Repetition had its way of converting things from unbearable to tolerable and then acceptable. The characteristic chatterbox mood of the market had been substituted with solemnity because of the previous day's incident. News had spread of the five bombings in Umuahia by Nigerian warplanes, hitting a Red Cross camp and vehicle, a hospital, and a market. The word was that twenty people had been killed at another market in the small village of Eziama Mbano, about twelve miles east of Orlu. Another two miles from Orlu, at Umuowa, the Red Cross headquarters for Biafra was completely demolished, even though it had large red crosses distinctively marked on the roof, on the ground, and on vehicles, and was flying an enormous flag bearing the emblem. The people's faith in the rebellion's strength and ambition had been dwindling, and the bombings proved its vulnerability and the folly of sending their sons and husbands to fight for the godforsaken cause.

The white reverend father from the Anglican cathedral in town was in the next stall, encouraging the women there to be steadfast in their prayers. He told them the eyes of the Lord weren't blind to their sufferings, His ears weren't deaf to their prayers, His arm wasn't shortened that He couldn't stretch it out to save them. Perhaps he underestimated the hunger for power that dwelled in the Nigerian heart. A moment later, he was preaching his message of hope to another pair of women. At the next stall, the trader and her customer were already exchanging opinions on what had happened at Eziama Mbano, based on what they had gathered from hearsay. The trader began describing to her customer how the plane had circled the Eziama Mbano market for about ten minutes, dropping bombs on the women and children, rotating her horizontally set palm in a circular motion and using her mouth for sound effects. For a moment it sounded so real, but suddenly, he couldn't hear her anymore—her voice was drowned in a sea of screams. Cletus began hearing a loud groan, what he later learned was the engine of the Nigerian Ilyushin jet. The terror on the faces around him was hellish, and at the sight, he let out a maddening shriek before bursting into tears. His mother looked up to the sky to catch a glimpse of the jets, and almost immediately, she was shoved over by a charging trader. She struggled to her feet and joined the stampede.

They hadn't gotten past the first stall when he heard the loud noise, and the ground trembled. After that, he heard nothing else and felt nothing else. The dust rising from the sandy ground was choking, so he couldn't smell anything, either. He could only taste the dust in the air and see the unfolding carnage. Some people headed straight for the bushes while some were running into the nearby police building. A few seconds later, a trail of smoke landed on the flag that stood atop the building, and it exploded into a raging fire. The burning flag still bore its emblem, that of the great rebel nation Biafra. Now everyone was heading into the bushes, but the ground trembled one more time, and Cletus saw drops of blood race past him. He looked back and saw his mother stagger behind him before dropping onto the sandy ground. His mouth opened to let out another shriek, but it was choked to silence by dust. He thought he heard his mother scream, but he wasn't sure. He stopped and tried turning around, but he felt strong fingers sink into his skin; they began pulling him away from his mother's body. He traced the fingers to a body and saw the pink face of the reverend father. The reverend dragged my father under the arms, just like he did to his Bible on Sunday mornings, and continued running. Cletus looked back at his mother for the last time, but he could see only her torso lying in an expanding pool of blood, trampled with the least degree of honor by her Biafran brothers and sisters. The ground trembled one more time, my father saw the reverend father clutch his rosary tight in his other hand, and then he blacked out.

"And after all of that happened before his very eyes," Aunt Kosiso concluded, "your father still opened his eyes and married one of them."

It was clear that as the imperial masters were kings and slave masters, so it was that tribalism was their unflagging horseman. And as observed by tradition in parts of Africa, the king's death must trigger the ritual suicide of his horseman, whose spirit would then guide the king to the afterlife. If the tradition was neglected for whatever reason, the king's spirit would wander the land and bring great terror to the people. When our imperial master died at independence, we failed to ensure his horseman justly committed suicide. Now the king roamed the land, in a spiritlike form less real and more apparent, entrapping minds and disrupting the balance of society by sowing ethnic hate. And through it all, no love was ever lost, and no love was ever found, because from the very beginning, no love existed.

I was never certain if it was wholly a Nigerian trait, but in every place in our country that I ever visited, most people in most conditions acted with the simple reason being that they should not. As Edgar Allan Poe, who never even set eyes on the beaches of Bonny, described it a long time ago, we were hounded by the imp of the perverse; it became absolutely irresistible that the assurance of wrong was the one unconquerable force that impelled us to its prosecution. What else would explain one of the world's largest producers of crude oil becoming a major importer of refined oil, or government contractors importing sand by the shipload into an African country? On the commoner's level, what else would make three-piece-suited men piss by the roadside, not into the gutter but facing traffic? And bringing the matter closer to home, what else would cause Effy to hold on to my figurines even after I admitted they were craven images of Yoruba gods?

The scare tactic had worked the week before, when Aunt Kosi used it against her. When Aunt Kosi went to pick her up from school, Effy's schoolteacher had reported that she was developing a keen fondness for boys. Aunt Kosi approached the issue with unusual tact.

"How many boys are in that class again?" she said as she served hot yams onto Effy's plate for lunch.

"Fifteen!" Effy replied excitedly, and obviously oblivious to her teacher's report.

"Just enough!" Aunt Kosi enthused. "You know you have started seeing your period, so if you allow a boy to touch you too much, you will just become pregnant." Effy looked puzzled, but her mother continued without even checking for her reaction. "And you know your father is a real Igbo man. Just allow twelve of those fifteen boys to touch you so you can have twelve children, only twelve! And your father would have to follow tradition and slaughter one goat by your waist to celebrate." For emphasis, Aunt Kosi crushed the butt of her kitchen spoon into the hot yams on Effy's plate, but with a subtlety that matched the tone of her voice. "Never mind the goat blood or the stink of the goat skin or even the twelve times you will have to go through labor pains, just keep your mind focused on all that goat meat that will be available for us to celebrate with." By the end of the week, Effy's teacher had to call in Aunt Kosi again. This time she was reporting that Effy had picked a fight with every single boy in class at least once within that week.

"Are you scared of a little blood?" I asked Effy on the afternoon I chose to implement my scare scheme. We had been watching *Living in Bondage*, a made-in-Nigeria home video. Most of the reviews about it were super: the disenchanting Andy and his ever devout wife, his ploy to murder her through juju for blood money, and how it was relatable to someone's father or another person's uncle. Aunt Kosi would never tolerate the slightest representation of anything that "sensitized our hearts to the devil," so we watched the video that Tessy had borrowed from Tobenna in the afternoon, when Aunt Kosi had gone to the market. Effy had threatened to report the matter if she was not allowed to see it with us. Tessy had no qualms about her watching if she agreed to wiping the backs of the television and the video player with a damp rag to keep them cool: Aunt Kosi always checked their temperature to know if and why they had been used in her absence, but as the hunter had learned to shoot without missing her children, the birds had learned to fly without perching.

Effy stood up to wipe the television down, shaking my question off, but I persisted: "You're scared of a little blood and juju and you're holding on to *Esu?* That's nice."

Later that night, long after the movie was over, when we were both alone in the bedroom preparing for bed and Tessy was clearing up in the kitchen, Effy inquired as if forced, "What's *Esu*, anyway?"

I smiled within but tried to match her level of disinterest on the outside. "The figurine you took from me, the one with the wide mouth, long and pointy nose, and the longer and pointier back of the head? The one covered with cowries from neck to toe? That's *Esu*."

"Nooo," she insisted. Her concern was creeping into the forehead creases on her babyish face. "What does it—*Esu*—have to do with blood and juju, is what I'm asking."

I was not yet sure I was in charge of the conversation, but I had to appear to be, so I acted like someone almost in charge, like Rhett Butler from *Gone with the Wind*. I squinted softly as I spoke, placed one hand on the other, and smiled with half my mouth. "*Esu* is a spirit, one of the gods of Yoruba juju. I don't know much about him, but when I asked my mother once, she said they said he was powerful, is *very, very* powerful, the link between heaven and earth."

"But what does that have to do with blood and the rest?"

"Well, she said he is the god of mischief, that he balances good and evil and makes sure they happen whenever necessary. If you have a car accident and drive into a wall but come out whole, then *Esu elegbara*—*Esu* is the owner of power—and if a truck rams you into the wall as you're stepping out of the wrecked car, then *Esu elegbara* also." She looked puzzled, but I continued. "When I asked my mother, she said that *Esu* once visited a village where the people had stopped praying to him, wearing his best cap, which was painted red on one side and black on the other. The villagers on one side of the road can't stop saying nice things about his red cap, and the neighbors on the other side of the road can't stop pointing out that even though the cap is as beautiful as they say, it is actually black. The argument turns into a fight that doesn't stop until the whole village is drowned in blood."

Tessy walked into the room as I said the final word, expanding my Rhett Butler half-smile to a full one in admiration of the dread all over Effy's face. "What's the story?" Tessy asked, and Effy replied as if the last five minutes of conversation had not happened: "Ihechi is making up stories for me because I told him I wasn't feeling sleepy," she said.

Now my whole face was dread-ridden, and she had the Rhett Butler half-smile on. But while I stayed up with Tessy discussing tapes produced by Lemmy Jackson, I heard Effy plead the blood of Jesus about a million times in her sleep.

The one thing all Nigerians have in common, regardless of how disparate in culture or location, is religious fervor. There were already hundreds of traditional deities even before the advent of Christianity and Islam, and those two still caught like smoke on cloth and were further tinkered with to create hundreds of other appropriations of faith. So I was not surprised that on Sunday mornings, the whole household took turns ironing the best from the bottom of their clothing boxes.

"Do you really believe in God?" I asked Effy as she fitted her dress in the mirror; she was barely four feet high, but she twirled every inch of it to dispel any myth that perfection was unachievable. "That out of the billions of people in this world,

He chose you to carry out a heavenly plan that could change life as we know it?"

"*Ehn*, I do believe in God. As a matter of fact, I think he chose every one of us in this world to execute some heavenly plan that could change life as we know it."

"No wonder nothing ever gets done in this Nigeria—we non-citizens of heaven procrastinate too much. Maybe heaven should get busy and stop depending on us to carry out their monkey business."

"You need Jesus!" Effy cried, her voice sounded like a puppy yet to be weaned. "I know you probably don't believe in blasphemy, but I do, so shush. A proper Holy Ghost baptism service would straighten you out."

Initially, I thought it was just sarcasm, but by the time the clock struck ten that morning, we were immersed in the desperate congregation, as only desperate people found God. I seemed to be getting a bit desperate myself, but not for God. I was desperate to be back in Lagos, to discuss vanities amid Afrobeat vibes and smoke with Mendaus and Pastor's son. I wanted Zeenat to exist in her entire person and not in my memories of her voice and laughter, or as skin crawling along my back and up my thigh in the lonely darkness of night. But chickens had not grown horns yet, and goats were not flying, so in church I was, a firebrand Pentecostal church which was just as out of place as a mosque would be in the predominantly Catholic Enugu.

We had come in together, but Tessy and Effy dropped into the pews in the back, and I followed suit as their parents went farther down the aisle to seek the unadulterated wholesome church experience. The choir's spirited ministration was still in procession, with occasional spittle-filled interjection from the preacher at the pulpit. And whether you paid attention to the lyrics or not, it was almost compulsory to bob from side to side in a two-move pendulum step just to keep up with the tempo of life in the room. Everything remaining still was inanimate. The violins and pipes could not be seen through the sea of raised hands, but their sounds bounced around the hall.

"Heaven speaks of your glory!" interjected the preacher, and the choir responded with a loud hum. "And the earth of your beauty!" he continued. "If I dance, it won't be enough! If I shout, it won't be enough!" The choir responded with a louder hum, and the congregation joined in this time. I looked at all the manifestations of absurdities around me—the man waltzing to the tune up and down the central aisle, hand in hand with thin air, the woman behind him rotating on a spot at no definite pace and making all sorts of guttural sounds, the elderly lady laying facedown on the floor, speaking into the terrazzo.

"You are the great and mighty God!" interjected the preacher. "You are worthy to be praised, faithful in all situations!" The choir hummed louder. "The joy of the whole world!" I caught a glance of Effy kneeling before the altar, the single stream of tears on her face reflecting the bright lights from the front of the hall.

Suddenly, the lead guitarist ripped away from the pendulum pace, and all other instruments faded into a supporting role as the raw sound of electric harmony shocked the congregation into a frenzy. My heart was heavy, acknowledging the presence of a higher power that my base knowledge of physics could not explain, and I felt guilty for not tendering enough consciousness to it.

I fiddled my hands in my pockets, trying to regain my swagger, and felt a cigarette. Without a single thought, I fitted the cigarette in between my lips and made for the church exit. The sound of worship overshadowed my every step, quickening the pace of my heart, and just before I took a plunge into the sunlight outside, I turned back one more time, long enough to catch Effy's teary face staring at me. I turned away from her, the church, that world, into one I was more familiar with. I pulled a lighter from the back pocket of my jeans as I walked onto the street and fingered the ignition for a bit, to no avail. I stopped midstride in frustration.

"You're shaking so much," I heard from behind me. "Have you never been to church before, or have you never lit a cigarette before?" It was Tessy. She was standing just outside the church gates, right by the side of the road, where a blue sedan was parked; with her was the ugly friend from the window-scaling night. She waved at the blue sedan, and it drove off.

"I light cigarettes every other day. It's just that lately, my other days have been few and far between." The lighter spat a blue flame in time to buttress my point. "I've just never been to this type of place."

"You complain when they have not even started," the ugly friend said. "You know how to make *moi moi okwia?* The level they are at inside is the level of going to buy the beans. They are still going to wash the beans, grind the beans, and wrap the beans inside the leaf before even cooking the beans. So I really can't understand where you are rushing to." We all laughed out loud. When we quieted, I offered my smoke to the girls, but they both refused.

"And both of you who are used to the *moi moi,* why are you not in there with the rest of them, buying and washing and grinding?" I asked.

"Well, it's hard to explain this in terms of *moi moi*." It was Tessy talking again. Her voice was lazy, and as she spoke, her left palm floated around her face as if ushering the words out of her mouth. "But let me put it this way: They prepare theirs with chunks of beef mixed with the beans, and I'd rather have mine with chunks of boiled eggs. So at that point of disagreement, we part ways."

The ugly friend attempted to reiterate Tessy's point. "I believe in God, I've seen too much to doubt His existence. For sure, He is not my best friend, but we talk every other day, as you would put it. Now, these men of God—apostles, prophets, evangelists, and all other names—a fair share of them have turned Christianity into a business. And since it's easier to brainwash an audience with one soul and one common need than it is to diversify an audience from different backgrounds with different needs, they carve out a section of the audience and tailor their own gospel to that part of the audience with one need. So now one prophet carries most of the businessmen, because his God is the Jehovah who protects the containers of goods on the high seas, and another apostle carries most of the young people, because his God is the Jehovah who gives university admission and success in examinations. Every problem now has its own man of God ascribed to it. But the saddest part is that half the containers still sink at sea or get impounded by customs at the port, and half the students don't get admission into universities. That's not the God I know, and that's not the God I'm looking for. I'm looking for the God who heals the sick, raises the dead, and answers when those who believe in Him call upon Him with faith."

"But if you know this God already, why are you still looking for him?" I asked.

"It's a paradox," Tessy replied. "To know God and still search after Him. If you are searching for God, then it means you already know Him because He is the beginning of all things. He is the one who puts in us that desire to search Him out in the first place." She added, "You know we didn't always come to this church. Our fathers were born Catholics. The only reason we still attend this church is because his friend claimed he got a miracle job a month after he began coming here, and it worked for my father, too, even though his own miracle job took a year before it came around."

"I'm just tired of Christians blaming God and not themselves," said the ugly friend, who seemed to have put together what was left of her serenity. "Wretchedness is creeping into all our lives, and we are singing and dancing. The church keeps breeding more millionaires to buy more vanities and fewer disciples to preach and pray."

"But you can't make a faithful man out of a hungry man," I said. "It doesn't have to do with just religion. No matter what you tell a man or promise him or even put in his hands, if it doesn't quench his hunger, he will still be forced to do whatever it takes to put food in his mouth before he goes to bed. Faith doesn't feed a man."

"Yes, it does," Tessy replied. "It just depends on where your faith lies."

The ash of my cigarette fell onto my fingers; I had not noticed it smolder away, since I had left it unromanced, and I made no efforts to blow it off. The spark Tessy had lit was burning in me hotter than anything on the surface could. My understanding of faith had been wrong for too long, but Tessy had finally gotten it right. It was not faith that fed a man but, rather, what kept him

searching for that fruit tree in the wilderness. It was that urge
in the wanderer to keep searching for the footpath through the
steep valleys and the impetus in a drowning soul to keep his eyes
fixed above the waves. It was not Mendaus's faith in Nigeria that
would change the lot of the people, but it was what gave him the
courage to challenge the authority that fashioned the lot of the
people. Just as there was no way Zeenat's faith in me alone could
have made me a better person, unless her faith acted in tandem
with my desire to justify her love which her faith in me created.
Faith in Ifá was not what gave my mother any victory but what
kept her fighting, and the loss of faith in everything was what
had knocked my father out of his own battles. I was more like
my father than I would have been eager to admit; I had no faith
in anything, I had no conviction, I was a fickle shrub with no
roots holding me firm to anything, an impending tale of woe if
perchance the wind of desolation crossed my path.

I had never witnessed the manifestation of masculinity in such a
real form until the day Uncle Adol bought a generator. He drove
into the compound unannounced, with the machine bound to
the Volvo, half out of the vehicle trunk like an erect penis peeping from its trap at the beginning of a porn flick. He strode
out of the car as ego-pumped as a Mandingo. Not expecting
to hear the hum of his engine so early in the afternoon, Aunt
Kosi had rushed from the kitchen at the back of the house to
the front veranda, past Tessy and me lazing in the living room,
clutching only her wrapper to her chest. We caught up with her
making her way down the front stairs, gaping awestruck at the
equipment her husband was packing. After we unpacked it and

turned it on, Uncle Adol's chest puffed as if the loud roar of the generator were adulation, the solution to our every problem, as if its noise did not make us shout so we could be audible in conversations, as if the energy required to pull the ignition cord would not ordinarily sustain me for a year.

Unlike Tessy and me, who got around more, Aunt Kosi had never seen a generator, only having heard testimonies from her braggadocio market-going mates. Now, understand she never put pressure on her husband to buy one, not necessarily because she was content or incapable of sufficient nagging but because a generator was one of those things you never needed until you had it. I mean, why would Aunt Kosi need to put on the generator so she could pick beans under a ceiling fan in the living room while watching television, when all her life she had been fine picking beans while listening to BBC broadcasts over the radio and sitting on the veranda in the evening breeze? It was simple: The luxury of ignorance catered to the absence of all other luxuries.

Depending on whether you decide to recognize the glass of water as half full or half empty, you could also recognize that as ignorance is the greatest luxury, so is knowledge the greatest misery. It was this misery that appeared to plague Effy. Ever since the night I'd told her the true nature of the figurines, the night she had proved so unbothered by the consequences of her theft, she had become a fragile pile of nerves that crumbled into a trembling avalanche of tears and terror at any mention of the gruesome. When she was reading the abridged version of *King Solomon's Mines* for her English class, she screwed up her face at any mention of Gagool's magic, and if the pastor in church spoke about hell, she wept fire and brimstone.

I had no clue her fear would drive her to get rid of the figurines. I did not notice when she bundled them up in a worn-out rag and threw them over the fence, and when I asked her why she was crying in the evening, tucked away in the bedroom while the rest of the family was watching television after dinner, she was not willing to confide that the figurines had somehow made their way back to the spot where she had hidden them before. I was not even aware when she left the compound the next day, going as far as the garbage dump three streets away to leave the figurines, and when I asked her why she was crying for a second consecutive evening, she hinted that she was having menstrual cramps. Not even *Esu* himself could have drawn my mind to think that she was crying because the figurines had found their way once again to the place where she had hidden them. And I never would have guessed she'd have the guts to douse the figurines in kerosene the next day and set them ablaze in the bush behind the fence. But when the figurines survived the fire and made their way back still, she cried to me, setting all of the truth free, so in turn, the truth could set her free.

Acquiescing to her bidding, I followed her to the other side of the fence with a shovel in one last attempt to get rid of the figurines. She picked a hard area of the ground—the harder it was for the figurines to get in, the harder it would be for them to get out—and I dug while she urged. I was exhausted at one foot deep, but she was not satisfied till I got to two. I finally stopped three feet down, not because she insisted—the slightly burned parts of the figurines, which I had never seen before, cleared any doubts I had about the veracity of her claims. I had become as terrified as she was.

Effy placed the figurines in the hole, keeping a steady gaze as I covered the hole with large fragments of caked sand and little pieces of coarse stone. And when we were done—me with my shoveling and Effy with her scrutinizing—we waited for a while.

"You only told me about the one with the beads and wide smile who used his cap to destroy a whole town," Effy said as we were stripping the leaves off branches of the tree under which we had found shade, almost daring the figurines to unearth themselves and fall under the wrath of our fear. The sun was pitilessly low, as if stooping to pay particular attention to our plight. "You never told me about the other figurine."

I remembered the carving of *Yemoja*, not the one that had been buried in the hole but its lookalike, albeit larger, that had sat in my mother's shrine from as far back as my memory served: the double-tailed mermaid, a tail held in each hand, with long thick locks that ran from her head into the hollow of her back and over her breasts to clothe her in the immaculate way that tears clothed sorrow. I could feel my mother speak through me as I explained the mother *òrìsà*. "*Yemoja*—queen of all mothers and protector of all children, calm as the tides but furious as the sea storm, she alone is the womb of the world."

Effy looked straight at me, unsatisfied. "But what's her story? The way *Esu* has his double-colored cap—how does she destroy people?"

"Not all *òrìsà* destroy people, Effy."

"So why did we bury her with *Esu*? I thought they were both evil."

"They're not both evil. Even *Esu* alone is not evil . . ."

"But he destroys people, and destroying people is evil." She seemed more confused with each query.

"It's hard to explain. *Òrìsà* are neither good nor evil. They have both good sides and bad sides. *Esu* destroys people but also helps carry blessings to people. And *Yemoja* is calm and kind, but when she's upset, she can destroy things."

She cracked a smile, and then it grew into a soft laugh which gratified me. "Your *òrìsà* behave like human beings. They can't seem to decide if they want to be good or evil."

"Well, you can look at it that way."

"Then why do you people treat them like gods?"

"Who says gods never had weaknesses?"

"I don't know about your gods, but mine doesn't."

I looked to the buried earth, and her gaze followed suit. Confusion resumed on our faces, and once again, our worries were at par. That night, the figurines did not return.

1993

Money is an unstoppable torrent of wind, and the wind blows all sails, whether slave ships or missionary ships, emissary boats or war vessels. That much I learned when Uncle Adol called me on a Sunday evening, not too long after I had arrived in Enugu, to let me know I would be resuming at the Enugu State University of Science and Technology the following day. I had finished secondary school just before I left Lagos, and all my university applications had been to schools in and around Lagos. But now I was in Enugu, and Uncle Adol had friends in the university who needed money to buy fuel for their cars and biscuits for their children, so I was given admission to study computer science. There had been no application on my part or consultation of my opinion, just a stern instruction from my uncle to put in my best effort, because securing my admission two weeks after the session resumed had cost him a lot.

Tessy, who was in her second year at the university, and I left home early every morning, when the mist stretched its hazy legs on the ground, leaving its footprints of morning dew on the grasses. It was a long walk to the main road, where we could get a bus to the university, up and down the little hills our fathers before had traversed, arriving at the road just as half of the yellow sun was lighting up the horizon. The house was not too far off from the 82 Division military barracks, and so the streets would often be recklessly littered with neat-pleat army gentlemen hurrying to whatever assignment they had been posted to within the city. Even though they seemed more easygoing than the Lagos zombies, having so many of them within close proximity was threatening enough.

Enugu was a smaller and less populated area than Lagos, which had rowdy bus stops polluted with the smoke and soot of thousands of yellow *danfo* buses with clearly defined, almost mathematical daily routes; like a pendulum, the buses had constant initial and final positions, and any change in the initial position would lead to a proportional change in its final position. Enugu had buses that simply scurried back and forth in search of passengers, each according to its own chaos theory, and if a bus started in a slightly different position, a search for passengers could completely change its trajectory.

The lecturers at the university taught fundamental mathematics and physics as well as introductions to computer languages and the rest, but I learned from Tessy the most. She was always eager to share the lessons of her previous year's experience, and I was more eager to listen.

"If you want to survive in this school, always give tax to whomever tax is due" was her advice for my first day. "Fear whomever fear is due, and honor whomever honor is due. Don't owe anybody anything except goodwill and respect. *Siiimple*. And you know why you should write that down on your brain like Scripture?" Before I could offer an answer, she replied, "Because it *is* Scripture—Romans chapter thirteen, verses seven and eight."

When she noticed I had started going around with some of

my new course-mates, she told me on our way home, "Always
try as much as possible to walk on your own—that way nobody
can tie you down to a particular clique, and you can fit into any
kind of group at any time, like water flowing from stream to
river. *Siiimple.*"

When we were walking together to catch a bus home after
lectures and some girls at the university shouted "Big girl Tessy,"
she whispered, "'Big boy' or 'big girl' is not a nickname, it is a
title. Nobody calls you a 'big' unless you earn it. *Shiiikena.*"

"What did you do to earn yours?" I asked naturally.

"*Ogini kwa?* Who killed Adol Igbokwe and anointed you my
father who can question me? You must be a hopeless goat. A
condemned Christmas goat is what you are. Did you eat your
grass this morning?" Her advice dried up for a while after that,
but eventually, she picked up again.

Between the business and the banter of learning and loafing,
there were the terrible crowds of students hurriedly moving to
and from everywhere. Terrible because in each concern-creased
and often panic-possessed face I remembered the terror of the
people trying to escape the carnage at the front of the Shrine so
many months ago. I could never avoid it in such a big university, so I had little to do but accept that I was destined to live a
haunted life.

Tessy's ugly friend came around often, and with time I
learned to call her by her name, Tobenna. With even more
time, I began to enjoy her company. She was in a state of delight always, having no regard for bad moods or ill twists of fate,
whether in her life or in others'. "Why feel special over nothing?
One person cannot have a monopoly on suffering," Tobenna
said whenever Tessy complained about her test results being too

low or not having enough money. "Everyone has their problems. There is as much to go around for everyone created as there are eyes and noses."

The only possible consequence to Tobenna's day, whether as perfect as white clouds in dark skies or as turbulent as the imminent storm behind the clouds, was a bowl of lightly oiled and heavily fished *abacha*, gossip, her joy of all moments and quick-fix solution to all problems. Tobenna was a smooth talker, slick as catfish, and for that reason alone, Tessy and I would end up at her one-room apartment every day after classes to share *abacha* and any other business, in that order.

My going along to Tobenna's was her only argument against her schoolmates who had been convinced she was a lesbian. She was the only one in her row of flats who never came out to play ludo, cook outside with the others, talk about pornography or some other variation of physical exertion, and did not have boys over for the weekends: concisely, a freak of nature. The fact that she preferred Ankara dresses to jeans and miniskirts did not testify in her favor, but she was hardly to blame, considering her "comfortable-but-not-rich" upbringing, as she always echoed. Even Tessy made jokes about her fashion, despite the fact neither Uncle Adol nor Aunt Kosiso would ever allow Tessy to dress in the manner she suggested to Tobenna. Tobenna knew it but never pushed the fact. That was the way they were: Both understood when to be crass and when to show candor. Their friendship was like that of the shore and the sea—not even the sailor whose life depended on their synchronization could separate the prisoner from the captive.

—

The city of Enugu, like the radiance of the yellow sun, reflected the innate passions of the soul but was never really alluring unless in its full, bright golden beam of barefaced ambition, which was typical of every Igbo man. The warm yellow that lay at the heart of the Biafran flag, fashioned into a rising sun, still defined its people a generation later, and so did the ideal it represented: a brighter tomorrow.

What had troubled me the most ever since I'd been in Enugu was that I was not sure if I was ready for tomorrow when I had not even let go of the past I had in Lagos. It was difficult enough fighting the evil spirits in my head when Uncle Adol came home with a new and improved VCR for Christmas, and everyone gathered around to watch *The Silence of the Lambs*, the film that had been the talk of the university, with its final scenes of the disenchanting Buffalo Bill teasing the earnest Clarice Starling, reminding me of the evening in front of the Afrika Shrine, the last night I saw Zeenat, and each one of Clarice's nimble steps resembled the ghost of Zeenat escaping my mind to haunt me in Technicolor.

That night, she escaped the world of Technicolor and sneaked into my arms, and for one just one more time her confidence was my pride, her smile my motivation. The first time I was ever with Zeenat, her body was my playground, and I was a lost child in frantic search of all the joy I could stuff into my heart before heading home. But that night it was an entire world, defenseless and in anarchy of all her efforts of self-control, yearning to be conquered. Our creation of world order was a noisy event, even though we barely spoke any words. Our sounds were in their raw form, undefinable by the words of any language: sounds of laughter and tears, capturing both joy and pain at interchanging junctures. I was much too grateful for the present to show greed by guessing about our future.

I remember hoping the night had not been a dream just before I opened my eyes. When I did, Tessy, made visible only by the moonlight coming in through the window, was sitting at the edge of the bed.

"You wet the bed," she whispered. "And with the way you behave, somebody would think your prick can't stand and your *yansh* can't shit."

She began to giggle, which heightened my confusion even more, until I felt around the bedsheet and discovered an unreasonably large portion of damp stickiness. "Ihechi, breathe easy," she added. "Don't be uptight all the time. Make a jamboree out of life from time to time." And when I thought she was going to laugh even louder, she stood up and got new sheets from a box in the corner of the room. I scurried into the bathroom to change out of my sticky embarrassment, and when I returned, she was laying the new sheets to the bed while Effy, who had woken up, stood weary-eyed, making incoherent grumbles. Then they both got on the bed and fell asleep as quickly as bloated drunks.

I waited for Tessy's jokes the next day, but nothing was forthcoming, not on the next day or even the day after. Almost two weeks had passed by when one morning, on our way to school, she asked, "What's her name?"

Even though the question was from a dialogue of cordial silence, I knew exactly what she was referring to the moment the words left her mouth, but still I feigned ignorance as I considered the lie to tell.

"The girl who made you dream, what's her name?"

I understood there was meant to be a level of trust, as she

had shared my troubles with me, but I also understood that however kind-hearted women might be, it was their nature to understand the irrational and pick problems with the rational. If for any reason I repaid her trust with lies and she doubted my next words, I would lose her friendship in a world where I did not have enough loyalties to spare.

So I began explaining to her how once I had been in love. How I knew it was love because no other word could justify what I felt for Zeenat. I had tried so many times to describe the way I felt with different words that would toss and turn Tessy if I ever suffered her to pay attention. And it had more to do with my shyness than anything else. I started with "friendship" but became the first to admit that Zeenat and I had matured beyond that. But with the way we'd started, it was not so difficult to venture under the safer umbrella of the word.

At some point I had toyed with the idea that I was probably just "attracted" to Zeenat, but that barely made any sense. I could not even say that she was beautiful, because beauty signifies unanimous perfection. But I could say, with the cleanest of conscience, how much I adored her pretty face—I slowed down when we walked sometimes, so I could fall a bit behind her or walk slightly ahead then look back at her, so I could catch a glimpse of her from different angles, and the way her eyes narrowed into a squint, and how her mouth shaped into a full smile whenever she saw me, or how she threw her head back when she laughed, and even though she did not always look at me when talking to me, I cherished the moments she looked me straight in the eye.

Now, I could tell I loved Zeenat, because I once heard the litmus test for love was if you could consider risking your life for a person. I could tell that what I felt for her was more than friendship, more than attraction, more than fondness, more than lust, and more than care. I had heard the most awkward comments over the years, good and bad, blessings and curses, from all sorts of people. They could never understand what we shared, but I could not blame them; a leaf not connected to the branch cannot partake of the fullness of the roots.

Then I explained how Zeenat had died, leaving me in the desolation of blind hope. I did not look up once to check for Tessy's reaction, even when I heard her sniffle and choke on her quiet tears.

And although she did not know to ask, I told her about the great Mendaus. How he was a troublemaker and liked to change things. He just didn't think he should go to school and get a job, like normal members of society, and he had his reasons—the unemployment rate was about seventy percent, and in his class of twenty-five at school, he was far from the top thirty percent, so even if he did manage to scale through university, it was statistically proved that he would be jobless by default. He believed if he made himself enough of a nuisance to the authorities now to effect change in the system, he could save himself from becoming a permanent nuisance to society. Though it was distorted logic, I lauded his foresight.

I told Tessy about everyone—my mother and my father, Pastor's son, and even Atonye—and the shitty fact that they were now all forced away from me, gone, fading memories. As if our emotions were drawn out on a children's library globe, Tessy and I kept drifting along a straight line in opposite directions—I, toward despair and she, toward empathy—till we reunited on the other side of the globe at a common point called unhappiness. And as with all reunions between two lost travelers on a similar journey, the sight of one brought hope to the other, like a lighthouse in the storm. And it was at this common point that we conceived, for the first time, an impression of genuine friendship, allowing tolerance to sprout from the solid rocks of unhappiness. On the branches of tolerance grow the most unusual gestures. There was no way I could understand the magnitude of Tessy's gesture when she declared, "Ihechi, breathe easy, after school today I'll take you to Madame Messalina. Madame Messalina has a solution for everything."

The gates of the house were imperial—in height, strength, and beauty—rising high above the gates on either side, and crowned above its prongs was a large golden sign embossed in the black wrought iron: XANADU. From behind the bars of the gate, I could see the house tower in greater majesty. Its grounds were vast with fruit trees, especially almonds, spread all around. The house was a marvel, rising to three floors, crowned with two domes at each end, and every inch of wall across the face of the building covered with marble or stained glass.

Tessy motioned for me to follow her as a crevice in the gray sky let out a spark of lightning amid the clouds. Her long-limbed frame swayed from side to side like the wild almond trees littering the compound as she moved in the rain, skipping over the little puddles of water. Right before the house, in a circled garden, was a statue of a woman in a long flowing dress with her arms raised to the sky. The headstone below the statue read:

Madame Messalina,
Kuhbla Khan of Nigeria.

I had asked Tessy about Madame Messalina just short of a hundred times since her first mention in the morning. She would start to explain, stutter, and then stop, so I still had no clue, but if what I saw was anything to go by, I knew the speechless awe Madame Messalina commanded as she—for there was no mistaking her when you saw her—walked out onto the second-floor balcony above us.

"How do you rate his lingam?" she cooed loudly, tilting her head upward and putting her hands on her hips in an obnoxious pose.

"But he's just my cousin, Ma," Tessy replied as they exchanged even more obnoxious grins and glances.

"Nonsense!" Madame Messalina exclaimed. "You're so young and pretty. A lingam anywhere is a lingam everywhere. I'll be with you downstairs in a wink." Tessy started to move inside and waved me on casually, as if we had not just witnessed such blatant display of gibberish chatter from a supposedly normal adult.

Inside, the house was littered with girls about Tessy's age, lying about in the living room, talking in low tones at the dining table, patting at their faces in front of large mirrors. They were all a bit too overdressed to be idly sitting around indoors, some as comfortable as chickens in their outfits while others picked and pulled at their clothes, but all waved or nodded at Tessy. And except Tessy and me, everyone in the room appeared to be of a complexion lost in the gray area of the lightest shade of Negro and the darkest shade of Caucasian. The absurdity twisted my insides; Jaja of Opobo was not murdered so his descendants would mate exclusively with the whites, and for those who couldn't achieve their Caucasian dream to bleach their Negro reality away. Tessy took a seat on one of the very long couches and started flipping through a magazine she'd picked up on her way in while I ogled on.

Then I heard the loud coo echo from the staircase: "The bus is ready outside to take you back to your hostels. Make sure you're all ready to go, the major general was very pleased with the way you treated his friends yesterday, so hopefully there will be more of that." All the girls got up and started scurrying about with urgency but no apparent purpose. "And don't forget to say your prayers before leaving," Madame Messalina continued. "Tessy, *nwanyi m*, I'm assuming you have something to discuss with me, you can wait till the sun sets before coming to speak to me upstairs." Madame Messalina began retracing her way back up the stairs before even arriving at the bottom landing; Tessy took her cue and followed her upstairs. When Madame was completely out of sight, the scurrying girls resumed moving about at normal pace.

When Tessy eventually came downstairs, she said Madame Messalina had asked to see me. She guided me up the first few steps of the landing and allowed me to discover the rest of the way, along the wide curving corridor leading up another flight of stairs and finally onto the balcony, where Madame Messalina waited.

"What are you afraid of?" she asked as I walked toward her, her voice now more woo than coo. Her skin was just as light as that of the girls who had left on the bus but for a few darkened patches around her cheeks and knuckles. The rest of her body was covered in a flowing white robe.

"Nothing, I don't know," I fumbled. "I just take a while to settle down when I meet new—"

"That's not what I mean," she interrupted. "Usually I would ask 'What's your faith?' or 'What do you believe in?' But they say the eyes are the pathway to the soul. *Nwoke m*, I see fear in your eyes, and faith cannot live under the same roof with fear."

Her tone was far from firm, but her intent was unflinching, and in that way, she reminded me of my mother. Both were powerful masters of their own worlds, but it also seemed that their own worlds were all they had—except that my mother and Madame Messalina could not be more different. My mother lived like the almond trees that stood guard all over Madame Messalina's compound. She grew in as many directions as she could and tried to bear as many good fruits to bless the world with as she could. She never worried about how she was going to end, whether she was going to be cut down by her *òrìsà* or allowed to wither away in old age; she just grew. Madame Messalina, on the other hand, was a wily old animal. You could tell from her every gesture that she had once ruled the forest, but she had retired to a cavern and was letting the younglings do her bidding. As a predator, she would care for only those within her flock. Unfortunately, I was not yet certain where I stood, so I did not know if I was to stand on my guard or accept the lure of her cavern. Animals like Madame Messalina never deviated from the script: Predator hunts prey.

I should have said something smart and assertive, like Mendaus, or replied to her question with a question, like Pastor's son. But I did what I did best; I thought and thought without actually speaking a word until someone spoke for me, in this case Madame Messalina.

"*Nwoke m*, we're all like a gush of water through our lifetime. If we keep moving in uncertainty, we will find out when our flow comes to an end that we have been everywhere but ended up nowhere, fading away into side gutters and seeping into the soil. But if we have enough conviction, we will make ripples and waves on the sands of time. We will grow into a river and define our own shores." She paused and moved to take a sip from the wine on the table at the far end of the balcony, and I followed her. "*Nwoke m*, when Tessy spoke to me about you in the other room, in all honesty, you struck me as water from the side gutters and not the rivers, and nobody likes to drink from the side gutters. Your mother still orders you around, and you have wet dreams when you miss your friends. To think I actually thought you were a man." She placed her hands on her cheeks in mock exasperation. "But she pleaded, and I do love her very much, so I am going to see if I can save you from yourself. You have one chance to prove to me you are a man. If you don't, back to the side gutters; but if you do, I can help you define your shores like I'm doing with the girls."

She picked up her glass of wine and walked toward me, placing her hand around my neck. "I know a lot of powerful people, and I can lead you through the right corridors," she added. I took to finger-fiddling. "You look so surprised; don't you believe me? Do you think I built this house and take care of all the girls out of my pension as a prostitute?"

She burst out in an outrageous laugh, and for a second she was cooing again. "You said it takes a while for you to settle before you meet new people, so go on and have your while. Let Tessy know if you want to play around the house, and she'll know what to do. By the way, I do have a friend in the civil service who could get a letter to Lagos and be back with a reply within a week, just in case you want to chitchat with your friends. At least that way you could put off the wet dreams, and I could put your lingam to proper use."

Tessy and I left Madame Messalina's house before sunset and got to church just in time to meet up with Uncle Adol, Aunty Kosi, and Effy as they walked in for the midweek service. Madame Messalina had her driver take us in her blue Mercedes, but Tessy insisted we get out two streets away from church and complete the journey on foot. After service, the Volvo was filled with inane chatter over *Rosa à Gabriel*, a Mexican television show that was currently running, so I could not talk with Tessy until after we got home and had dinner.

"What's a lingam?" I asked Tessy. She was squatting to wash a severely charred pot in a basin of brown soapy water. She gave her usual chuckle, which I now realized was a spawn of Madame Messalina's obnoxious laughter.

"Don't be silly, Ihechi. If you did not know what a lingam was, you wouldn't spend so much time in the bathroom on Saturday mornings," and she chuckled again, louder this time. "Don't worry, when you die, you can ask Vātsyāyana why he did not just write *The Kama Sutra* in simple English."

"She said she was going to put my lingam to better use."

"Did you think Madame Messalina would help you with your issues and ask for nothing?" Finally, she seemed as serious as I was. "Oh! So, you want all your bottles full of wine but your girlfriend drunk, *okwia?*"

"I should sleep with that old woman so she can help me deliver a simple letter? When it's not like I cannot find my way to the post office again."

"And have those illiterates use your letter from the depth of your heart to wrap their smoke, *ehn*? Besides, it's not like she's going to sleep with you, *oh*, maybe she'll just have you run errands for her and her friends."

Aunt Kosi came in from the back door with a heap of starched shirts in her arms, and Tessy gave me a stern look that choked my reply. "The way you people always follow one another about, if you weren't cousins, I would have thought Ihechi was discussing plans to visit us with his father and a crate of hot drinks." Aunt Kosi bounced her jolly laughter against the walls as she left the kitchen.

"Just tell that woman my lingam is mine to use as I please. I don't need her, or her major general, or her friends in the civil service who deliver letters."

"Can't you see further than your letters? Madame Messalina can help you get on your feet. Ihechi, it's either you choose to get beaten by the sun or flogged by the rain, or else you will die of hunger under the comfort of this roof."

"Is that why you sleep with all those old bastards?" I looked into her eyes and saw the frailty in her ignorance. "And Tobenna knows about this, so that's what both of you disappear in the middle of the night to do? You're too intelligent to let these people feed you lies, too beautiful to let them take advantage of you."

"You think you're any different from the old bastards I sleep with?" The charred pot dropped from Tessy's hands and clattered onto the floor as she stood up and pushed me away, her hands trembling in rage. "All you men are empty; your words are empty; your hearts are empty. You'll offer the whole world, but your sense of generosity is so empty that the best you ever give is good intentions. But good intentions never fed me, and good intentions never kept me warm. So yes, call me a whore! But don't judge me—aren't we all whores for a better life?"

Aunt Kosi and Effy rushed into the kitchen screaming holy obscenities. Tessy stood glass-eyed, trembling, and in no position to tell a story. I walked out of the kitchen before the explanation was required of me, leaving behind the barrage of questions and Aunt Kosi's allusions to my Yoruba heritage as the cause of fracas. I went to the bedroom and seethed in the shadows. All forms and shapes were cast on the bare ground outside the window by the half-moon up high, a short crescent, as if the galaxy were smirking mischievously at all that had happened. The night air had a chill, so I clutched the pillow close to my chest and wondered if the moon gave the same demeanor to my family and friends in Lagos. But then it dawned on me that I had no reason to wonder idly when I could write to ask. I fetched pen and paper and wrote under the moonlight:

Dear Mendaus,

It's been about five months already since I left Lagos and about five months I've been planning to write with some explanation. But I've only just learned tonight that actions are the plainest truths and explanations often confuse more than they could ever hope to enlighten.

So these are the actions as they happened: After the bonfire at the Shrine, my mother panicked and sent me off the next day to Enugu. I'm staying with my father's family now. My uncle has no care in the world for anything other than

simple stuff; my aunt is more tribalist and naive than I ever thought possible; and as for my
cousins, I think one is a prostitute and the other
is a priest-in-waiting.

I heard a groan in the springs of the bed, followed by a slight
movement at the other corner of the bed. It was Effy. She had
been asleep and I had not noticed. I paused in the sway of my
slight cursive for a while and watched her watch me. She reminded me of myself so many years ago, a shadow ever present,
an observer ever silent. I wished very badly for her to deviate
from the perilous path I was just returning from. My muscles
tensed as she maintained her fixed gaze on me and I battled the
urge to cudgel her head, in my father's devil-incarnate manner,
to bring my point upon her: This world has not the courtesy to
ask your opinion on anything, and opinions should be spoken
with or without warrant because it is the silent and lifeless that
get pissed on. But she stared for a while and then stared some
more until her body yawned and returned her head to its pillow.
I poured myself into the letter with renewed urgency:

> This place is strange to me. It is without all of
> the sincerity of words and motives, no matter
> how favorable or not, I was surrounded with in
> Lagos. Everything I do gives away how different
> I am, so I don't need to be told I'm walking on
> thin ice. I would have preferred if everyone was
> as cold toward me in their actions as I'm sure
> they are in thought. At least that way I'd know
> around whom and to what extent I need to be

careful. But instead they are all very warm, so it's easy to forget I am on ice.

I still think about every one of you I left in Lagos, and more often than convenient, I especially think of Zeenat. Her death finds a new way to haunt me every hour; lonely walks are just as much torture as crowded streets. And it's only at night that I become familiar with more sensual thoughts of her. Certainly, I know that even if you and I never share a laugh or a story, a beer or a smoke, or another moment in each other's company, memories of Zeenat are something we will share forever.

Till we see each other next, may the rift between us be bridged by letters, let these words absolve the grievance of my leaving, and let the drops of my oceans of emotion that they capture be proof that my leaving was never anything hateful. Forgive me for all of the suffering I have put you through, but I promise you I did not suffer any less.

Think of me kindly,

Ihechi

I folded the letter four times and slipped it between the pages of one of my school notebooks on the dresser. The next day after school, I headed straight for the post office.

Tessy was right about the post office. I waited endlessly for a reply, returning three times a week to ask about a letter from Lagos. The only success I managed in that entire endeavor was being able to bang on the clerk's desk hard enough to awaken the ever slumbering civil servant.

Even after I admitted that Tessy was right, we still saw eye to eye over little after the incident of Madame Messalina's house. We still went to school together and exchanged our different accents and laughter in conversation, but her accented sentences were not as long and frequent, and her laughter was not as loud and genuine, as before. And I did not follow her around after school, except when she stated we were going to Tobenna's flat and back without any diversions.

Tobenna still came around occasionally in the dark of the night to lure Tessy out of the house. Tessy still folded naira notes under my pillow when she returned just as before, and I would wonder what home had been torn apart, hinge after hinge, by her footsteps as they danced to the bedroom or parlor or wherever it was she did what she did that required my purchased silence. I was not sure if Tessy thought I would tell on her and genuinely believed her money could assure her peace of mind, or if she was just giving me a share of the spoils.

There were two types of Enugu people: those who intolerably adhered to the traditional past, and those who flung themselves into the open arms of civilization. The men were in their red caps and beads, with the former often feathered, the occasional bald head, which whispered wisdom, and potbelly, which echoed wealth. Or they wore fancy hats hanging loosely from every angle of hip-pop Afro-punks, strangling gold chains, and pointed shoes. The traditional women were glorious in their wrappers with their hair braided or knotted into befitting crowns, while the modern women adjusted their kinky hair into flowing manes, and adjusted their psyches as well, because they walked as confident as lions. While a lot of the young were stuck in a social limbo, the rite of passage into full-fledged adulthood seemed to be that point of decision when you put the fork in the road behind you.

I unwittingly acquiesced to the potbellied ways of the past because my separation from Tessy and consequential loafing around the house made me prey to Uncle Adol's alcohol-tainted yarns every other evening. After he arrived from work and had his siesta, he would send me to fetch a small bottle of dry gin from the bar a few streets away. Then he would walk to the edge of his veranda and pour out splashes of whiskey on the ground in between the bottom of the staircase and his Volvo for his ancestors to partake, and then he would offer a cap full to Aunt Kosi, who would always refuse, before indulging himself. And as he drank, he would begin his story for the day to whoever did not steer clear of his sight.

The first time I fell victim, he defended strongly his stance on drinking in the sanctity of his home and not irresponsibly at beer parlors, as his father, my grandfather, always did. Many years ago, by the setting of the sun every day on that very same veranda, they—my grandmother, my uncle Adol, and my father, Cletus—would all converge to tell exaggerated stories of how their days went. The boys took turns to go and fetch my grand-father from Mama Nkechi's inn, the local beer parlor. And if they set out a moment too late, they would come home father-less, only to have their father knocking away at the front door well after midnight. Each and every one of such nights followed the same procession. Their father would stand at the corner of the room almost theatrically, allowing the flickering flames of the candle on the center table to create a shadow on the wall behind him, enlarged in both size and terror, oblivious to his wife's silent tears and his children's absorbing gazes from their bedroom window. Then he would go on a wild display of ranting.

"Look, Ezinne," he would tell my grandmother, "the moh-rah-lee-tee of law can be tampered with, but the moh-rah-lee-tee of justice cannot change," adding emphasis on any word containing more than three syllables. Then, after setting the stage with his unchanging opening statement, he would go on into the night about the "nah-shun-nah-leests" or the "proh-greh-seefs" and how they "mean business" about one thing and "fake it" about the other. When he started speaking in languages nobody else could understand, my grandmother's silent tears would be transformed into loud intermittent sobs.

"I guess she knew people only started speaking in strange languages when they had been afflicted with terrible madness by wicked witches in the village looking to curse those who had attained wealth far away and refused to return to share the fruits of their labor," Uncle Adol explained in her defense. In the morning, the bright sunshine would wash away the sins of the night before, as they would all continue life without showing the slightest hint of discord, like servants in a king's palace.

"He ate so little but had the fattest belly," Uncle Adol would continue to me, as if oblivious of his own fat belly. "Even his breasts were protruding. And as his breasts grew larger, other women juices—you know, those juices in women that cause them to nag—started growing inside him." And then he would laugh, almost off his chair, then force a shot of whiskey down my throat. "Sometimes I wondered if our women ancestors had such strong blood that could overcome the gender barrier and cause women juices to start growing in men like my father. What else could explain all those women behaviors in my father?" In an hour we would both be drunk and teary-eyed from laughter.

Soon enough, our bond grew over more bottles of whiskey, and sometimes he would even permit me to offer our ancestors their portion of whiskey before we started drinking. Sometimes Aunt Kosi would bring out roasted cashew nuts on a huge tray for us; she always looked grateful that I had come to rescue her from her husband's opinions and stories. Uncle Adol told me how he would go off to catechism classes after school while my father worked the chores with their mother for the rest of the day: He had found the Lord Jesus and my grandmother was pleased. She had lofty dreams that her first boy would grow up to become a well-known reverend father who would walk side by side with the white men sharing communion, praying for the sick and doing other great things. And maybe one day she would be recognized as the one who had birthed such a great man of God and be regarded around town as some sort of Virgin Mary.

On the days when there were no catechism classes, my father would go on with the rest of the children of the dirt road to do the troublesome things children usually did. But he did not go out to play much, because unlike his brother, he had neither the temperament nor the spiritual serenity to stomach being taunted as a drunkard's son, even though almost every other child they knew was a ward of men who either shared or helped sponsor his father's habits; besides, none of the children in the neighborhood were really much like him.

"We were all paw-paw seed-brained fellows, you know," Uncle Adol said as he pressed his forefinger to his thumb so I could visualize his point. "Our thoughts of ambition before they went to bed each night were never more than waking up early enough to catch the morning-ripe almond fruits before they hit the ground. On the other hand, your father dreamed of having the prestigious life of a doctor or soldier or even an international drumbeater, like Chris Anyogu from Orlu. Chai! The ladies really loved Chris Anyogu." Then Uncle Adol went on talking about Chris Anyogu for the next hour, and the fame and prowess of his band and their ballads. While, on a low key, I wondered if it was humanly possible for any man not of Yoruba heritage to attain the tempo of percussions set by the fuji bands of Egbeda.

When there was no money for whiskey, Uncle Adol would settle for bottles of beer, and the stories would continue. Though he and the other children would not understand, Uncle Adol later admitted, my grandmother encouraged her younger son in his wild dreams. "She said it was that kind of thinking that would make him a great man like Nnamdi Azikiwe, who sat down with the white men like an equal and even rubbed the tops of their heads when they laughed over jokes together," Uncle Adol said, deep in thought, with his eyes to the ground where he splashed his alcohol, as if every word he spoke had been relayed to him by our ancestors. "She gave him one of our father's empty squadron bottles and told him that any time he had a new dream, he should write it down and bottle it so he would have it forever and never forget the destination he was working toward. So he put his little dream of becoming an international drumbeater down on paper and bottled it. A few weeks later, when he saw a group of soldiers at Mama Nkechi's inn break up a fight and inflict brisk discipline on the culprits, he dreamed of becoming a high-ranking military official so he could put into people the polite kind of fear that cowards like to refer to as respect. And as soon as the piece of paper floated to the bottom of the bottle, he was already dreaming of becoming an official driver to a white man, so he would be able to get close enough to understand for himself the mysteries behind the color of their skin."

I laughed, not at my father's childish ways but at memories of times when I also saw things in only black and white; when I used to think things were either good or bad and my father was only loving or unloving. I laughed because now I understood not just black and white but gray. I understood not just blue and green but turquoise, too. That red was not one color but scarlet, burgundy, carmine, maroon, and rose. And that there was much more to life than what met the eye. It was strange hearing stories about my father that portrayed him as this jukebox of dreams and embodiment of hope, an anathema to the defeated soul I knew him to be. How much of my father did I really know? He fed me, clothed me, put a roof over my head, paid my fees, and spat out his life's frustration at me. Finish. And I had been comfortable with that all my life. I had never cared to wonder if he was religious or fetish, compliant or rebellious, dream-laden or genius enough to have schemed to be so desolate from the very beginning. And as he had never bothered to share, how was I to avoid falling into the same potholes?

In the solace of night, when our glasses were dry and our hearts were sober again, I would bother my mind to no avail, trying to figure out how and when things went wrong. But somehow I was sure the end of the truth would eventually spill out of Uncle Adol's mouth; it was just a matter of how many more bottles of whiskey I would need to suffer before then.

The rainy season came around; when it rained, we would still drink out on the veranda. Aunt Kosi would come out with Effy because they liked playing with the rainwater. Uncle Adol and Aunt Kosi had picked up from one of the many churches they had frequented over the years that the rain was Jesus' gift of fertility to the world. They believed that, just as the rain made the outstretched leaves of the plants fertile, so it blessed the human hands. Aunt Kosi would guide Effy's open palm under the edges of the flooded roof so the droplets would fall into it and prepare her womb for the due time. Effy would give in to the rain because, I think, she enjoyed the attention and not because she actually cared about her due time.

On the days the rain began very early, it would take Uncle Adol much longer to get home. The day he took the longest, he stepped out of the muddied Volvo just as the cold sweat around the bottles of beer Aunt Kosi had me prepare for him dried up. He announced, before his wife queried him, that a stop at the post office had delayed him. He made his way up the stairs to the veranda and collapsed on the chair that had been set out for him without bothering to remove his damp suit.

"Ihechi, there was a letter for you," he said, shaking the bottles of beer as he tossed his briefcase on the table and flipped it open. "If I had known you knew your way to the post office, I would not be going all the way there. Those people give hardworking civil servants like me a bad name."

The letter he handed me had no name, but the address was all too familiar. "I think it's from your mother, *okwia?*" he asked, and I nodded in reply to keep from telling an outright lie before remembering to utter "Thank you, sir." I ripped open the letter and held it close enough to avoid any puck-nosing.

Hello Ihechi,

How are you doing? It is exactly six months since the bonfire, as you call it, Zeenat's funeral, as I like to look at it. I remember Mr. Thomas digging mounds in the grass patch behind the house for the maize and pepper seeds when Zeenat and I went running to tell him we would be out at the Afrika Shrine for all of that evening. Since then Mr. Thomas has roasted a whole harvest of maize for the house and has started cooking our stew with his own pepper, and oh yes, I still haven't heard from you.

I have been through the most terrible circumstances these last few months, as you would guess, especially considering the fact that no one has been here. After my dad went to cause drama at the police station when Zeenat died, his friend the police commissioner came around and was just giving everyone stupid sarcasm and unnecessary stress. All for me to get into the books, trying to cool off from the protest gizmo that was on television, just to have my mother create a collage of emotional antics all over my sanity because she thinks I'm the cause of Zeenat's death. I'm sad, disgusted, irritated, annoyed, everything in all.

Today also makes it two months since Pastor's son was driven off to a theology college all the way in Hawaii—that's meant to be somewhere in America. His parents had had enough about the church complaints on his behavior when he was meant to be preparing his white suits to take after his father on the pulpit, so his punishment is this exile till he can find again "the joy of salvation."

So, basically, living without you this last year has made me live within myself, my dreams, and my potential. In the fury of all that happened at the Afrika Shrine and to Zeenat, I shelved my admission to do mass communication at the University of Lagos in exchange for political science so I would be eligible to work part-time at this popular campaign group everyone used to talk about—the Democracy Union. Joining the union was the worst decision I could have ever made. I work so hard for so little pay, and all they gather to do is complain. The office is a hellhole; the other executives are devils who orchestrate misery from afar, and the other volunteer staff are little demons whose larking about invades the tiny peace and tranquility I try to muster out of my existence. No wonder why your people say the beautiful ones are not yet born. Nobody bothers for anybody here, they're all just trying to solve their own personal issues. Everybody's selfishness has caused us to keep plunging deeper and deeper into futility. It's just like the story Fela told us at the Shrine about the end of the world: The blind man who hears the chaos but refuses to ask for a guide beside the lame man who sees the chaos but refuses to ask for assistance—they both perish as fools because they refused to work together. And it's really not that I can't do anything on my own, it's just that I can't do everything on my own. This dream could have been realized so easily if you were all around, together complementing each other. Would it actually have hurt you if you had refused to go to Enugu and hung around when I actually needed you? I'm tired and quite pissed off at you. YES, AT YOU!!! I'm sick of complaining, really, very sick, because it would seem like I'm always nagging, and I never get satisfied. But I'm your friend and I have to be always true to you and this is honestly how I feel, I'm not saying this for pity, so don't get it wrong.

My eyes fluttered as I fought a barrage of tears and I stood up without touching the bottle Uncle Adol had kept aside for me.

"*Le kwa* Ihechi of yesterday, *oh*!" yelled Uncle Adol as I walked away. "Is that how you stand up and leave when your father is talking to you?"

"I'm sorry, sir," I began, but was more caught up in keeping away tears than fashioning a lie. "My stomach, sir," I continued just as he was about to speak again. "Purging, sir," I said, just before I started to appear silly. And then I ran off into the house, nestling in the solitude of the room where sobs would not be heard, to conclude the letter.

I'm finished being petty, so now, more impor-
tantly, I have a few questions I need to understand. So first, I'll start with a few why's. I want
to know why you agreed to leave even after everything that happened just before and why you
stopped communicating. I also need to understand the how's. How could you ignore the af-
front in Zeenat's murder and the need to avenge
it in any way possible? How could you go to bed
even the first night knowing her body was lying in a gutter? And last, I will need to know
the when's if I'm to ever call you a friend again.
When will you be back to Lagos so we can make
a difference, for shit's sake? When will you realize that we can run from our fears forever, that
we are all doomed in this country if we sit silently, because a multitude always suffers if one
man, any at all, fails to think?

You know I just realized how much I miss
all you guys; it's saddening. Like it has been six
months and I'm still like this! I think the whole
not talking to anybody about our gizmo just
makes everything worse. IT'S SAD!!! I almost

feel like crying, I swear. Atonye still comes around from time to time, but it's not the same. She met some guy who wants to marry her and take her abroad, so that should explain it. My dad is out on his travels, as usual. And my mother has been around for the past month, playing all these films that Zeenat made me watch on the VCR all evening, and I'm just going crazy . . . yeah, crazily sad. I'm hungry at the moment and I'm having ulcer pain but I'm too depressed to even eat. Oh well, life is unfair.

Mendaus,

The pissed and shat on.

The last words of the letter made my face a waterfall. I had anticipated Mendaus's reply but had never braced for the impact of its heavy blows. The true words crushed my mind just as the letter itself crumpled into a tiny ball within my clenched fist. I looked up to hurl it away when I saw Tessy wince at the door, as if she feared being my target.

"I'm sorry," she said, almost without any feeling.

I tried to reply in equal calm, but my fluttering eyes betrayed me. "What for?"

"I'm sorry you're hurting."

"What if I'm not the victim? What if I'm the one who did the hurting?"

"That's unlikely. You're not smart enough to hurt someone knowingly, even if you wanted to." I would have felt insulted if I did not believe she was right, and we both laughed it off. "Even if you did, hurting whoever it was obviously hurt you, too. And I'm sorry about that." She came closer, put her arms around me, and smothered me in a hug.

"Why do you care?"

"*Ehn*, because I've taken so much from the men of this world that I feel I have to give something back. You know, like how rich people steal from us and do charity work because they feel guilty . . ." She trailed off into her usual loud chuckle. "Or maybe because I really care for my baby cousin no matter how much he hates to believe it."

She made to pry the balled-up letter from my fist; I did not struggle, and so she read it.

"You know you're going to make up your mind to return to Lagos sooner or later?" she said when she was finally through. "If you're waiting for my father or your mother, you'll be waiting forever."

"I know. But I just don't know how."

"Well, for a start, you're going to need some money."

We stared at each other silently for about a minute, and I was sure we had been thinking the same thought all the while when she smiled after I asked, "Is it still possible to go back to Madame Messalina?"

Uncle Adol neither spoke to me nor permitted me to have drinks with him for the following week, but Tessy told me not to bother. It was an unwritten decree that whenever he was angry with whomever over whatever, he would go an entire week without speaking to his victim; if it was Aunt Kosi, the punishment would include his eating outside the house for the week.

True to Tessy's word, after the week of silent punishment was done, we resumed booze and banter as if the calendar had simply omitted a week of the year. I asked him about the happenings leading up to the civil war, the stories Aunt Kosi had told me of my grandmother's death, and how they survived through it all. He would dodge my questions when he could and at other times blatantly refuse to recall, so I relented.

The next day, however, Uncle Adol did not bother to get out of the Volvo when he returned from work and asked me to get into the passenger's seat. When Effy tried to make a fuss about coming along, he said we were making a "quick dash to church," and she quieted as he pulled out of the compound before Aunt Kosi had even made it out of the kitchen. But we drove past the church and, in due course, onto the main Obiagwu road. I peeked into the wide-open doors and windows of the Siamese-twin-styled bungalows. Petty traders conducted business, groups gathered around black-and-white television sets, lovers groped each other: People were engrossed in their own worlds with such blissful inattention that I thought maybe that was exactly how all lives should be lived. There was the mouth of a dirt road after every few blocks, lined with furious *okada* riders and careless bare-bottomed children, leading to who knows where, and each one mystified me differently. We drove past it all and past the dreaded road that led to the 82 Division military barracks, past the state museum Tessy had warned was not worth my time, past the wired fence of the Polo Park, then turned onto the road where the fence met with the arched gate. The grass on the large field was slightly overgrown, but little children still chased through it, while furious boys gathered to kick footballs around. The only ones who appeared concerned about the overgrowth were the grazing horses, but all their diligence made little difference.

Uncle Adol guided me to a large canopy that watched over huddled tables and chairs. The waitress, wearing a straight single-strapped dress with bright yellow flowers, despite the tender chill of the early evening, smiled at our table and brought a bottle of something from the bar without being told, and Uncle Adol smiled back. Then he rushed down two glasses of the whiskey before our chairs got warm, and he brought up the previous day's discussion of his own volition.

"You know, this matter always turns my belly. But if I don't tell you these things, nobody will," he started. "I am sure they would never teach you these things in all those schools in Lagos."

"I have learned more about Nigerian history from Fela records than from school," I replied, and he shook with laughter, spilling the whiskey in his glass.

"You know, if the lion never learned to tell his own stories, the story of the hunt would always glorify the hunter. In fact, these hunters have cleaned their hands and wiped their mouths and would prefer the hunt to be forgotten altogether." He laughed heavily once more, slowing into a loud wheeze before beginning his story.

Shortly after my grandmother died, news spread quickly that the Nigerian army was closing in on Enugu. My grandfather, already engulfed in despair and in no condition to put up a final stand with any of their zealot neighbors, took his two sons and headed toward Abakaliki in Ebonyi with the intention of sneaking over the border into Cameroon.

"You know the worst thing?" Uncle Adol asked with his bottom lip still pressed on his glass. "The worst thing was not even our war. Almost all of us in Enugu had lived there all our lives. Same as Nsukka, Umuahia, Aba, Owerri, in fact almost all of us living in Igbo land. We had not offended anybody. Few people had or even wanted office jobs back then. People just wanted to farm the land their fathers passed on to them and feed their family. But instead we were witch-hunted from our own very land, and our farms were burned."

"But you know," I tried to offer from my shallow pool of knowledge amassed over the years from rivers of adult conversation never intended for my ears, "they said the Igbo people . . . they said we were greedy and overambitious, trying to get our hands on everything. And that's why other people hated us."

"Who was greedy and overambitious, Ihechi?" he asked in all seriousness. "Is it the innocent farmers in Ikeduru or the drunk palm-wine tappers in Udi or the traders in Onitsha who were greedy and overambitious? It was the deserters! The ones who left us to go and find money in Lagos and then avoided their people back home like cockroaches once they started earning peanuts! The ones for whom the cooperative society in the villages gathered money to send abroad but refused to come back to develop the community after they collected their education abroad! Some of them even felt too big to take a wife from the village that brought them up! It was when their so-called *paddy mi* and *aboki* started calling for their heads that they remembered they had family back home. It was their war, not ours, but they put the target on our heads."

As my grandfather and his sons scurried to leave Enugu with the herd of fleeing Biafrans, they were blocked by a troop of army recruiters. My father escaped amid the terrified women and children as they scattered into the bushes, but my grandfather and Uncle Adol were not as lucky. A few weeks later, Uncle Adol was deployed to the Biafran marines stationed in Port Harcourt, while my grandfather was deployed to the military remaining in Enugu to hold off the impending Nigerian army. That was the last thing known of my grandfather and everyone else known to have stayed behind in Enugu.

More drunkards had started trooping under the canopy: the idle townsmen who came to sample the fresh palm wine tapped in the mornings and afternoons and the old men, who were most likely unemployed degenerates but maybe were retired gentlemen, discussing the newspapers over dark foaming beverages brought in from town. A live band had begun performing under the next canopy. Uncle Adol looked disgusted by all the loudness. Me, I did not mind the music. I was not used to highlife, but it was genius. The keyboardist directed the flow of the music as the men with the Ogene, the Igba and Udu, and the other contemporary percussion maintained a steady tempo, playing with the music only at the end of a repetition, allowing the bass guitarists to infuse unpredictable oddities that made the ear squint in craze. The whole performance was orchestrated by the lead performer, who meandered through the merry band of drunkards as he blew on his saxophone. His voice was not perfect, a strained baritone that seemed to imitate the verbosity of sexual climax, but in its imperfection, it captured the very passion that was highlife.

"If a people loses its brothers, that's a tragedy for one generation," Uncle Adol said as he struggled to stifle a tear for the first time. "But if a people loses its humanity, that's a tragedy for eternity. Anyone who survived the war would tell you we were not defeated by human beings. Human beings could not have put their brothers through what they put us through, when our only crime as a people was refusing to lay our heads on the guillotine in the north and the west."

"And the world did nothing? They let you get forced into sleeping in the same bed as your father's murderer? Into letting it all go just like that, without holding anyone accountable?"

"There's a limit to what can be achieved by force. You cannot murder or torture or bomb away hatred from the hearts of people gathered under the banner of a mutual grievance. You can keep their mouths silent but never their hearts. And hope the hatred gets buried with them and not shared among their children."

About five years after they had been separated, well after over a million Biafrans had perished, General Ojukwu—the Biafran arch-secessionist—had gone into exile, and General Yakubu—the Nigerian head of state—declared, "No victor, no vanquished." Uncle Adol came to answer a knock on the door of the house just a few months after he had moved back, the only house on the street that had made it through the war unscathed, only to open the door to my father, Cletus. My father had gone with the fleeing women and children to a makeshift refugee camp set up on the grounds of a large Catholic church by a white priest. Out of sheer luck, he had made it into the care of one of five Catholic priests in Biafra at the time who knew of the Caritas International Biafran refugee project. Before the week was out, Cletus and more than fifty young Biafran refugees were airlifted by Dutch mercenary pilots to Britain from a landing strip tucked in the valleys of the hilled city of Enugu. It was the second time in the first six months of the war that he had found succor in the arms of the Catholic Church.

Sadly, succor did not last for long. But I would not find that out till the next morning, when Uncle Adol was having *moi moi* and *akamu* on the veranda while I washed his Volvo in preparation for the day. Parked at Polo Park, the car had sunk into a soft marsh of grass, and all the tire rims were muddied.

"I'm sure you would have rather stayed home if you'd known all this cleaning came with a trip to Polo Park," he said in between bites of *moi moi*.

"I enjoyed the drink and the band, and all I have to do is wash the tires," I replied, wiping beads of sweat off my forehead. "The gains outweigh the losses."

"Well, I enjoyed the drink, but I hated the crowd and the band. Your aunt does not like when I talk about the war, because when I do, it's hard for me to sleep at night. So I took us out yesterday because I was tired of her scolding." He laughed with his mouth wide open, exposing half-crushed morsels. I could understand her concern. Uncle Adol spoke with a passion I had not witnessed since I'd watched Mendaus speak out on the buses and at the Shrine. Biafra was dead to the world but still very much alive in him. But bitter was the poison of such unrequited love for Biafra, and the burden of harboring something so toxic would have to be shared, ultimately.

I asked when the laughter quieted, "Do you wonder sometimes how your life would have turned out if you had made it onto one of those planes that flew children abroad?"

Uncle Adol played with his fork for a while before coming up with an answer. "Yes, I do. But don't get it confused; some of them faced their own torture, which was worse." He saw my confusion and continued. "Well, see your father as one. He arrived in London and was placed with a Nigerian family who had escaped before the war got out of hand, a very wealthy family. They were part of a group carrying out campaigns with some ambassadors Biafra had appointed, you know, to help put together money for the people who were not lucky enough to make it out. Your father had just finished secondary school, so he used to go around with them; they would make public speeches and discuss matters with important white people privately, and to be fair, they gathered a fortune." Uncle Adol's voice slowed and his eyes narrowed as he spoke. "And then they shared the fortune among themselves. Not one shilling returned to Biafra."

"That's not possible," I said, and I truly believed it.

"Well, at that point he could have stayed to make a fortune and tried to save his family, or he could have been honest and tried to save his country—but he had to let one of them die." Uncle Adol had forfeited the rest of his breakfast at this point. "He left the family and his share of the fortune and tried reporting to the British authorities, but someone must have gotten to them first and told them a different story, because your father was deported right after the war and returned to Lagos to begin his life afresh."

My chest was heavy. I exhaled deeply to free the congealing stress in my left breast, and my mind went back to my father, broken in spirit and in mind, exiled from the domain of my concern and love for so many years. I wondered at what point he'd broken finally. Was it a slow and gradual process or a single and fatal fracture of the soul? Could I have helped nurse him back, or had I just trampled on his broken bones all my life? He, as we all are, was just another desperate artist judged not by intentions or gifts he kept hidden but by the colors he eventually lay down to define his existence. He was not of the few lucky artists who would have the colors of their soul come down as presupposed as rain showers on a windowpane. No, he was one of the many unfortunate artists who endured phases of detachment when the colors did not smudge as imagined and nothing about the work went according to plan, just as unfortunate as Mendaus and I were.

The only thing that could rescue the artist at that point was a fresh pair of eyes to offer a second opinion, and woe betide him if those fresh eyes were jealous or dishonest, laden with ulterior motives. My mother was my father's fresh pair of eyes when he returned to Nigeria, as Uncle Adol later continued, full of love and good vibes. She was too late, though. My father was already stuck in his ways. Like a sour fruit fallen from its tree days before attaining sweet ripeness, he could never be made better and could only become worse. At best, he could be managed for what he already was.

Slowly, I began to fear that I was resigned to a similar fate. I had spent my childhood probably as he had: told how important it was to gather wealth, acquire a wife and family, and at the very least make a name for myself. Those were the three hallows of Nigerian manhood. How could a man love if he remained with a barren woman or none at all? How could he follow his passion if he remained poor? How could he be called a man if his name was not respected? All other things were worth considering only if they existed along with the three hallows.

But I had also wondered: Are there not men created with love and passion for art, beauty, and truth, just the same way there are men predestined for wealth, family, and fame? If there was no one who revered beauty, who would checkmate those who exploited our lands in pursuit of the three hallows? Who would cure those who were afflicted with hate if there was no one who loved? And what else could resurrect the parts of us that die every day if not the cultivated passions of our soul? Surely the balance of society could be shifted if people, whether one or in thousands, were made to cut against the grain of their souls just to find peace with the majority. My father had been frustrated away from his passion when he was deported back to Nigeria. That forced shift in balance, not the war or any other issue, was the juncture of failure in my father's life, and is the true crisis of Nigeria's history.

"Well—" Uncle Adol was about to speak again when Aunt Kosi came out to clear the breakfast table.

"*Ahn di m*, was there anything wrong with the *moi moi?*" she exclaimed. Uncle Adol hardly ever left his meals unfinished.

He shrugged and replied, "I cannot spend the whole morning sitting around over food." He thanked her for the meal with a pat on the top of her head and turned to leave. "The sun will shine on those who stand before it shines on those who kneel under them."

I quickly dabbed my dry rag all around the wet car and followed my uncle and aunt into the house, allowing the sun, now fully birthed to the glory of the dawn, to adorn itself on the polished panels of the Volvo. It was almost time for Tessy and me to leave for school, and I had something I had been meaning to do since the previous day, Uncle Adol's stories making the need all the more urgent. So I got to it.

Dear Mendaus,
    I have never forgotten you and everyone else and miss all of the best memories—the football,

the beach, the shrine, the conversation, and the silences in equal measure. It haunts me that I could never say a proper goodbye, that I could never hold you up when the sorrow was too heavy. I should have put up a fight with Mother to stay, but as I had been all my life, I was a *mumu*, a zombie. I cannot be sorry enough but I am sorry still.

I think about Zeenat every day and still see her in my dreams. But I was not as you were. I could never have spoken a word well enough or made an action brave enough to avenge her. If anything, being so far away in Enugu has brought me closer to being the sort of person who could make the kind of difference you seek. In this place, I finally figured out how passive I have been, and even though that's neither an apology nor a solution, it's a discovery of the problem, which I think brings me a step closer to redemption. I have never stood up for anything in my whole life, not even myself. I mean, Zeenat would never let anything mess with her happiness, and Pastor's son would juggle a football in the middle of Third Mainland Bridge at midday without any second thoughts if he felt he had heard God whisper the idea into his ear. My mother has devoted her life and, sometimes I worry, her sanity to Ifá, and I've met people in Enugu who would sell the only clothing they had if you promised to fill their pockets with money. But I don't have any passions. What's the point? I'm human, so I'd suffer anyway. And till that changes, I'd probably just be like you and believe, with all I have, in better tomorrows.

Regarding better tomorrows, making a difference here in Enugu or with you in Lagos, it's something I want to contribute to. My grandparents' memories deserve it, my father's failed efforts and broken dreams insist on it, and Zeenat's death justifies it. But if there is a god, my mother's or Pastor's son's or any other, I swear to it that I just don't know how. I saw you on TV that night and still remember your words. I guess you were right—we need someone to carve out a path to salvation. But that also means some of us are destined to wait and follow the well-trodden path after it's been set.

Your friend,

Ihechi, the ashamed.

Mendaus's reply took another eternity to get to me. The long wait for the letter coincided with the seemingly longer wait I endured for Tessy to pick the right time for me to return to Madame Messalina, and the weight of it all whetted my doubts. Tobenna had visited in the night twice since the wait began, but on both nights, we were expecting Aunt Kosi to deliver Effy a beating, and woe betide Tessy and me if we were missing. Then one night, Tessy woke me up from sleep, dressed up in one of those many dresses she wore only when Tobenna came knocking at the window, and asked me to put on my clothes quickly. There was no briefing, no preparation, nothing. We escaped the house and compound quietly enough, and then the night was torn mad with our footsteps as I raced after her down the dirt road. Out of the darkness ahead, a pair of vehicle headlights appeared twice, each time for barely a second, and Tessy steered in that direction. She got to the vehicle first and exchanged words with the driver, who asked about Tobenna, and she shrugged off the question. We got into the backseat and nothing was said from then on, even when the driver dropped us off at the large gates I could never forget.

Madame Messalina's house was empty as death in the darkest hour of night when we arrived. We accessed the gates and knocked on the door; a dreary-eyed girl, who did not know Tessy by name but knew her well enough to call her madam, answered and asked her to forward her interests to the "Stray Dog." We moved through the large house, which became less quiet as we progressed, an occasional string of laughter or wave of cheers echoing toward us, till we arrived in a hallway with light and noise at the other end. It all seemed to excite Tessy, who hurried forward and urged me to follow faster.

The high dome of the room we entered enclosed a circus: unclothed skin with stretch marks by the thighs and dark patches by the knees, birthmarks that would rather be hidden, and scars here and there, skin seamlessly fitted tight around bouncing buttocks and slightly loose around the stomach, skin donned as confidently as the latest fashion. There were three of them moving about the room in whatever direction was pointed out by Madame Messalina, and another three on the floor seated amid Ghana-must-go bags, calculators and notepads in their hands and loosely bound naira stacks strewn on the floor around them.

Even more curious were the three men positioned around the cash-counting girls on the floor like village masquerades stalking a lost girl who had wandered into the bush at the forbidden hour. Two of the men were seated and had assumed the nature of kindred spirits, frolicking away the night despite being dreadfully watchful, while the last man, pacing and squatting and hoarding all of the tension in the room, appeared to have just broken free from the evil forest. He was short, but somehow his miserly length managed to support an incredible potbelly, leaving little room for his neck and legs. He had incredible discipline over everything that concerned him, be it within or without, except his tongue, of course. I would soon discover that he replied to questions not with answers but with stories.

"Major General, are you having any issues?" Madame Messalina asked from afar as he quibbled with a girl who had taken him a drink.

"I want a straight straw," he replied, pointing at the pink loopy straw that floated from the cup on a tray. "With a straight straw, when I sip my drink, it gets to me right away, but with these fancy straws, it takes about five seconds going around these loops before getting to me."

"But it's more fashionable. When last were you in Lagos?" one of the seated men countered. "I thought you liked ethics? Or attics? What's your word again?"

"Aesthetics?" Tessy suggested

"Aesthetics!" he echoed. "Of course, yes!"

Tessy faked a sigh. "And what would you ever do without me?"

"It won't be the end of the world. I'd masturbate." Everyone laughed, even the girls counting money in the middle of the room. "But you see, more than I like aesthetics, I like to get my drink exactly when I want it. Not a second more, not a second less. It's too stressful to have to remember to sip my drink five seconds before I actually want it, don't you think?"

"I think you should be more open to new things," Madame Messalina replied. "You've been wearing starched shirts and leather loafers every day since I met you over twenty years ago."

"It's called structure! I live a well-structured life. If I woke up today without planning to meet the love of my life, and by divine providence I came across an angel of a woman, I'd tell that angel that she would be the love of my life, but she would have to book an appointment to meet me like everyone else, because everything, even love, has to be structured."

"That's the major general, paranoid as a housewife," Tessy whispered into my ear underneath the laughter that had engulfed the room. "He can't trust a log of wood alone in the same room with his money."

"I can't trust my money alone with itself; I didn't pluck it off the tree," the major general boomed across the room. "It's the dividends of independence my father debated the British for while the rest of the country was tilling soil. So you haven't seen me in how many weeks, and you're still gossiping there? C'mon, do that thing on my neck that you used to do."

"*Aburo*, don't be angry," one of the seated men said, looking in my direction. He was the only one without a girl. "When I was in school, we used to say, 'If you're old enough to go with a girl to a party, then you're old enough to have your girl taken from you at a party.'"

"Alhaji, you never went to school," retorted Madame Messalina, and everybody laughed out loud.

"*Aburo*, leave these people alone. Come and sit down on my lap, let me tell you about law and medicine and engineering."

"Alhaji, he's not a chewing gum boy," Madame Messalina intercepted again. "This is the boy who is meant to go on your excursions to Lagos."

"No, nah!" he shouted. "This one would be a waste if police caught him and hung him naked from the fan to—"

"No one is catching or hanging anybody, Alhaji," said Madame again. She seemed to be the conjunction between everyone's sentences. "Allow this one; your own is coming later."

"I thought you said he objected to the idea," Major General said.

"Well, I hear he wants to honor the memory of a girl," Madame replied.

Major General's pupils widened, and he clapped his hands with each question: "You want to do this for vagina? For pussy? For *toto*? For *punani*? Oh, you little ignoramus, there are a million places in Nigeria you could get *punani*, a thousand places you could get free *punnai*, and hundreds of places you could get free quality *punani*. So, you can't be actually making life choices over simple *punani*?"

Alhaji nodded in agreement.

"Major General, you do realize there is a difference between a girl and her vagina, *okwia*?" Tessy said. She might have noticed the shame in my face at the thought of Zeenat, or maybe it was the shame she felt from knowing I was aware she had told Madame Messalina as much as I told her in confidence.

"Let the boy speak for himself." This voice was different. It was the third man, who had been silent all night long. He looked toward me. "We don't care what you do, just as you shouldn't care what we do. But you have to understand why we need to know you're here for the right reasons. You know they say, 'If the forest lets in the ax just because it is made of wood, the forest will fall.'"

I remembered my conversation with Tessy that had led to my second chance at working for the major general; I was silent and thoughtful for a while. "I am here to make some money so I can move back to Lagos." The room remained as if I had not said a word: All mouths remained shut and all eyes remained fixed on me. Alhaji said something inaudible; Major General grunted in response.

"Alhaji believes there is no point in hiding from you what you will know eventually," said the major general. "All you will be doing for us is delivering packages, sometimes letters and other times parcels, sometimes to Lagos and other times to Niger. All in all, you will be our messenger, and you will be made fat for it."

He sounded way too cool, in way too much control over the room. He was the person in charge, regardless of whether the other gentlemen in the room chose to call themselves his acquaintances or subordinates. I tried to match his aura, so I played the coolest move I knew: nodding slowly as he spoke and brushing the back of my fingers on the side of my face, just as Marlon Brando did when acting as Vito Corleone, the godfather, in deep thought.

"How regularly do your shave your face?" Alhaji asked.

My hand subconsciously stopped moving against the virgin stubble on my chin and cheeks that had started growing out only a few months ago. "About once a month," I replied.

"Ah! *Aburo*, never again," Alhaji rebounded. "You look like a teenager."

Madame Messalina and Tessy laughed with their heads cocked backward, as they always did; they were probably the only people in the room who knew I was actually still a teenager. Tessy went to meet the major general, and he quieted for the rest of the evening, except when she put her face to his neck and his voice boomed. The rest of the men remained distracted with the other girls, and I remained in the corner. Occasionally, they would snap out of their halcyon and remind each other about less important issues. Madame Messalina caught my gaze from a distance, and she meandered around the room, appropriately apportioning glances of approval and twitches of reprimand to her girls, before finally ending up where I was.

She whispered into my ear, "I know all this is new to you, but you really can't ignore all the beauty around the room. Get off the wall and live for the moment." She sipped on her drink between every few sentences, as I had noticed Tessy do occasionally. "Never forget: Be as generous with hellos as you are with goodbyes, because the only difference between a bride and a widow is time." She placed her hand on my chest, feeling for my heartbeat, and then ran her fingers down to the buckle of my belt. "But let's leave the lessons for later; tonight is for hellos, and you, *nwoke m*, are the bride."

With her hands wrapped around my belt buckle, she led me into an adjoining room. It was dark, and she did not bother to light it. Her actions echoed my thoughts in soft caresses of melodious motion, like a backup singer getting in sync with the lead's harmony. I leaned against the wall for support in the dark and she leaned in to me. I put my hands on her waist and she guided them lower. I licked my lips and she kissed them. And then, deviating from what my fantasy was scripting, she took a solo performance.

"I love you, too," I said to her in a hushed tone. She paused for a moment, looking at me, confused, but I was lost for words to explain. In all her years and after all her men, she could not understand that oral consummation was the most intimate form of sex, with every attention to detail being paid to pleasuring your partner's organ of adoration and none to your selfish cravings, as selflessly intimate as love itself. That was the first night I was with a girl other than Zeenat. It was the first time I tried to picture Zeenat's face in my mind but found the memory fading.

Part 3

1997

Graduation from university and growing up had a lot of twists. All through our childhood, we dreamed of dressing up in suits from eight in the morning to eight in the evening, working the most important jobs for money, only to mature and realize that what gave us the most happiness was the exact opposite. Our expectations were rarely in tandem with reality. I never would have seen myself exchanging sweat, spit, and semen with a woman my mother's age. And even if I had envisioned it in a bizarre dream, surely I wouldn't have seen myself enjoying it time and time again.

The first time we had sex in her room, Madame Messalina shut the windows and turned off all artificial ventilation so the room was airtight. "Thinking of this moment has had me sweating for two days nonstop," I complained. "If you don't put on a fan, I'll melt in your hands."

"That's why your skin is glowing so much," she consoled as she pressed her skin against mine underneath the cool sheets.

"You mean that's why my skin smells so much."

"The smell is a short-term sacrifice for the glow." Her hands guided mine toward her breasts. "Imagine if you didn't sweat and all the disgusting things that cause the smells stayed in your body on and on."

"So that's your secret to defy age?"

"Exactly! I found the fountain of youth, and you know why most people never find it? It's because they're looking for a place where they can drink purity and live forever, when really, it's a place where you forsake all your impurities so you can live forever."

"But there's no forever. We all live and we all die, impurities or not."

She wrapped her hand around my lingam and buried it in her warm, wet yoni, pushing into me again and again, ever slowly and ever firmly. "Does this feel like a moment or does this feel like forever?"

I satisfied Madame Messalina's needs and she satisfied my curiosities, but we were never an emotional fit. I'm not sure she needed me to be. After our affairs, I collected a thick brown envelope and explored the streets of Enugu. Another twist to life after graduation was that you had to make more deliberate attempts to meet women: know enough current affairs to discuss politics with a lady in line at the bank; dress up enough to look sexy but not so much to appear overly horny or just plain degenerate-won-the-lottery. Guys didn't just run into girls who had something to say first, like on campus or in Madame Messalina's house.

The bookstore in the business district of the city was the closest semblance of a university campus, frequented by a few guys who preferred an easy way out of socializing. Bookshelves climbing the entire height of the room were set up to form spacious rectangular cells that had raffia chairs and tables arranged in the middle. Guys who would not come alive amid the cold and insincere streets of Enugu found the bookstore a more conducive habitat to let their hormones roam, checking out and purchasing literature and music, walking about, occasionally making conversation with a stranger who appeared to share a similar taste, such as Amos Tutuola's *My Life in the Bush of Ghosts*.

The lady was returning a paperback copy while I was about to buy one. She was like Eucharia Anunobi in *Glamour Girls*, everything—from her bright cropped clothes and bold makeup to her dramatic gestures and pop-star demeanor—seeking attention, and her beauty in motion justified all the attention she got. That day she got all of my attention, beginning with a smile and a handshake, then a conversation. She thought Tutuola's writing was crass, and the thoughts behind it laden with a childish sort of naïveté. I had never read the book but, knowing the history behind it, had respect for the brazen spirit of a man who had no history and fantasy of his own choosing to tell his story for himself. We then battled over the sexes. Chinua Achebe or Buchi Emecheta? Fela Kuti or Sade Adu? We did not find common ground till our interests traveled abroad and we mutually consented to the dream-woven prospect of Whitney Houston and Luther Vandross creating an album together.

I spun the key chain to my new Peugeot 505 around my index finger and asked for her name and address, one right after the other. She withdrew a little magazine from her bag, then began scribbling just below the frayed edges. I recognized the familiar frowsy fellow gracing its cover page: the browned and curled knots of the Afro tapering down to thin sideburns that reached out for a thick goatee like the fingers of Adam reaching out to the hand of God in Michelangelo's famous fresco; the glasses frames looked larger but of the same style as when I first met this man almost twenty years ago, although the scar that ran above his right eyebrow was new to me.

"What's your take on him?" she asked when she noticed me staring at the cover page. "Is he Mendaus the menace, as the government papers suggest, or Mendaus the messiah, as the people's papers say?"

"I know him only as Mendaus Mohammed," I replied curtly.

"I don't know many people who know his second name, not even the government papers."

"We grew up sharing smoke, most of the time from the same joint. I tend to have history with a lot of these people in the news." She smiled, but I kept a straight face; I had perfected my Rick Blaine in *Casablanca* face a long time ago.

"Go on, don't be modest," she said. "Blow your trumpet, connect with your inner Smokey Miles."

"What does Smokey Miles have to do with this?"

"Smokey Miles . . . the jazz instrumentalist . . . connect the dots."

"Smokey Miles wasn't a jazz instrumentalist, that's Smokey Robinson."

"I'm not stupid. I know Smokey Robinson, he was a pop artist." She was giggling now.

"The pop artist was Sugar Robinson," I argued.

"Isn't Sugar Robinson the boxer?" she corrected yet again. "Or is that the pretty singer from that movie *The Color Purple?*"

"No, *biko*, that's Shug Avery." I had lost my Rick Blaine face and was giggling, too.

"Wait, so who is Smokey Miles again?"

"I don't know. Some jazz instrumentalist is what you said. But what does that have to do with anything?"

"Oh, yes! You were meant to blow your trumpet like Smokey—Miles, not Robinson."

"Carry go with your palaver," I said, pushing her away gently, but when she made to leave, I held on to her arm. She gave me the magazine with her number on it, and after talking for another half hour, we parted ways.

I spent the next half hour flipping through Mendaus's interview in the magazine. The bold quote below his picture on the first page was Mendaus's typical intellectual jargon, the sort that appealed to the pseudo-intellectual elites who patronized our publishers: "I am an artist with no muse, all I have is myself. I do not seek anyone's validation; everyone who is worthy is dead. Don't tear down my symphony because you were brought up on ballads. You don't have to crown me king, just acknowledge my kingdom."

I did not know anyone who could aptly describe the crude affairs of Nigerian politics with art and symphonies except Mendaus, not one person at all who could do so without appearing mad. But Mendaus was not bonkers-and-raving mad; he was subtle-whisperer-of-the-town's-secrets mad, the type of mad the town rulers feared. And in Nigeria, there were many town secrets and rulers. I searched the article for the fearful secrets he was spewing on the occasion.

MAGAZINE: What do you think are the prime needs of the eighty million plus Nigerians living below the poverty line in the villages, towns, and even Lagos? Food and water or housing and education, some dare say tribalism?

MENDAUS: No, not at all. I know hunger and thirst are painful, but food and water can wait.

Being homeless isn't a mother's dream, but housing can wait, too. Missionaries gave us these things for centuries, and after that philanthropists gave them to us for decades. But what we need more than all of that is leaders, leaders who would walk among the evil for the sake of the greater good, guide the minds of the people, and show them how to uplift themselves.

MAGAZINE: That's an interesting perspective. And how close do you think our present leaders are to providing these solutions?

MENDAUS: We don't have leaders, we have politicians. Politicians have nothing to offer but words. They are victims of privilege of the system, so why would they want it to change? A revolution is in the hands of the people.

MAGAZINE: Are you suggesting a civil uprising is indirectly the prime need of the Nigerian people? If the people cannot afford to pay for things with cash, they should pay with blood?

MENDAUS: Not at all, this is far from a call to arms. It is a call to break free from cults of personality that are stealing our bread and placating us with crumbs, to curb our dependence on Western culture and be brave enough to depart from the twilight of our traditional culture

because the only worthy culture is the culture
of self-learning. The window of opportunity is
open now. Light a fire to illuminate your mind,
let the passion of your soul fuel it like dry wood,
pass it on to as many torches as are ready, and
when the time comes, we shall use this fire to
raze the walls of oppression to the ground.

Typical Mendaus. His rise to fame had coincided with my
rise to fortune. We had both attained greater heights riding on
the shoulders of giants. I started working for the major general
about a year before the 1994 presidential election that was meant
to see the peaceful transition of power from military regime to
civilian rule. I had never known whose side we were on, the military or any one of the civilian groups sharpshooting for power,
but it was not my job to know. My job was to serve as the unseen
and unheard courier between the major general and his allies.
I never knew any of the allies, but that was not my job, either.
All I had to do was tuck brown envelopes into newspapers and
drop them on tables in hotel lobbies until whoever recognized
his consignment came to collect, or picking up briefcases from
the landings of empty staircases in multistory buildings.

All of this occurred after the campaign organization Mendaus was working with—Democracy Union—registered as a
political party for the 1994 election, about the same time they
were releasing public statements condemning the military, and
just before the group's activities were suspended by the military
regime and its most prominent members indefinitely detained
in police custody. It was Mendaus, previously unknown to the
public eye, who led the protests for their release. It took a week

for the military to coerce the detained Democracy Union members to identify the unknown noisemaker and almost a month before the media knew. But all they had was a first name. There was no surname or address or personal detail that could aid the hounding of the rebel, just threats. It was sometime during this period that he was dubbed "Mendaus the menace."

The election eventually came and passed as freely and fairly as the watching world had hoped, to the dismay of the foreign press, who had dreamed up Pulitzer-worthy headlines and metaphors for the bloodshed and carnage they predicted. But as we were Nigerians, it was beyond possibility to let any ray of spotlight shining upon us to go unbasked in, and so we entertained the world. A petition was made by some unknowns to have the elections canceled; a court without due jurisdiction dribbled the country's entire legal practice and upheld the petition, then passed it to the military regime, which—never failing to be the star of the show—annulled the election results with such aplomb that you would think they had strategized the move from the very beginning! And the audience went wild . . . with riots in the streets, searching for blood and fire to quell the bitter betrayal on their tongue. Houses were looted, cars were burned, and government workers were targeted for murder.

Chaos ensued, and journalists scurried across and within the borders to script the inferno, one level of the Nigerian hell at a time. And as Dante looked to Virgil for guidance through the perilous paths, so did a few journalists take to Mendaus, who had an opinion on every fire lit or smoldered in the name of justice. More than anything else, it was his natural showmanship that fueled his flight to fame. I was watching the BBC via cable when a British presenter covering the riots in Lagos asked

Mendaus to describe the riots in one simple word, setting him off on a tirade: "There's no name to this cause other than justice. If there's a name, there's something for the enemy to attack and distort. You give it a name, and they'll spread lies and misconceptions about that name before truth is done tying its shoelaces. Just live out the cause, and at worst they'll attack your person, but your cause stays untainted. If there's a name, it becomes a religion, a cult, then it needs a chief priest, a leader everyone can look to for guidance. Having anyone above equals is brewing egoism and jealousy. Egoism and jealousy mixed together is self-destruction. Without a name, there's freedom to have a parallel structure where everyone learns from each other. No chief priest, no ego, no self-destruction." Ironically, this was the speech that earned him the moniker "Mendaus the messiah."

On one other occasion, he had strayed off topic during a radio interview, digressing from a critique of the military regime's tyrannical attitude toward political groups to give an enchanting eulogy of Ken Saro-Wiwa, who had been hanged on the orders of the military government. Mendaus went on to refer to Saro-Wiwa's Movement for the Survival of the Ogoni People as a model political group in the stand against military dictatorship in Africa. Since then, I had followed his articles and interviews with steadfast discipleship, to the major general's amusement.

"That Mendaus chap, a lot of what he says is true, and he is bold. He's like a Rottweiler in a cage, waiting to be unleashed on the thieves in the garden," he said, and I smiled, my chest swelling with pride on Mendaus's behalf. "But you know the thing about Rottweilers in a cage, they just assume that the louder their noise, the better their chances are of escaping their cage. And I can't judge them, because they're animals with pitiful brains. I only get upset when humans, people like that Mendaus chap, think like animals with pitiful brains. Barking in the cage gets the Rottweiler shot by the thieves in the garden. And usually, the loudest dog gets shot first."

The bubble of pride in my chest popped like a balloon that had strayed too close to the sun. The major general put the truth plainly, without making any extra effort to convince me, resting assured that my disbelief of the truth could not make his words any less true.

Not much was ever said about the major general's person, and as soon became the norm, I never asked questions. But since he played a rather significant role in the latter stages of my life, it is only fair that I gather a few sentences to explain him and what we did. He was a power broker and I was his left hand, bearing the shield that protected his image from public scrutiny as his right hand prodded the dagger of power. If he had told me he was much older than he looked, I still would have guessed he was in his mid-forties. In ten years, he had elevated himself from police officer to supplier of retired police arms to warring university confraternities, and then supplier of these battle-tested university confraternity members to local politicians for "canvassing grassroots support," until he eventually monopolized the distribution chain and was supplying politicians and government appointees across the entire eastern region. There was no way I would have deciphered all of this from the start, but it did not take too long to figure out after I began receiving and sharing his envelopes and briefcases, and attending public functions on his behalf, overhearing people discuss him in whispers, urging each other to seek his support in search of an appointment or to stay wary of him lest he dealt with them like a Mr. So-on-and-so-forth, who was always either dead or out of the public eye.

The major general's office was filled with a large number of *tatafos*, both to our cause and to my story, so I would not delve into their details. It is necessary to know only that there was a table in each corner of the room, occupied by the ignorant, the lazy, the big-breasted, and the gluttonous. And as they were all unoccupied almost every day, it was quite obvious that they were all retailers of idle chatter, connoisseurs of high-society gossip, each taking pride in their own collection. It baffled me that the major general suffered to have them around, much less pay them. But as a titled chief in his village, he was expected to do something for the village youths. So, the *tatafos* massaged his Igbo man ego.

If there was one thing that could publicly subdue his Igbo man ego, it would be his Igbo man religiosity. He swore to God at the slightest doubt of his integrity, was a patron of the Anglican Boys' Secondary School, and had severe financial commitments to the building of the diocese's new cathedral, never minding the fact that he bought Rolls-Royces for the last two bishops of the diocese. It was quite impossible to estimate how much his spending on God translated into his love for God if you were not aware that above and beyond all things, even God, the major general esteemed cash. He regularly espoused that cash made up for all shortcomings, and so whenever he disappointed any of his three hallows—God, Madame Messalina, or his wife—he made up for that by doling out cash. It is easy to come to terms with his strong belief that cash was the solution to Nigeria's problems; if his cash seemed to appease God, what were a few millions of petty Nigerians? This is why I traveled to Lagos, with a suitcase of clothes for a week and another full of naira notes, and planned to speak with Mendaus in person for the first time in about five years.

I had been back home to Omole in the past year, but there was still a disconnect between my mother and me. I had read all of the letters she had written to me when I was in Enugu but replied not once. She had accepted me with open arms anyway. My silence did not stem from anger or revocation of love. It was because I had spent all of the time, until my departure, believing we were symbiotic, each able to survive on the other's love regardless of the challenges posed by the habitat. Sending me away was her declaration of independence, and keeping away was my equivalent. Simple! My father had also left for good a long time before, and she hid the pain well. Even though there were a few lines on her forehead and streaks of white in her hair, and her arms were more flab than firm, it was nothing unusual for a gracefully aging woman.

This visit was different because Effy was around to bridge the chasm of words and thoughts. Effy had received admission into Queens College, Lagos, exactly two years before. Her school headmistress in Enugu had come to deliver the news personally to Uncle Adol and Aunt Kosi on a Saturday afternoon; they usually had a few students make it into Queens College and Kings College every year, but Effy had been the lone admission that year. Effy was ecstatic; she had never been among the best students in class and managed to write the entrance examination in Lagos only because she had lied to her parents that the trip was compulsory for every student in her year. Uncle Adol was satisfied because the fees were affordable, while the admission provided the luxury of bragging to all who bothered to pay attention that his child was schooling in Lagos. Aunt Kosi was miffed. How could it be that she had fasted and prayed for her youngest daughter's future as diligently as she had, and God had fashioned His will for her to be cast into the midst of the Yorubas?

Aunt Kosi could not fight Effy going to school in Lagos—Uncle Adol would be convinced the witches from Udi had possessed her soul to torment him—but she could fight Effy living in a boardinghouse with Yoruba strangers. And so Effy lived with my mother in Omole and left for school from there every morning, because the devil you know is better than the angel you do not know. She had grown as tall as Tessy in the last few years, only skinnier and darker-skinned; she was still as witty but less talkative. I imagined the latter was my mother's effect on her.

"When are you going to come to Enugu to see my place?" I asked my mother as Effy served dinner for everyone seated around the table.

"*Okporoko.*" She picked up the dried stock fish Effy had just dropped in her egusi soup. "You will turn into this *okporoko* if you are waiting for me to start entering airplanes at my age. My heart cannot take it." Effy stifled her laughter, and I could tell she had been rubbing off on my mother, too.

I took a stroll out of the house after dinner to pick up wraps of smoke from the street vendor's son. Before I'd left for Enugu, he'd been too little to be allowed to wander away from his mother's kiosk, and so he'd watched us play football from across the street. Since then, his mother had built a proper shop of concrete and aluminum. And as she was not literate, he was in charge of writing out receipts and supplying the neighborhood smoke. In that same vein, everything else in Omole had changed. Within ten years, young aspiring couples had transformed into upper-middle-class families, empty plots where children played into duplexes, and dirt roads into tarred streets. I walked down to the end of the street, where a gully served as the boundary between Omole and the rest of the world, and I could hear pigeonholes on the recently erected metal gates clang open as I walked past them, allowing cautious night watchmen to observe the unknown stroller. Far away in the distance, yellow headlights of vehicles on the expressway descended slowly on each lane like angels on Jacob's stairs. The heaven beyond the horizon was on the other side of the Third Mainland Bridge that lay at the foot of the expressway: Lagos Island, Victoria Island, Ikoyi, and Lekki—their big banks, finance firms, headquarters of oil companies servicing the Niger Delta fields, local branches of international corporations, and thousands of smokescreen businesses for nameless crooks. By the next morning, these angels would be summoned again to worship and praise the world's unified deity—capitalism. And in a few nights, I would be worshipping the deity's nemesis at its revered temple—the Afrika Shrine.

I'd heard things had not changed much, but the nostalgia still choked me because I had not been there since the night Zeenat died. It was a Sunday afternoon, and the sun hung oppressively low over the Shrine, streaks of sweat held back by my brows like a river dam as I waited outside. Music had not begun playing inside, and so there was barely any activity. Mendaus and I had agreed to meet early in the afternoon to get all of the discussions out of the way before the evening groove. There was no crowd yet, and the vanity vendors were just setting up their stalls; under one such I was seated when Mendaus's slender figure approached in a checkered blazer and plain trousers, trailed closely by a woman and none of the usual entourage that would accompany anyone who had mustered a bit of wealth or fame in this part of the world.

"I never thought I'd see you put on a suit," I said as he came closer; to judge by the look of surprise on his face, I suspected he had not recognized me until I had spoken.

But he covered up well as I stood to embrace him. I went on, "And this your hair, still as tight and tacky as ever. Not even the limelight could trim or straighten it."

"I have to flaunt it if I was born with it. I mean, if Cindy Crawford can flaunt her body, I can flaunt my hair. Yes? It's almost as if we have to wear trim hair to be recognized as sane nowadays. By the time we have children, we'll need to be stinking rich to be validated as human beings."

"You haven't changed a cell, always making a civil rights movement out of everything."

"My hair is a lifestyle choice; you're the one making a movement of straightening it." He stared me in the eye. "Unfortunately, I'm still the same guy. I still read a lot and drink as much as I read. I still fall in love instead of fucking and moving on, like you did with Zeenat." I flinched, and he smiled coyly at the girl by his side. "I still eat pussy."

"But you . . ."

"No *wahala*. I was just teasing about Zeenat." The ice thawed as we made small talk, and when the conversation was warm enough, I unveiled my agenda.

"I must admit you've made a lot of friends in the media. I follow your articles and speeches. They give you a lot of credit, and deservingly so," I said. His attention was firmly knotted to my string of words despite the girl by his side toying with his sleeve. "But the one being carried never knows how far away the town really is."

"Ihechi, you're confusing me. We're not gray enough to be using proverbs yet. So right now am I the carrier or the carried?"

"The carried."

"Why can't I be a carrier? You still think I'm a weakling, don't you? I do fifty push-ups a day now."

"You're the carried because you're trying to wage a war you don't have the resources to win. The media have you looking like the messiah of the Jews, but which of them are going to stick their necks out for you when Pontius Pilate sentences you to death? Which of them are going to give you guns and spears? And by the way, I used to do fifty push-ups a day when I was in secondary school."

"I don't need guns and spears to win this battle. And I do a hundred sit-ups apart from the push-ups."

"For crissake, I don't mean actual guns and spears. I mean, you can't face the system without any money. And even if you did two hundred sit-ups and push-ups a day, I wouldn't bet on you going toe to toe with a teenager."

"Oh, I know teenagers who would knock you out. Who says I needed any money, though?"

"A revolution has to be financed."

"Our revolution is of the mind, not material."

"And that's fine with me, but is your mind bulletproof?"

He chuckled; this was the first time I'd ever been in the

position of winning a debate with him. About a dozen people ran out of the Shrine, and for a moment, Mendaus and I were distracted, but then he continued, "I know you didn't come here to offer me guns and bulletproof vests, you know better. So what is it you're offering, really?"

"I know people who are willing to work with you if you're ready, people who can expand the spread of your propaganda, people who can stir up grassroots support for your cause all over the country in regions where your name has never been heard, strong people with influence in the present government who could ensure your protection from government reprisals and turn your popularity into political clout."

"Who are these people now?"

"You know I can't tell you that just yet."

The people who'd run out of the Shrine had clustered together, and some of the vanity vendors were being sucked into the black hole of tittle-tattle. Mendaus continued still: "I understand, but no harm in asking, right? You could at least tell me why me, out of all the pricks in the government's *yansh*."

"You're a man of words, so I'll borrow an idea from Aristotle: Every great curiosity begins from wonder. These people have seen, and are very amazed by, I must say, what you can muster on your own. It's only natural that they wonder what more you could do with the right investment, especially because they are capable of providing such investments."

"Aristotle can take a seat. We've had wise men in Egypt who argued that every great curiosity begins from frustration, and I agree with them because a content man never wonders what could be better; that's what frustrated men do. So, now, Ihechi, why are your people frustrated? They already have influence in the government, so it's safe to say they dine with the military, but what is it they really want that they cannot have despite all their power and influence?"

"The same thing you want. We are all trying to make this country better in whatever way we can. And sometimes whatever way means doing things together."

"I don't buy that. They have money and protection and influence, they don't need a figurehead to make whatever change they have the capacity to make. Unless a figurehead is actually what they need. They don't necessarily need a revolution, just the revolutionary, a puppet, a poseur."

"Don't be ridiculous, Mendaus."

"Are you part of this scheme or are you really ignorant to what's going on? I don't know who these people are, but they want a civilian coup, not a revolution. It's the power that's driving them."

"But it's power that makes the decisions," I said. "Good intentions never changed the world. For all you know, you still have a lot to learn. And these individuals can teach you a lot."

"I'm tired of their type, all these teachers teaching me nonsense. All along they have taught us about the power of the individual—fill 'my' wallet, feed 'my' family, teach 'my' children. The only time these individuals remember the community is when they can benefit from the community and never vice versa. This lie they taught has chained us to the floor. And the only truth is that when the upper class is pushed to the wall, it is not individuals but our community that is hassled, our community that is murdered—and if God tarries, our community that is delivered in the end."

There was a loud shriek from the cluster of vanity vendors,

and then everybody dispersed in a wailing frenzy, some with hands above their heads and others sprawled on the floor with limbs akimbo. Mendaus and I turned simultaneously. The girl beside him stood up and I followed, but Mendaus was the first to walk toward the cluster, and ultimately, we all followed, hoping and gliding to catch up with his lanky strides. None of the wailers answered our "What's happening?" and "What's going on?"

At the center of them all was a radio on a stool, loud enough to be heard over the wails. Just as we got close enough for the blaring noise from the radio to become audible, we heard: "The immediate cause of death of Fela was heart failure, but there were many complications arising from the acquired immunodeficiency syndrome."

One of the vanity vendors, palms plastered to his cheeks, gave the first of a million eulogies: "It's not true. Fela will live forever. He can't die."

There were not many people who believed in Fela's efforts to progress the harmony of the world more than Mendaus, and the fall of the iroko tree crushed the little grains of sand that carried the tree atop their shoulders. Mendaus was devastated, and so the news ended our conversation that Sunday, and I left the Shrine looking to reorganize my proposition and come back stronger whenever we spoke again. But I had one more job to do before leaving Lagos, a package to deliver to an Indian at a beach resort in Lekki. This was my umpteenth delivery to him and we had grown cordial with time, so he insisted I stay around to share a bottle of wine as he complained about his problems with the local boys. They had barricaded his new construction site and beat up his engineers, demanding he give jobs to five of their colleagues-in-arms and pay a monthly stipend to their boss before work could be resumed. And all this after he had given the traditional chieftain, local government chairman, and ministry of works representative "money to buy fuel." The problem was very much beyond my comprehension; those were things he should have done from the very beginning, without the need for coercion, but I could not say that out loud. I went on to blame the government for everything and then fabricated an experience similar to his but more gruesome, so he did not go to bed convinced that he was in the predicament because he was seen as a white man, a *maga*. But my greatest feat of the night was urging him to drink away his sorrow and subtly refilling his cup until he passed out and I could slip away.

It was about 8:45 p.m. that Friday when I left his resort at Lekki. The major roads were still congested with endless traffic of the tired working class streaming down clumsy lanes like ants marching toward the anthill. There was an accident on a side street that had brought the service lane to a standstill, so those who usually traversed the route had to wait till the gathering ants uncertainly dispersed or drove farther down, searching for an equally uncertain alternative. Most drivers chose to wait it out. But the last thing I wanted was to be stuck in traffic on a side street too obscure for traffic vendors with their polythene packaged snacks or iced drinks in trays and coolers firmly balanced on their heads like an extra appendage, no matter how fast they ran. I drove past the side street and kept to the service lane, driving slower so I would not miss the turn my memory suggested was somewhere close by. Impatient horns began sounding behind me as bright headlights blinded the rearview mirror, causing the crystal pendant of *Yemoja* hanging from it to sparkle. The events leading to the pendant being hung from the mirror crept into my head, and I smirked.

It was about five months back, during one of my trips to see my mother. I had barely arrived from the airport and was anticipating the pounded yams being prepared as my mother jammed pestle against mortar when the doorbell rang. I knew it was the neighbor who lived in the large new duplex opposite the house, who had been so keen to remind me on my first trip home in years that the estate they lived in was intended for middle-to-high-income earners. And that the pounding of yams, grinding of pepper, and other low-income habits practiced regularly by my mother behind her wide-open gate and low fence were an inconvenience to all other residents, an eyesore that reduced the value of their property.

But on that occasion, some other demon sibling of arrogance had possessed my neighbor.

"Ihechi, my fren!" my neighbor exclaimed in his Ogbomosho accent, thrusting his arm into the doorway and pulling me out by the neck. "Do you know what a V6 engine is?"

I was quiet and unsteady in my steps, feeling my body growing weaker with each step as I moved farther away from the pounded yams being served on my plate at that moment.

"I guessed as much, my fren," continued the neighbor, who had correctly taken my silence for ignorance and was now pointing outside the gate to the front of his house. "Well, each of these engines in those two cars, which I just shipped in from Germany, by the way, are state-of-the-art specimens of the latest automobile technology. Do you understand what I'm saying, my fren?" We then pretended to inspect the shiny metals and tubes beneath the hoods of the two new cars.

"But all this is not exactly why I called you out of your house, my fren. You see, with all that has been going on, I've taken the liberty to recruit a night watch to be overlooking our street and all our property we leave out here when we go to bed at night. So, since we are civil gentlemen, and it is all our property being secured, I believe it is logical that we should split the night watch's salary."

I looked at the two new German cars, his old French car, and then at the Japanese car I had just purchased for my mother the month before, and interrupted my neighbor before he could continue.

"Is this one of your jokes, or are you being serious?" I asked before substituting silence for ignorance, as my neighbor had done moments ago. "First, if I had any spare change, I'd rather invest in a yam-pounding machine, as you've always suggested, instead of suffering my mother to spend her evenings bent over pestle and mortar. Second, unlike you, all my mother owns that is of any importance to her fits perfectly into her house. And finally, if anybody was crazy enough to steal my mother's car, I'd consider it a deed of community service, because clearly, anyone hopeless enough to overlook all your cars and steal this Japanese car needs more help than mere mortals can offer." I walked over to my mother's car and opened it, removed the chain with the *Yemoja* pendant from around my neck, and hung it from the rearview mirror. "And just in case, *Yemoja* right there is all the protection my car needs."

The neighbor moved out a few months later, and my mother said the last time she saw him, he was talking about an aptitude test he had written for a new job in a taxi. She didn't ask too many questions.

I turned onto the alternative road and tried to negotiate the Japanese car through the narrow lane, made even smaller by the double-parked vehicles along the entire length of the road. The digital clock on the dashboard displayed 8:50 p.m. There was no way I could make it home in time to see Effy before her nine o'clock bedtime. Knowing that my mother would not enter the kitchen to start preparing my dinner after nine, I lost every incentive to make it home that night and considered stopping off at Mama's place, a tender euphemism for the new pub that had just opened in Omole, or maybe even the gentlemen's cabaret, another tender euphemism, this one for a local strip club. Better the cabaret, because at least I wouldn't have to bother about arriving home saturated in a musk of alcohol and cigarettes.

I noticed a blockade along the narrow road and slowed down a bit. There were three uniformed men standing behind an improvised roadblock of vehicle tires, very unorthodox for both the time and the location. Two of the uniformed men approached the car, one on either side, as I slowed to a stop and wound down the window.

"Good evening, sir," the uniformed man by my window said a bit too calmly. "Abeg you for like comot that car and submit all your better things for here."

I was far more confused than my facial expressions could convey, and maybe the uniformed men mistook it for stubbornness. The policeman on the other side of the car spoke: "My colleague would not repeat himself, sir; would you please step out of your car and submit all of your valuables?"

My first coherent thought was "Is this a robbery?" and without thinking, I uttered it.

The uniformed man at my side pulled a gun from his back

and smashed the butt into my forehead. My eyelids fluttered from the pain, which was as familiar as it was unwanted, like that glutton friend who always knocks at your door just in time for dinner. My vision blackened.

"Pocket dey empty," said a voice from beyond the darkness, husky and blurred. "Wallet dey empty. Make we just dump am for gutter?"

"Money dey dashboard," a second voice whispered with more subtlety.

"Oya carry the leg, make I carry the hand," a third voice joined in, softer than the previous two.

"O boy, wait first. Make I off the guy shoe first. E go size me," said the first voice once again.

"Allow allow. E be like say I know this guy." I wasn't sure if this was a new voice or one of the previous, tenuous under strain.

"So make we no thief the money? You dey crase abi?"

"Allow. I know this guy. Na sure guy. We no need thief the money. The guy go dash us." The tenuous voice was now adamant.

"As long as we go still chop the money. So make we leave am for here?"

My eyes opened slowly and surveyed the four men around me in police uniforms. Before I blacked out, I heard the tenuous voice one last time: "Baba no now. We go carry am reach headquarters, make e wake up small."

When my eyelids fluttered open, like feathers around a chicken's buttocks blowing in the wind, it was impossible to figure out which of the absurd scenes of my environs had woken me: the dank stench of the bare mattress I lay upon, the rhythmic crank of the ceiling fan above my head, the furious keyboard clicks by the young boys peering into computer screens lined up by the wall, or the metallic squeak that suggested a bouncing spring bed hidden behind the dirty curtains opposite the computer screens—all were contending for chief absurdity. A hand supported me up as I surveyed the room and handed me a clear cup of water. I raised the cup so that it was between my gaze and the lightbulb at the side of the room to inspect the uncountable fingerprint stains on the glass for a while.

"I don't want to sound like those bad guys in action films, but you know if we were trying to poison you, we would have done so a long time ago instead of waiting for you wake up."

I took a half-gulp, and the sweltering vapor from the lukewarm liquid burst through my nose, choking me into a cough. "This isn't water?" I asked, inspecting the glass again.

The room erupted in laughter for a few seconds, and then the computer chaps resumed focus.

"Vodka?" I suggested.

"Yes," the action-film bad guy replied. "But not any brand you have tasted before, I'm sure of that."

"I doubt it. I've done my fair share of vodka sampling in my time."

"This is only the second batch of this combination I've ever made. I distilled in the kitchen above us with potatoes from my own little farm in the backyard."

I doubted his claims and sipped a little more of the vodka, as if I could somehow verify his claims with my palate. I heard a woman cry in a slow ascending tone; everyone except me seemed unbothered. Then the metallic squeak from behind the curtain came to a sudden stop, and almost simultaneously, a stark-naked fellow emerged, struggling to put on a pair of jeans.

"He is our very own chemist on campus. First-class chemical engineering graduate from the University of Lagos," said the formerly naked fellow, as if he had been part of the conversation from the very beginning. I now recognized his tenuous voice. "Ihechi, right? It took me a while to remember your name."

I was sure I'd had no identification on me in the car. I drank a bit more vodka to jog my memory.

"You don't remember giving me this?" he continued, pointing to a little but thick scar running across his eyebrow. "It's okay. It's always the challenger who remembers the fight, never the champion. I'm sure if we played a sharp game of football, you would remember me. I was always the champion on the field, and you were always the challenger."

"Maradona?" It all came back suddenly. "Or is it Bee Money?"

"I can't remember the last time I was called any of that." His pathetic American accent was thankfully absent. "It's Capone now."

He had aged exactly as I would have imagined if I'd been tasked to: thick arms with sleeves of scars and dark spots, muscled out from his head through to his torso and thighs and calves, with barely any hair on his body except a few klutzy strands sparsely scattered on his cheeks. He told the room a great tale of how we had gotten into a dangerous fight with all sorts of weapons, and after he had danced through my flurry of attacks and landed a number of hefty blows on me, he had been distracted for a second by the prettiest girl he had ever seen, which was enough for me to catch him with a solid right that knocked him out. I reminded him that the pretty girl's name was Zeenat and she was dead. The whole room toasted vodka to her memory. Then he apologized for his friends knocking me out with a gun, as casually as he would have if he'd scuffed my shoes.

"You should thank God I was with them tonight," he said in between sips. "It could have been worse."

"I should thank God my childhood buddy grew up into a pistol-whipping robber?" I had intended my remark to contain the same wry humor that had pervaded the evening; instead, the room fell into an uncomfortable silence, and a few heads supposed to be focused on computer screens peeped over their shoulders to see what would happen next.

Capone threw his cup of vodka into the air. Naturally, my eyes fixed on the soaring projectile, and in that split second, I heard a loud slap on my face before feeling the sting as I recovered my balance on the floor, careful not to graze any of the broken glass. Capone threw his weight on me and forced a grip around my neck, pressing a large shard to my cheek before I could take my next breath.

"You scare so easily," he whispered as I felt blood drip down my cheek from the tip of the shard. "See how all your veins are jumping out of your skin. I could bleed you dry with my thumbs."

All eyes in the room remained fixed on him, even when he slipped off my shivering body, even when he laughed and poured himself more vodka in a fresh glass, even when he dispelled the intrigue and walked out of the room, guiding me along with him. The cold breeze on the balcony stung the open wound on my face.

"You understand, *abi?* The reason I have the loudest voice around here is because I'm the most feared. I would draw blood from any one of them if they disrespected me, and they know it, so it must be the same with you. We still be guys, *abi?*"

I stared away his apology but tried to take control of the situation before more disrespect was assumed. "I thought you were just a yahoo boy. How did it get to the point of armed robbery?"

"Don't you even judge me," he replied instantly. "A man does what he has to do to survive."

"Aren't there better ways to survive? Anything is better than armed robbery."

"Better way? Can you remember I always got better results than you in primary school? The only difference between us right now is that your parents could afford to put you through university and my mother couldn't. It's not because one of us is smarter or better at heart."

"You've made enough money to get away from all of this and put yourself through school."

"But who would pay my mother's hospital bills while I spend four years rotting in these shithole local universities? And I could afford to go abroad, but my mother would be dead from loneliness before I got halfway across the ocean."

From the balcony, a myriad of deceitful shadows were cast down on the street by the half-moon up high. The night air held a chill, and I clutched my shirt, now wet with sweat, closer to my chest. Capone handed me a dry towel from the balcony banister and continued. "And after I finish school, what next? There are more jobs in backstreet Lagos than in high street Lagos, and backstreet pays better. Those boys on the computer make thousands of dollars every month from the clients they scam abroad; all of them were jobless computer science graduates before they came here. From the robbery on you alone, the boys gained thousands of naira in cash, and your car will sell on the Cotonou black market for thousands of dollars. No high street job is that profitable."

"What do you mean 'the boys gained'? I'm not getting my car back?"

"Your car should be the least of your worries. If our unemployed doctor had been around for the job, they would have cut you open, taken your kidney to export to Malaysia, and stitched you back up tidy for some more thousands of dollars." His reasoning knocked on the door of my conscience, but there was no budging; I would never understand his justifications. I had always heard but never understood that survival on Nigerian streets was like a game of chess, and no pieces were spared en route to checkmate. I guzzled the rest of my vodka at once.

"I know what we do is unpleasant," he continued, and I laughed at his understatement. "I mean, we all had lofty dreams, but we ended up worshipping the disciple when we could find our Jesus."

"Worshipping the disciple? More like giving the devil fellatio."

"I'm going to hold my cup and sip like a real gentleman, so you'll think I'm not confused and I know what fellatio means. But if I'm to be honest with you, I'm not ashamed of what I do. I lie, I steal, and if I have to, I kill. It's no big deal. It's so honorable when people kill for love or for their god. Well, money is my true love, it's my god. Why is my killing any less honorable? People can say what they like, but I'm fine because I know they wouldn't think the same if they were sharing my profit."

"So you think people are vexed about armed robbery because you don't give them a portion of the money you stole from them in the first place? I think you've been having too much backyard vodka."

The chemist joined us on the balcony, derailing our train of thought. "The bride is ready for marriage," he announced.

"So let's take her to church," Capone replied. There were loud cheers from inside, as the computer scientists had been listening for his reply; in a second, they had vamoosed from the room, hurtling down the staircase at the end of the balcony.

"Will your *padi* be following us to church?" the chemist said, looking at Capone.

"I don't do church," I intercepted. "I'm not a Christian."

"Neither are we," Capone replied with a smile as he showed me down the stairs.

My mind had not been bothered about my exact whereabouts while we had been upstairs, but my curiosity was piqued as the whole lot of Capone's boys filed through a maze of unpainted concrete buildings cramped beside each other as far as sky met ground. A few of the boys paused to pick up big brown cartons from the floor below, and then the merry marauders continued uninterrupted. There was barely enough space between the buildings for walkways, which remained in perpetual darkness because the moonlight could not filter through the thicket of dense face-to-face concrete flats. The overused and undermaintained drainage had clogged up, so the narrow walkways were damp with sewage. Occasionally, these walkways intertwined with the corridors of people's homes, causing the boys to skip and hop above and around trays of *garri* set out to dry.

All until the waves of dilapidated high-rise buildings filled with lowest-income earners slowly subsided onto a shore of sandy beach littered with nylons, plastic bottles, and a million tiny seashells. Atop the stretch of beach sat unending rows of wooden sheds serving as makeshift bars with little or no furniture, just four walls and a roof full of loud people and louder music. Each shed was linked to another by a continuous stream of humans dancing from one to another. And each stream was upended only when an open dance floor served as a dam, containing the stream and creating from it an electrifying energy that powered the vibe of the thousand-man groove.

"You may now kiss the bride!" Capone screamed above the blaring disco, and his long line of boys opened their brown cartons and twisted open the corks of green bottles, kissing them with a low, smacking "muaah!" before becoming one with the crowd and distributing their brew to anyone who cared to taste.

"Is this church?" I asked.

"Church?" Capone retorted. "This is Sodom, the biggest *gbedu* in Lagos." It had been forever since I'd heard that word in use, but then again, it had been forever since I'd been in any scenario that demanded its use. *Gbedu:* a social gyration involving loud music, unashamed abuse of currency, excessive smoking and drinking and eating and intensive frolicking.

There was none of that hip-pop obsession that had taken over the popular nightspots in Lagos or Enugu; it was strictly African dance-hall tunes that rocked the stacked speakers, and people had turned up to dance, not to pose with expensive bottles of cognac as they nodded out of sync with the beat without saying a word to anyone. It had none of the passion of the Afrika Shrine, where optimists came to find succor and pessimists came to validate their disdain for whatever; Sodom was a haven for transparent thrill seekers.

"Where are your car keys?" shouted a girl Capone had shuffled over to dance with.

"You want to dance in my car?" he replied.

"Slow slow, Maurice Greene," she said, breaking the exchange of questions with an actual reply. "I'm tired of trekking in this Lagos, it's not good for my complexion. I want to contest for Miss Nigeria next year, and I don't want to have to bleach, so from tonight I only dance with men that have cars to drive me everywhere I need to go."

"Only fair girls ever win that thing," said a girl dancing with her. Apparently, they were friends, so I shuffled over to make it a quartet. "It's too late now, even bleaching can't save you. I keep telling you if you want a man with a car, go and stand on Awolowo Road by midnight with those other girls."

"You want her to trek some more because she wants to stop trekking? That defeats the whole purpose of wanting a man with a car," I interjected.

"At least being black is better than having tribal marks," said the first girl, pointing at her friend, who had three horizontal scars drawn on each cheek, man-made evidence of her Yoruba heritage.

"You would think tribal marks would be an advantage in a Miss Nigeria pageant, oh," her friend defended with faux hurt. "I mean, anyone from Africa can be black, but only a true Yoruba queen could have my kind of marks. I don't know what those judges are judging."

Capone fumbled with his pockets for a few seconds. All of a sudden, he thrust his fist into the air, dangling the keys to my

Japanese car. "And look what I have here," he announced, sending the girls into a cheering frenzy. He stuffed his hand into his pocket once again and withdrew some rumpled naira notes that, earlier that night, had been neatly folded in my pockets. He placed them in my palm. "Use these to have some fun." And he disappeared into the crowd with the giggling first girl tucked under his arm.

The tribally marked girl danced closer to me. She smelled like my mother's kitchen, fresh fish and spices. Even with her artificial hair extensions and long acrylic nails, it was not hard to guess her day job. In a few hours, when day broke and she had to set up her market stall, we could be standing in front of each other, separated by a table full of fish in any of Lagos's open markets, and she would not dare look me in the eye, let alone place her arms around my neck and grind her waist on my groin like she was doing under the moon. The realization of the truth stilled me slowly: It was the same with Capone. We had grown up in the neighborhood but had never really come from the same place. We had been headed to different destinations, and even if he'd wanted to tag along, the high society I was still finding my footing in was strictly by invitation, and the gatekeepers did not take kindly to unexpected guests. He could only pull me down. They could only pull me down.

I took a few steps away from her and flipped through the money Capone had tucked into my palm and confirmed that it was more than enough to take a taxi from anywhere to anywhere in Lagos. I began walking back toward the concrete buildings we had come from, not once looking back at Sodom, leaving the tribally marked girl staring at me in frozen confusion like a pillar of salt.

—

There are two types of people. The first people know they are not born with enough; they have a definition of enough, though, and they work, to withered limbs, to attain this defined standard. The second people believe they are not born with enough, even though sometimes they actually are, but more crucially, they have no definition of enough, and so they seek to keep amassing wealth without any sort of discretion, leaving nothing to chance.

As birds of the same feather nest together, so do people of the same type cluster together. In Lagos, the first types usually were on the mainland, and the second types were across the Third Mainland Bridge, West Africa's longest, on the islands. The second types are not attuned to grunt work, so they import the first types from the mainland; these imports cannot afford to live on the island proper, so they settle in the outskirts, where land is cheap—Ikate, for example, where Capone and his boys found a hiding place.

The first types were content but ambitious; the second types were in a never-ending pursuit of a seemingly elusive utopia. These two were the same people on the exterior, but in their minds, they could not have been any further apart. I had been born of the first type, and though I would not realize it till much later, I had become the second type through my association with the major general. Maybe if I had realized it earlier, I would have been better prepared to allay my mother's temper when I stumbled into the house a couple of hours before dawn, sweaty and exhausted and without the Japanese car in sight. She hooted and tooted for an explanation.

"Ihechi, these people you're working for, don't they have a

conscience? Why are they keeping you outside till this time? Are they the first to give work? The people who release their staff at five o'clock, do they have two heads?"

"Mummy, this has nothing to do with my boss. I had some other things after work that delayed me and took longer than expected."

"What rubbish, other things? Is it money? Is it woman? If you die now, money and woman that you're pursuing would continue as if you never existed. Soldier come, soldier go, barracks go remain."

I looked on, captivated by my mother in her theatrical element while she employed the full space of the living room as her stage. I tried to lighten her up. "*Ehn*, because soldier would leave barracks tomorrow does not mean soldier should not parade for barracks today now."

She was having none of it. "What have I done to deserve this? Why has *Esu* picked me to make a laughingstock of? Ihechi, you're not the first tribulation I would pray my way out of."

"So why do you keep praying to *Esu*, who never answers you? I know you were afraid for me, and I'm sorry, but it's okay to be afraid. You don't have to run away to those logs of wood every time you're afraid. They've only ever torn us apart."

"Listen to yourself." Her voice was irate. "You've started talking back at me when I'm talking to you, *abi*? You've been drinking as well? I can hear the smell of the hot drink in your mouth."

Perhaps I should have denied her last accusation immediately, but I exhaled onto my palms and placed them close to my nose to detect the pungency of the alcohol on my breath. "Are you not happy to see me here in one piece?" I digressed. "I just want to rest my head properly. You could continue all these questions by morning."

"Did your hot drink put you inside an accident?" she continued, her voice beginning to flare in as much concern as anger. "Is that why you came home without the car? How many times will *Esu* deliver you before you stop all this foolish rubbish?"

If I had realized that she did not really care about the car, that having me safe and happy around her was more than enough for her, I would have known better than to reply. But I did not know better.

"I would get you another car. And for the last time, I don't believe in *Esu*. *Esu* is a fraud. The entire notion of Ifá is a fraud."

My mother's face was frozen, the model of a terrifying scream stuck in a particular second in time, like a video hooked on the VCR coil. She tried to forcibly press play on her scream, but she could only rewind and get stuck on that particular second, taking a deep gasp and getting stuck in her scream again. Then she clutched her chest, still gasping for breath as her body slithered to the floor. I caught her just in time to break her fall, resting her body, now as stiff as sorrow, on the cold ground. Her face was stuck midscream, but in her eyes a thousand words were being said by the second, hundreds of synonyms for pain and fear and uncertainty resonating with every blink.

I ran out to get the car but remembered halfway out the compound that the car was gone, so I ran back in. Halfway in I remembered there was nothing helpful inside the house, so once again I scurried outside, banging on the gates of neighbors and screaming on the street. I could see the night watchmen of the large houses on our street light their lanterns and peep through pigeonholes, but every single one of them shut their pigeonholes and dimmed their lanterns after a few seconds. I sped back into the house, but my mother was gone from the living room floor.

Spirited away? Ifá doesn't rapture. Perhaps phantasmagoria, a lucid dream? Yes, that, until loud incantations pierced the silence. The voice, so tender but the tone so severe, guided me through corridors. All the way I stumbled through shadows and echoes, arriving at the door to the room that was my mother's shrine. Beyond the door, Effy, somehow awoken from sleep, crouched over my mother's body with the *opon* Ifá—divination tray—in one hand and *iroke* Ifá—tapper rod—in the other. The tray and rod were adorned with carved images along with artistic representations of the deities my mother believed determined the comeuppance of every human existence. Effy tapped the end of the rod on the tray with a rhythm that was to invoke the presence of my mother's *òrìsà*, her ancestors, and *Orunmila* himself.

"*Onigbowa aye*, the one in control of the earth," Effy was shouting as she slipped something between my mother's lips. I'd had no idea that she could speak Yoruba. "*Alare na ode orun*, the middleman between heaven and earth." Then she cast a beaded chain onto the ground and whispered into her fingers as they settled. I could smell the burning flesh of whatever little animal she had sacrificed before I came into the room.

I tried to get through to my mother, but Effy shoved me back. "*Fimile*, leave me alone." Her eyes wielded fire. "*Elekun n sunkun, Esu n sun eje; Esu* is shedding blood when the owner of the problem is shedding tears."

"Don't you fear God anymore?"

"Fear God? But I'm not a Christian," Effy replied.

"You're an Igbo girl; you can't worship a Yoruba deity."

"And yet nobody seemed to mind when I used to worship a Jewish deity."

"Stop all this nonsense! Your mother's tummy would be turning, wherever she is."

I forced her aside and lifted my mother off the floor, her body looser than when she was in my arms just a few minutes ago. And then slowly, her hanging head turned toward me and her lips parted, whispering, "Ifá be praised."

"You're alive?" I asked in disbelief.

Effy echoed, much louder, "Ifá be praised!"

"The last time I was home, he queried me about not getting married yet," said Tessy. "But when I brought out the bottle of whiskey, we spent the rest of the evening laughing about how silly a question it was to ask. My mother was livid."

Since I'd moved into my new flat off Upper Chime Avenue in New Haven at the start of last year, Tessy had made a habit of spending her Saturdays with me. She would first go to Ogbete market to buy all sorts of foodstuffs and condiments, then make her way to my place to prepare the meals that would be packaged in old ice cream tubs and stocked in my freezer to cater my stomach through the next week. On occasions when I was just returning from a trip to Lagos, she would also clean out my flat. When she was done, we would spend the rest of the day laughing over interesting updates in each other's lives or the lives of people we knew. The people we were currently talking about were her parents.

"If you keep pushing her buttons," I replied finally, "one day your mother is going to blow up and pestle you into a bloody mess. After all, she has an extra daughter."

"Honestly, half the time she looks like she's going to bust up in a fight at any given moment. But her scarf is my gauge; as long as her scarf is still on her head, I know I'm safe." It was a classic Aunt Kosi move to remove her scarf from her head and tie it around her waist any time her aggravation was about to transcend into aggression. Tessy was on her feet, striding across the room and gesticulating energetically. I tossed a few roasted peanuts at her head as a tender reprimand. Tessy went on, "And if she ever found out that her extra daughter was now a pagan, all my past sins would be washed away, and I would finally, deservedly, be conferred a saint. Then, if anyone was going to get bloodied with a pestle, it would be Effy."

Earlier in the afternoon, I had told Tessy about Effy's conversion. More than anything else, Tessy appeared ecstatic that Effy, like her, had failed to live up to their mother's pious expectations of them.

"I don't want to be within a fifty-mile radius of your mother when she finds out," I said.

"No worries, she might never find out. At least I don't plan on telling her." She was now diving at the roasted peanuts I was still tossing at her, trying to catch each one with her mouth. "And bigger secrets have slept under the same roof with her and she never found them out."

I knew she was referring to her window-escaping escapades of her university days. I never would have guessed things would change so much, so quickly. Once she'd graduated from university, she had managed to sever her relationship with the major general and had only a cordial one with Madame Messalina.

More remarkably, she had used her final payout from the major general to open a large boutique that was bested in stock only by Eastern Shops in the entire Enugu. I knew she made more than enough money to move out on her own, but she still regarded her parents' reputation, even if not their opinion. A woman living outside her father's house if single, or outside her husband's house if married, was unequivocally equated with prostitution and a disgrace to her family.

"What's your take on Effy's conversion?" I asked. "Hate it or love it, your way of thinking is cut from your mother's cloth, but you don't seem as worried as she would be. Why?"

"Money matters? Yes. And maybe I can be uppity about petty things," she replied as her eyes rolled. "But we know my mother is a chronic overreactor, which I'm far from. I know Effy's issue is very serious, but what would screaming and skinning her do? Panicking never solved anything in this life."

I remembered how my mother had panicked and fainted the night I came home without the Japanese car. The same way she had panicked and sent me off to Enugu so many years ago after Zeenat died. Maybe panicking was an adult thing we were not yet privy to but ultimately destined for. Or maybe their apprehension was a consequence of all the tribulations they had endured as a generation, pressures that Tessy's and my generation never experienced and therefore could never be shaped by. Whatever the case may be, we lived in a different time from our parents. We would never understand them, and they would never understand us, not because understanding was impossible but because both sides of the divide never asked the questions that would make understanding possible, the kind of questions that empathetically inquired opinion and not the kind that brutally enforced it.

"Madame Messalina says she's looking for a new lingam because you won't have her time anymore. I'm not in the position to judge, but I think you should find someone to settle with. You need it more than I do."

I shrugged. "It would not matter tonight." Major General was hosting a grand party later in the evening. It was not celebrating anything in particular, but he could afford it. Tessy had also been invited, although she had declined because the venue was his house, and she had no desire to be ogled in contempt by his wife all night long for her past sins. "There will be much bigger fish in the ocean. Major General has many important friends coming."

"Don't rubbish me. Fish is fish; a bigger fish is simply the fish that is not scared of swallowing other fishes. And all you men would swallow anything in your path to down a pant."

I squinted in faux disgust. She read right through it and stuck out her tongue at me. After half an hour of goading, she agreed to drop me off because I knew too well I might not be sober enough to drive myself home after one of Major General's parties.

Popularized by the Yoruba moniker of *Owambe*, this type of party was the big brother to the *Gbedu* parties of Sodom. Men wore traditional garb with the necessary insignia to indicate their chieftaincy titles. Women wore similar garb, color-coordinated with their spouses, and heavy weights of gold unashamedly borrowed if not proudly possessed. Money was not spent; it was thrown into the air while dancing. Loud music was substituted for live music from dozen-men instrumentalist troupes, and excessive alcohol for excessive food.

Major General's house was not as large as Madame

Messalina's, but it was more beautiful, more of a fruition of lavish taste than lavish spending. His garden was filled with decorated tables under a large tent. Trays of food were lined underneath another tent, awaiting the commencement of the buffet, and the aroma of the cow being roasted at the back of the house pervaded the air as the guests began trooping in by sunset.

If the major general was a grand composer, the lavish house his grand stage, and the party his grand symphony, then I had been handed the duty of conducting the orchestra. My few years in his service had made me aware of his every like and dislike, and I was to ensure that the former prevailed while the latter was confined to the barest minimum.

"Make sure table seven always has at least two open bottles of champagne," I barked at one waiter. The major general needed the minister seated at that table drunk by the end of the night, when they were to talk. "Not so much for table five," I added as the waiter sped off to inform the rest of his colleagues. The major general also needed the chief justice sober enough to overhear the crucial gossip that was scheduled to be discussed loudly at the table beside him by the irrelevant from the office.

By a cup of wine to midnight, all the guests had departed well merry. The waiters did not need supervision tidying up the garden, so I sat alone at a table, contemplating whether to spend the night or have one of the major general's drivers take me home. The major general himself was at a table at the far end of the tent with a company of friends. They were the usual suspects: Madame Messalina, Alhaji, and the third man. Alhaji caught my gaze and waved me over. I feared the worst but walked over nonetheless.

"*Aburo!*" he hailed as I drew closer. The stench of alcohol on his breath slapped my nose, and I wondered how the rest of the people on the table were coping. "Will you not come and sit on my lap?"

"Alhaji, that's Ihechi, not one of your chewing gum boys," Madame Messalina intervened.

The third man tapped Major General on the shoulder. "At this rate we will have to make him a coffin to keep him in a sitting position when he dies. If we don't bury him with a boy on his lap, his spirit will return to hunt our first sons."

"Your first sons would be safe from even my spirit if we managed to take over from the military regime. They would be living in between New York and London and would never have to set foot in Nigeria again. And you know spirits cannot apply for visa to enter airplane," Alhaji replied, laughing louder than everyone else.

"No one is ever going to take over from the military," I added, sensing that my opinion would be more tolerated in the present mood of banter. "I would dump all my sons in the military after training them to plot coups from the cradle."

"There would be no need for that because the military is planning to begin a transitory process into democratic rule in the next two years," said the major general. I fell silent, weighing the possibility of his claims. He went on, "It's what we've been scheming to take advantage of for the last few weeks."

More silence. Then Madame Messalina said, "We'll have to set up a political party and contest in elections and all that palaver."

"Tonight's party was for attendance taking. We had discussed this idea with a lot of people, and those interested were meant to confirm their alliance by showing up today. We had a decent turnout." A decent turnout had included the chief justice, a few serving and past ministers, and more than a dozen traditional rulers. "And that's why we needed you to pinch that Mendaus chap for us. He would have made a good spearhead for our plans."

"Mendaus has ties to some other political group, but I don't think they're at all aware of any transitory process."

"And that is because when the iroko is being cut down in the forest, it is the wise who would look out for what direction it is falling," Alhaji replied.

"They're not aware because it's still in the planning stage, whispers in the corridors of power," Major General added. "And the fact that this group Mendaus has ties with is ignorant of these plans is one of the clear reasons he cannot get anywhere with them."

"Why can't one of you spearhead our campaign?" I asked, placing extra caution as I pronounced the penultimate word. "Mendaus is popular, but it would take some effort to get him into office."

"What would I do with the office? What would any of us do with the office?" the third man asked, chuckling. "*Ah*, if monkey wear suit and tie shoe for leg, how monkey go climb tree to pluck banana?"

The rest of the table laughed this time around. The major general stood up and circled the table. Coming to a stop behind me, he placed a hand on my shoulder. "Politics is an art, and in art, the main players who determine what is what are the artists and the patrons of art. Now, the artist gets all the fame, so naturally, everybody wants to be an artist, the head boy of the new school of thought, the one who is celebrated. But the truth is there can't be any grand artist if there isn't any grand patron. Behind every champion is a godfather. And we are the godfathers, the grand patrons of this art of Nigerian politics."

"*Beeni!*" Alhaji shouted with terrible excitement, and he stoned the rest of whatever was in his cup down his throat.

"Come, Ihechi," Major General said. "It's late already, and you should not be staying up with these men lest you pick up their dirty habits. Let me see that you get home."

We walked in silence away from the garden, and when we were some way off from the tables and tent, he said, "We've chosen you, Ihechi."

I looked at him for a second, confused, to say the least.

"Well, not all of us. It was Messalina's idea when you couldn't get us Mendaus. Alhaji had some objections; he thought if you could not get Mendaus, how could you be trusted to get the office. I think he just wanted us to choose one of his chewing gum boys instead. But it's more or less settled now—when the transitory process begins, and the time comes to run for office, you're going to be spearheading our campaign."

"I don't understand. I never . . ." My head felt dizzy. I placed my hand on his shoulder to steady myself, and then it turned into a full embrace.

"I've placed your prick in Venus," he whispered into my ear. "Don't start lusting after the nymph peeping through the window."

I laughed, and he laughed as well, and I wiped away the tear that had escaped down my left cheek.

"Where did you park?" he asked.

"I didn't bring my car."

"Go into the house and ask for the key to the new Beemer."

More tears escaped down both my cheeks. "I'll have it back first thing in the morning, I promise."

"Bother less." He was already walking back toward the tents and table. "It's yours."

What happens when a dream is gifted though it was never really desired? I never could have known beforehand; nobody prepares for such incidents. Then again, the realization of dreams that were never desired always seems inevitable. Fate always has the end of such stories scripted from the beginning, leaving nothing to the choices and chances of the helpless dreamer. The joy of it— the prestige and power that came with the opportunity—was also the burden, the danger that faced anyone who had ever squared up against the military regime under any guise. Still, the major general had maintained that I was not "squaring up," because every move being made had been sanctioned by the military regime.

Tessy came over the next day, having already received the news from Madame Messalina. She brought along a cake and a bottle of wine.

"I'm not sure I'm in the mood to celebrate," I told her right at the door, even though I could not keep from smiling.

"Me, neither," she replied. "But it was the polite thing to do."

"You don't think I should go ahead with it, *abi?*"

"How could you even think that? Have your mother's idols been chasing you in your dreams or what? I'm not in the mood to celebrate because I have cramps. Take all these things from my hands, and take all that nonsense thought from your mind, too."

"Everyone is so sure I'm right for this except me," I said. We were now in the living room. She had collapsed on the couch and stretched out her foot for me to rub and relax her. I did not enjoy it, but I was used to it.

"You're looking at it from the wrong angle," Tessy said. "This is not just about you. You know how many generations of Igbo men and women have been waiting for an Igbo head of state? They would get their goats and chickens to cast votes for you if they have to."

"And what would the generations of Igbo men and women do when the military regime has me tied to a mop stick and shot down by firing squad? Would they get their goats and chickens to mourn me, too?"

"Never. Our forefathers would have died in vain if that happened. The souls of all Igbo children massacred during the civil war would not stand by and let that happen."

"And let me guess, my mother's ancestors would cajole the whole Yoruba land to vote for me as well, plus their goats and chickens and cows. Thank God the Yorubas have cows, those are more votes."

"Now you're thinking straight! And the Hausas would throw you their votes once word is out that you lost your virginity to one of their long-lost daughters."

I remembered Zeenat. She had been the excuse for all this freedom-fighting mess Mendaus and I had gotten into, and now, at the brink of achievement, she was nowhere to be found, her memory the butt of a joke, her name a second thought. Had we been lost from the very beginning, or had the recent taste of power distorted our sense of direction?

Mendaus once said, "Words, sounds, and actions are too

loud to conceal the secret of this world, so hush-toned messages are best conveyed in colors, and black and white shows the well-known facts." The truth about anything, anywhere, and anyone was black or white, tending either away or toward bringing balance to the world. Just as the truth of da Vinci's maddening genius and Delacroix's passionate romanticism was undeniable in their pencil strokes, how blatantly we could see the truth of Idi Amin's brutal megalomania and Nelson Mandela's unconquerable soul when blessed with power. When the truth of my soul was examined in its black and white at the end of my story, all I wanted was for everyone who spared a second to look upon me to be pleased with what they saw.

I thought I heard Tessy apologize for her comment on Zeenat, but I could not be sure, my mind was so far gone. It returned back to my body when there was a resounding knock on the door. I crept to the peephole, as I had formed a habit of doing, and spied on my visitor. It was the girl I had met at the bookstore nearly two months ago. We were engaged in an undefined thing that appeared more serious in her mind than in mine. She had been to my place a few times but never unplanned. And there was Tessy on the couch, feeling at home, while I stood by the door in singlet and knickers, contemplating a suspicious scenario. I could easily say Tessy was my cousin, but, albeit the truth, it was also the most clichéd excuse ever used by a caught philanderer. I damned the worst and opened the door. Her gaze was wide and glassed out as if just shined with tears; I could almost see the anxiety on my face reflected in her eyes.

"I heard the news," she said slowly.

"That's impossible, it only just happened!" My anxiety turned to confusion. "How did you find out already?"

"It's in almost all the newspapers," she replied, and she shed a tear as she handed me the magazine in her hand.

I tried to imagine why the major general would have leaked the news to the media so soon, but my eye caught the headline at the bottom of the cover page and my heart chilled. "Impossible!" I screamed.

MENDAUS, THE MURDERED?
Mendaus Mohammed shot down in Lagos streets
by unknown gunmen

I had no belief in any divine deity; I placed no trust in any acclaimed omnipotence, omniscience, and omnipresence. But I had beliefs about them. I knew of the hand of God clearly intervening in my father's life to deliver him from the civil war. I knew of the tenets of Ifá being instrumental to the sustenance of my mother's fragile health. I did not doubt their existence and powers, but I also did not doubt the exaggeration. Still I found myself mouthing words of prayer intertwined with recitations of the *Odu* on my flight from Enugu to Lagos.

As always, I went to Mendaus's old house in Omole for information on him; Mr. Thomas, the old and loyal house help, knew little. I was given directions to a hospital I had never heard of in Egbeda, a part of Lagos I could not remember ever having been to, and so I did not bother trying to find it on my own. I hailed a taxi and mouthed more prayers and recitations as my heart inclined to leap out of my reclining body in the backseat. I shut my eyes to attain peace, and slowly, my heart rested and my mind wandered.

It returned when the unpaved road began to bounce the taxi, the sleeping dust rose as the impatient tires disturbed it, choking me and wetting my eyes. The concrete bungalows were shabbily clumped together just as mud houses were; the doors to the houses were separated from the road only by the gutters, and the gutters were filled to the brim with still, brackish water.

A bit farther down the road, the still water began to move as a woman stood over the gutter, her skirts lifted to her thighs, pissing as she conversed with another woman across the road. Some men gathered around draft boards on narrow benches, while others just pivoted on chairs and sky-gazed. The children were happy, boys kicking about unripe tangerines and girls clapping and singing *tenten*. Farther down and a right turn later, the taxi stopped at a large church to ask for directions. He spoke to the gateman for a moment and returned to tell me that the hospital I was looking for was within the church premises but behind the main building.

An ambulance came hurtling down the bumpy road and made a screeching turn into the church compound. The gateman jigged after the vehicle, and I followed their trail. The hospital was almost as big as the church itself and had a large red cross above the entrance. A bleeding man was hauled out of the ambulance at the front of the hospital by the driver and a panting security man while a nurse jogged behind them. I followed the trickle trail of blood in their wake into the reception, stopping to take a seat while they rushed into an inner room. A doctor and a few other nurses rushed into the same inner room about a minute or so later. The ambulance driver and gateman exited soon after, and then the receptionist returned as everything seemed to get back to normal pace.

A pastor in purple with a white collar arrived at the hospital with a few other people just as the receptionist finished mopping the trail of blood off the floor. Two elderly women waiting, who had returned their focus to the news bulletin on the television fixed to a corner of the ceiling, became visibly apprehensive. The receptionist, after speaking to the pastor and his entourage, went into the inner room and returned with the doctor, who also spoke to the pastor before withdrawing once again to the operating theater. Very soon, the pastor's entourage formed a circle in the middle of the waiting room and an ad hoc prayer session was held; God's Holy Spirit was invoked, the chains of the devil were broken in faith, and a feeling that all would be well was generally restored.

I walked up to the receptionist and asked to see Mendaus Mohammed. Her head jerked, her eyes darted all over the room, and after overcoming a stutter, she denied having any patient by that name without even consulting her records. I insisted she check her records, and she walked briskly from behind her desk and went to whisper into the ear of the pastor, who was visibly irritated to have his prayers disturbed.

"What's your name?" he asked, walking up to me, looking just as nervous as the receptionist.

"Ihechi," I replied. "Ihechi Igbokwe." I had underestimated how huge his frame was when he was at the other end of the room. Now that he was just a meter away, I had to look up to him to meet his gaze. His nose was fluffy and his cheeks were round; there was something altogether familiar about his face.

"Pastor's son?"

He smiled at my words and engulfed me in an embrace. "It's Pastor now, Pastor Enoch. How did you find this place?

The only one who knows he's here is Mr. Thomas." He realized the answer to his question as soon as the words were out of his mouth. "Come with me."

We navigated the inner room and through the corridors beyond and came to an unnumbered door behind which Mendaus lay with bandages on his head and over his right arm and shoulder.

"*Chineke!* Are you fucking okay?" I exclaimed with my palms over my mouth. Pastor Enoch shot me a hard glance, and Mendaus sprang up from his bed, shaking the IV stand that was attached to his bandaged arm.

"Nope, I'm definitely not fucking okay. I think okay is cheating on me. Okay is fucking someone else, and it could be anyone in this world. But one thing I know for certain is that I am definitely not fucking okay."

"You're getting better already," Pastor said with a laugh to Mendaus, and then he turned to me and continued, "When he first came in, all he did was moan and pass out. There were two bullet holes the size of almonds, one in his arm and the other through his shoulder. He lost so much blood, it's a miracle he made it."

"The head wound?" I inquired.

"Oh, that's where he gashed his head on the concrete when the bullets took him down. He fell from the top of a car. It was at Tejuosho market. I warned him when he told me about the crazy idea." The magazine article had said he was shot by unknown gunmen when he was speaking to an open crowd, but during the tenure of the military regime, we had come to understand, though never spoke of, the synonymy between unknown gunmen and military murder squads. The only mystery was that military murder squads never missed.

"This is the path you turned down my offer for? You're not going to be useful to anyone dead," I said.

"I'm not going to be useful to anyone as a puppet, either," Mendaus said to me.

"So, what's your scheme? You'd talk the military out of power, persuade them to see common sense, and feed the people with at least the back bread of the loaf instead of just the usual crumbs."

"As pitiful as you're trying to make my case sound, I did earn a few bullets for my efforts," Mendaus replied. "What have your efforts gotten you? Why don't you do all the things your bosses need me to do?"

"That's exactly what I intend to do." There was a brief silence. I continued, "A transitory process from military to democratic rule is going to be initiated, political groups will be asked to register as parties, and there will be an election."

"Nonsense," Mendaus sneered. "It wouldn't be the first time they would be promising an election."

Pastor's son was more patient and more interested. "The Lord indeed answers prayers. Where did you get this news from?"

I hesitated a bit. "The people I work for. They know a few people who say the news is legitimate. They're already putting together the caucus of a party."

"You really can't be buying all of this pretentious nonsense." Mendaus was much louder now. "Okay, even if it is legitimate and elections are going to be scheduled, how come some people are given prior knowledge and allowed to make prior plans? It's just recycling the same old corrupt system and maybe even the same old corrupt people. How am I the only one who smells a rat?" He looked around desperately, begging to see a glimmer of acquiescence in any of our eyes.

Pastor's son dropped his gaze to the floor. He was distracted by something. "There's a spirit in this place?" he said.

"Nobody has time for your trances and prophecies," I said, irritated. Mendaus's irritation was more visible, but he at least kept quiet about it.

"I don't mean the Holy Spirit," Pastor's son continued. He went to Mendaus's bedside and started searching through all the containers on the side table, sniffing their lids. He stopped when he picked up a plastic bowl, dipped his finger into a clear liquid, and placed the finger on his lip. "I don't know how you keep getting your hard drinks in here, but if you try it again, I'm going to dump you at the general hospital. Don't you know your body is the temple of God?"

He stormed out of the room with the plastic bowl in hand, and I laughed away his empty threat. Taking Mendaus to a general hospital would be the same as chauffeuring him to the doorstep of his assassins.

But Mendaus was unrelenting in his debate. "Stop moving with this same old crowd," he said to me. "These people would never risk changing a system they benefit so much from; the change is in the hands of us who have nothing at stake. Politicians are violent in their words and reformist in their attitudes, but revolutionaries are reformist in their words and violent in their attitudes. We—you and I—are revolutionaries. They are politicians. How will the people we are meant to lead separate the wheat from the chaff if we all bundle ourselves in the same sack? Come with me and let's fill our mouths with the sharp truth till it slits our throats and kills us."

"You really can't be this naive," I replied. "All those books you get theories from don't have the answers to our problems." My palms returned to my face and I took the nearest seat. "The people don't want love and unity, but if you fill their stomachs, they will lift you in their arms and wage war on anyone who speaks against you. You know the philosophies of every country in the world but your own. You don't pay attention to past experiences."

"But the past in its entirety is flawed! All these things—tribalism, religion—they are distractions. What we need is vision, vision to wage this propaganda war. We can teach a generation that all Nigerians are equal regardless of tribe or religion or social status."

"Mendaus is a Hausa name," I said. "You can't just stroll through Igbo towns and villages and inspire change. Your name alone renders your opinion irrelevant."

"It's the same with religion," Pastor added. I hadn't noticed him returning. "If you go to the north today with one cow and a bag of rice for every living soul, they would sing praises to your name until the call to prayer sounds from the mosque and you refuse to kneel. Your head would roll on the floor before any of the cows you came along with. Nigerians are greedy, and the only thing greater than their greed is their piety. You can't teach that away. Hate it or love it, it's not going anywhere."

"Don't rubbish me with talk of tribes and religion. What religion? What tribes? A Yoruba man, when the Yoruba man was still great, was only as strong as his òrìsà. But now the Yoruba man has no òrìsà, their blacksmiths removed iron from their doors and replaced it with wooden crosses. Igbo women burn their chi and pray to the portrait of Cesare Borgia because the white people told them it was the face of Jesus. Igbo fathers re-fuse the wisdom of their ancestors hidden in proverbs, so they don't make references to what you call heathen and pagan; and the Hausas would die for an Allah whose name was used to murder their ancestors in a supposed holy war. Is this the same culture and tribes you still hold dear? You swallow all the lies of the foreign world and spit out their wisdom and truths."

I almost laughed him off. Nigerians are very superstitious people by nature, but I would have least expected it from Mendaus. A hundred years ago, farmers would leave vegetables and yams on a table in the road, far away from their presence. A number of pebbles representing the worth of the foodstuff would be placed by it, alongside an insignia of any òrisà to show they were protected by the gods. Passersby would trade these foodstuffs with the farmers in absentia, replacing the items on the table with money, which the owner would retrieve at his convenience. Theft in such scenarios was unheard of. This was order maintained by superstition. Nowadays a lot of delusional people swindled our nation with modern-day superstitions that foreign philosophies, cooked up for altogether different political and cultural climates, were the solutions to all of Nigeria's problems. Mendaus had been swindled.

"It's the person wearing the shoe who knows where it pinches," I said. "We are our own problem, our own scourge, and we are our only solution. You can blame imperialism and all that other textbook piss, but every injustice we ever suffered from outside our lands was first perpetrated by us. You know why? Because tribalism and all these other things you title rubbish don't need your endorsement to exist."

"You're as genius as your bosses and their friends, who have had the resources for who knows how long but haven't changed a damn thing. That's your way out? Why haven't they filled the hungry stomachs of the masses with bags of rice and beans?"

"I'm not arguing that these people are perfect. Who knows? They might be the devil. My argument is 'Aren't we all?' Whether we like it or not, we're human, we've been bitten by the incompetence of the corrupt system that governs us, and the venom is within us. Save your self-righteous nonsense. Besides, it doesn't have to be an Armageddon of the rich against the poor. The middle class—everyday people like you and I—can strike a balance, broker a peaceful transaction of societal equality."

"The middle class?" he asked. "You mean the few selected by the upper class, one out of every thousand, maybe hundreds of thousands, to make the poor believe there is still hope of crossing over the society's divide? Stooges like you?" Mendaus pointed directly at me. "They dress you up and teach you to act like the upper class, then leave you stuck in limbo, just near enough to the banks of the lower class to allow you belief that someday you can help each and every one of them make the crossover, and just near enough to the upper class's gates to appease their conscience without having to lose or share their wealth. You are stuck in the divide forever; if anything, you can only retrace your steps, but you'll never break past the gates."

"Look at the both of you, at each other's throats," Pastor's son said. "What for? Leadership? Power? Power that is not even yours? If Jesus had picked His disciples from Nigeria, there would not have been anyone left to betray Him. They would have all left to start their own churches. Everyone wants to lead, and no one wants to follow. If the two of you aren't going to join each other, you're going to have to beat each other."

"I'm done with this," Mendaus said. For the first time since I'd come into the room, he tilted back in his bed. "You can help yourself out whenever. I need to rest and get out of here as quick as I can because I have a few diems to carpe."

"That's if more bullets don't carpe your diem first," I whispered under my breath as I headed toward the door.

"Wouldn't that be a treat? I'd be able to meet Zeenat when I'm dead and regale her with all the foolishness you've been spewing."

"Go to hell!" I walked out and slammed the door behind me, hearing Mendaus's cynical laughter and reply—"I don't believe in a hell"—as Pastor's son reopened the door to come after me.

"God help us all," Pastor's son said with arms raised.

"Amen!" I replied.

"Good to see you're on the right side now," he said as his hands came down on my shoulders.

"I'm not some kind of devil," I said as we walked back to the reception from the depths of the inner room. "I believe there's a supreme deity. I don't just agree with any of the alternative options the world has set out for me to relate with Him."

"That's exactly the same opinion the Bible tells us the devil has about God," Pastor's son said.

"Imagine that," I replied, "a preacher condemning a lost man searching after God."

"How could I condemn God's chosen vessel?"

"I'm God's chosen vessel now? It would have helped my argument if you had mentioned that back inside the room. Where does your God stand in all this politicking?"

"I'm the mouth of God, not the mind of God. The important thing is, whether it's you or Mendaus or someone else coming with the change we need, God planned it all over twenty years ago when He sent you guys into the world. And if He's been planning this change for over twenty years, I think I can trust Him a bit not to mess things up. We know that all things work together for the good of those who love God, to those who are called according to His purpose. For those He predestined are those He would call. Those He would call are those He will justify. And those He justifies are those He would glorify. If God is on your side, who can be against you?"

"The least His Omniscience can do is offer us a blueprint to follow."

"As with every other matter, Jesus' life is the blueprint. That should go without saying. That's the purpose of all His trials and tribulations. Jesus created an empire without armies, warfare, or money. He offered undying love, He confounded us in the mysteries of an invisible God we could never understand but still could trust, and He inspired the love and loyalty of the world even in death and for centuries after. He was the prince of peace and never promoted the use of force in the propagation of His empire, and today His empire still stands. If that is not a worthy blueprint, then I do not know if anything could satisfy you."

We had arrived at the reception, and my mind was silent. The room had emptied of Pastor's son's entourage as well as the two elderly women, who had been there for most of the evening. The receptionist had fallen asleep with Sidney Sheldon's novel *The Other Side of Midnight* blanketing her face. Pastor's son stretched out his hand to shake, and I embraced him. He placed his Bible in my hands as I was turning to leave.

"Travel well," I heard him say as I was going through the

hospital door. "May you never walk where the road waits, famished."

I left the hospital feeling pity, more than anger, toward Mendaus. There was nothing to be angry about; bastards were a prevailing people in Lagos, and I was used to them, so I could not be vexed by them. The majority of these bastards were neither ideological bastards, as in Mendaus's case, nor were they born out of wedlock, as in the more direct meaning of the word. Rather, they were the sinister scoundrels who incensed everyone they came across till their victim boiled over with unbridled fury. Like the taxi driver I hailed on my way back from the hospital who deliberately took me on a much longer alternative, once he figured I was not sure of the route, all so he could hike the fare. I paid the sly bastard with a grimace. Or like the receptionist at the hotel I had checked in to, who personally went to pick up the laundry of some British guests yet refused to provide any answers on why mine had not been delivered to my room. I had no words for the condescending bastard. And especially like the woman who attended to me at my insurance company, convinced that my Japanese car had been secretly sold and not stolen because I had not filed a police report as soon as it happened. Audacious bastard, she would not grant me the benefit of the doubt at the expense of compromising her quarterly target with a shady payout.

I purchased another Japanese car for my mother, a new version of the old model that was stolen, with my own money. I drove down to Omole at about noon and met Effy near the gate; she had a bucket of water and a well-stained rag draped over her forearm. Her eyes narrowed as I stepped out of the car; when she noticed it was me, the tightness loosened, and a smile spread across her face at viral speed. I walked up to her with open arms and she jumped into them, tilting me half a step backward.

"You like carrying work on your head." I ruffled the edges of her braids. "I can't remember ever washing the gates when I was still around."

"Is that our new car?" she asked. She smiled and held my arm as we entered the compound. It was littered with empty plastic bottles all the way from the gate to the house door.

"Did you have friends over?" I could not hide my worry.

"It looks like the old Japanese car," she continued with her unbowed smile. "Your mother says Japanese cars look like German cars until you get into an actual German car."

I lost my footing as my rubber soles slid on spilled liquid, and Effy held up my arm just in time to keep me from crashing.

"What exactly happened here?" My eyes had lit up, and the fire of joy in hers dimmed, ushering in a cloud of silence.

"Some people from the church down the road, some prayer warriors, they came here yesterday evening."

"When did my mother start throwing parties for prayer warriors?"

"Party? They came to pray at our gate, and when nobody came to open it, they began throwing holy water and olive oil over the gate."

"Rubbish! Why didn't you call the police? Is my mother okay?"

"They were angry because of the dog that burned in the backyard. Our neighbor there"—she pointed to the massive duplex on the right side of our fence—"saw it through his window and came to create a scene with his church people."

"But it's none of their business what we burn in our own compound."

"It was their dog." She stared into my eyes plainly, as if her last sentence had not been said at all.

I heard my mother laugh from inside the house and then her soft aging voice: "Ihechi, is that you?"

I got into the house and bent to press my forefinger on the floor in greeting, and when she had blessed me, I asked with lips stretched into a forced smile, "I never knew you had a taste for dogs. Or is it just the neighbor's that was catching your eye?"

She laughed even louder than before. "What am I burning dog for? *Yemoja* does not demand dog, nor *Esu*. It's Effy who has chosen *Ogun* as her patron deity."

I recalled my mother's Ifá teachings through my childhood. *Ogun* was the *òrisà* of iron, of conquest, of creativity, and every year he required the offering of a dog from his devotees. Whatever could have made Effy decide on devoting to *Ogun* was beyond me, but it was too late to cry over spilled milk. I shot her a stern gaze, but her gaze somersaulted over it, landing on the opposite side of the room.

"When are you going to become a man and submit yourself to one *òrisà*?" my mother continued. "No one gets a mouthful of food by picking another person's teeth."

"You were aware? You let her steal your neighbor's dog and burn it while he was watching?" I seemed to be alone in my bewilderment; expecting them to see reason beyond this point was akin to waiting for a canoe on top of a tree in the middle of the desert.

"I did not steal it," said Effy. "It was wandering on the street."

"And she did it especially for you. She had a dream where bad things happened. She did it to protect you."

"Protect me? Would *Ogun* cross over to where I am in Igbo land to intervene if *Amadioha* of the Igbos declares his will?" My bewilderment suddenly became contagious. "And even if he could—"

"Even if he could?" Effy exploded. "The lion would never let anyone play with his cubs! *Ogun* can do all things; he is the one who goes forth where other gods have turned."

I laughed because I remembered telling her that story in Enugu, of how the *òrisàs* journeying to the world of men had been disenchanted by the chaotic chasm that had grown between the sky and the earth. All the deities had sought a way through without consequence until *Ogun* forged an ax from iron ore buried in the womb of the earth and cleared a path for himself and the *òrisàs* following him.

I followed that tale with one of how *Ogun* had gone into battle with his devotees against their enemies, his waist stringed with three gourds of war. He exhausted the first gourd of sperm, the elixir of creativity, in decimating the enemy camp with arson. Then he emptied the second gourd of gunpowder, the pulverized seeds of war, as he turned their folks into folklore. The last gourd of palm wine was guzzled as libation by himself to himself to the point of drunken rage, causing the *òrisà* to destroy everything in his sight, foe and friend alike.

This was whom Effy had chosen as patron deity, an *òrisà* who had as much tendency to uplift as to pull down. In a country so blighted by military excesses, the last thing I needed was to include another militarized power into the equation. I could do with his renown in leadership and creativity, but *Ogun* was too volatile an *òrisà* to be trusted absolutely. But were they not all? Like my mother's beloved *Esu*, who was as quick to mischief as he was quick to aid. And if the almighty *òrisàs* were actually as volatile as ordinary men, why should they accrue more trust and devotion than mere mortals, since they were just as likely to disappoint?

"Yes, even if he could," I reaffirmed, "he is a deity; he does not need my compulsion to act, and I trust him to make decisions for himself like the adult that he is."

I felt the sting on my cheek before I realized my mother's palm had cracked on it. She had managed to propel herself from the chair just long enough to strike my other cheek before recoiling to the chair. Her body quaked like the ground beneath a masquerade's feet, and her eyes watered.

It was amazing how I was deprived the liberty to decide simple things for myself, such as my belief or nonbelief in whatever deities I chose, but the hopes and aspirations of the future of the nation were heaped on my shoulders with careless confidence. My parents, from the beginning, had staunchly believed my fate was theirs to dictate. And it was no new thing; they did not know better, so they did to me what had been done to them. There was always a general set of expectations laid out for entire generations, and because the promised reward was usually riches and happiness, no one questioned being forced down the path.

After our national independence, it was the era of the civil servant and government appointee. Then it was the era of the doctor, engineer, lawyer, or any other titled professional. And now we were to adhere to new rules. In short, one generation fails and then tries to force the ones after them to live the dreams they cowered from and share the perspectives they wished they had held firmer to. They do not recognize that the world changes and the people after them have new dreams and perspectives.

I hoped to change the topic. "I got another Japanese for you. Maybe next time it would be a German." I handed my mother the key. She hesitated but then took it, looking from me to the key and then back before flinging the key straight at the space between my eyes.

"If you really cared, you would come around more and see that I can hardly walk, talk less of driving. Maybe when you get a German, it will be to drive my casket to the mortuary."

"Don't talk like that, death listens."

"You can talk any how you like to me in my own house, but I can't do the same to you," she said, laughing again. I was well past fearing for dementia. "I don't know who you are anymore. I have only one child, and it's not you. You have not taken after me. Even your mad father was never as mad as you are. You're a bastard."

She kept on laughing. I moved toward her and placed my arms around her and she fought back, her hands and elbows digging into my chest till they were stiff in my embrace and her laughter turned into quiet sobs. I picked up the keys to the new Japanese car and walked out of the door. Effy ran after me.

"You can't listen to her. I swear, she has been saying a lot of strange things lately," Effy argued. But it was not the words that pushed me away. It was the sincerity in her eyes, the confines of her soul that had come to the fore; it was the hate I had seen that pushed me away.

"I'll come back in the evening," I lied. "Let me just give her time to cool down."

Effy smiled. "I'll tell you about my dream when you return."

I hoped for her sake that there was a deity somewhere who would watch over her and deliver her from the madness she was unknowingly meddling with.

1998

A body brimming with life by dawn is returned to dust by dusk; all the while, the corpse never knew the maggot devoured it. Of all the lessons I learned from the major general, that was golden. Some men admired the lion for its strength and bravery. Others looked up to the eagle for its vision and individuality. But the major general revered the maggot because it was thoroughly efficient; you never saw a carcass half-rotten and abandoned. And the only thing that matched its efficiency was its invisibility; you never saw maggots arrive or depart or in transit. They were available only when necessary and hastily lost in oblivion when the job was done. Nothing was more paramount in Nigerian politics than efficiency and invisibility. In that world of distrust and ruthless ambition, success was a destination, not a journey, and you could neither be seen traveling toward it nor afford to fail along the way.

My earlier courier jobs for the major general and his friends had hinted at the need for efficiency and invisibility in unclear terms. But the lesson echoed more significantly after the choosing, which made it necessary for me to relate more closely with them. The method to their maggot madness was simple enough—their every move and appearance had to occur for a definite reason that played a part in achieving a greater goal. Outside of these necessities, they existed in total isolation from the public space. This was the first principle of political godfatherism: invisibility. When they needed to obtain relevant information, they purchased the integrity of the individuals who possessed it, and when they needed to share relevant information, they purchased the creativity of journalists. When they were called upon by higher powers in government, they sacrificed profit to come to the aid of the nation, and when they needed the higher powers in government for minor favors, they tinkered with the supply of one or two consumer goods to create a scarcity and the public strike action and protests that ensued, ultimately leading to the government calling them to the round table; at this juncture, favors were bartered.

Invisibility did not mean just being unseen and unheard but being unnoticed. The way to being unnoticed was to recognize the stance of the person with the most leverage in the room, usually the representative of the military regime, and to align with it. If they were invited to a dinner by the head of state and he held his fork in his right hand and his knife with his left, the principle of invisibility demanded they do the same. If he referred to the Federal Republic of Germany as East Germany and West Germany, they were to follow suit, and if the need to discuss Zimbabwe arose, they were to show proactiveness and refer to the African country as Rhodesia. Aligning with ignorance was one of the perks of allowing your country to be ruled by illiterates.

Sometimes the paradox of invisibility translating to outright flamboyance occurred because being unnoticed translated to fitting in. And in the environment of Nigerian politics and upper-class living, flamboyance was the norm. Not just in one-off appearances but as a lifestyle. The flashier the attire of the person, the bigger the person's car, the longer the car's entourage, the greater the number of armed policemen in the entourage, the greater the number of titles these armed policemen saluted the person by, all translated proportionally to how much a person fitted into this absurd environment. The objective of the charade is neither comfort nor happiness but, rather, a chronic addiction to recognition that is captured in Nigerian parlance as *Shakara*. The less *Shakara* a person displayed, the more the person was prevented from being comfortable, to the point that even a passing glance could not come across without a judgmental undertone.

The major general and his friends were efficient in their *Shakara*, as in all else they did, unstoppably efficient. It was the second principle of political godfatherism: invincibility. Efficient meaning not that they were in control of all the decisions being made but that they ensured all the big decisions swaying in their favor. Some favors, however, required more coercion than others. The transition program by the military regime was one such favor, in the works for almost three years.

After the annulment of the 1994 democratic elections, the major general and his friends had sponsored pro-democracy organizations that incessantly staged protests, invited and guaranteed the safety of international news agencies that showed interest in the fracas, and ultimately hiked the prices of many consumer goods, bumping the cost of living to unbearable levels that swept the trade unions to the streets. In a few weeks, the oil industry that lined the nation's foreign-exchange coffers was almost grounded. Instead of inviting the major general and the other power brokers to the usual round table, the military regime struck back by arresting trade union leaders and taking control of their offices and assets. The pro-democracy organizations were infiltrated with bribed informants, and their key members were arrested indefinitely. The power brokers united in sabotaging multinationals operating in Nigeria; these multinationals ran crying to their governments; their governments came at the military regime with blaring voices and arms in the air. It was shortly afterward that the transition program became hot gossip.

Eventually, the gossip cooled and was gradually being forgotten. The major general and his friends constantly offered private words of reassurance to the multitude they had gathered under their banner, but there was very little indication in the public space that their claims were any realer than pigs with horns. If they had just claimed pigs existed, they would have been fine, because the military regime had in truth announced a transitionary program, but they did not describe what sort of transition it would be. Optimists, like the major general, hoped for open democratic elections. Realists not blinded by vested interest knew the same sinister people at the helm of the military regime were looking to contest and rig their election to office in a staged national referendum.

We were also aware of these prevalent rumors, but our determination prevailed higher than all else. A party-sponsored, pro-democracy rally was arranged in Lagos, to be the first of many. Prominent trade union leaders and civil rights activists had been scheduled for attendance, as well as a few traditional rulers who had sworn to show up and brave any backlash from the military regime. However, the bulk of the masses were the unemployed and the street hustlers who would leap to the moon for the slightest stipend.

Alhaji had hinted that I was going to talk for a few minutes at the rally, so I had been stuck awake all night, pondering what to say. The crowd would expect fire and brimstone from anyone who was going to come within a five-meter radius of the microphone, to flaunt a deep knowledge of government impunity, and to pass a sentence of their eternal damnation. The observing journalists would want quotes from Nietszche and other things more attuned to Mendaus. The more refined audience, following events over radios and televisions from the safety of offices and living rooms in Lagos, would expect staunch declarations that, when handed power, our party would transform Lagos to London, Nnewi to New York, Gombe to Geneva, and Port Harcourt to Paris. But if I could script the future, I would rubbish all of such transformations. I would preach neither capitalism nor socialism—in fact, I would burn every instituted temple devoted to Adam Smith and Karl Marx.

I would not have an African civilization that would be an annex of Europe and America in administration and culture. That was Mendaus's dream. I would rather have modern versions of our great cities of centuries ago, like Zaria and Ijaiye, where wealth was defined by the abundance of the community, not the profit of single individuals, where both largesse and famine were endured communally, unlike modern cities, where dozens starve on the same street as one man's dog with leftovers, but the street is heralded in greatness because of that one rich man. If I lived and died a million times, I would prefer a progression to the present past, with morality determined by communal values, not by the sentiments of the deepest pockets. But I did not know how to shape these ideas into a speech, let alone muster the courage to voice it.

The morning of the rally was spent setting up the stage and sound system at the Tafawa Balewa Square. As soon as that was done, loud music started blaring and a few of the idle gathered. I was with the major general and his friends, seated in the stands behind the stage. The traditional rulers and other dignitaries were relaxing with us in the shade, made even more reassuringly comfortable by the retinue of armed security men patrolling the stands.

Actual musicians began to climb the stage as the blaring music turned into live performances and a few more people gathered. Food hawkers noticed the crowd and came around to milk any lactating pocket. Then actors, comedians, and football stars from the World Cup team showed up on stage, and the crowd kept growing as each personality handled the microphone.

Finally, a party leader got to the microphone; he asked the DJ to play back some of the earlier performed songs, danced *galala* to the beat for a while, and spent about five minutes repeating some of the comedians' jokes. Just before the crowd had completely forgotten why they were gathered, he went on a forceful tirade, throwing questions to the crowd, demanding to know the names of their oppressors, of those who held on to power without the voluntary empowerment of the people, of those who plundered their resources like the spoils of military conquest, of those who had arrested and locked up their neighbors without charge, all the while never actually mentioning the names of the culprits himself. The people were not as discreet. They shouted the names and positions of members of the military regime; they cursed and jeered and made a riotous noise.

Even with all the noise, the gunshots fired into the air at the far end of the Tafawa Balewa Square rang loud and clear. All eyes searched frantically for the exact position of the shooters, but white fumes of tear gas were rising every few meters apart. A few hefty armed men in police uniforms mounted the stage and rammed the butts of their guns into the astounded faces of the party leaders. The policemen tried to make their way to the stands where we were still seated, but our armed security came to the fore, causing a deadly stalemate, with weapons drawn on both sides but neither galvanizing the courage to start a gunfight in such open space.

The crowd refused to disperse, splitting into many factions and confronting the police, tossing stones and glass bottles at them. The policemen, without helmets or shields, scuttled through the rain of danger and retaliated with all they had: bullets, batons, bare knuckles, boots, and belts, all purchased with their victims' taxes. Their bulletproof vests read POLICE IS YOUR FRIEND.

The guns blasted in a continuous spree and the batons swung unendingly, but the dispersing crowd stopped in their tracks and gathered around, their backs to their uniformed assailants. Their forlorn faces stared down at a little boy in a school uniform sprawled on the road, his gaping head pouring blood and brains. The crowd stood still, even the police officers. More people gathered, and revenge festered in the cluster of the angry mob. There were cries and yells in pidgin and Yoruba and a medley of other languages. Slowly, they encircled the policemen, the radius reducing drastically by the second until the circumference and the center were one.

Tires and kerosene were thrown into the melee, and a bonfire was made of three policemen. Every other man and woman in uniform turned on their heels, stripping off their clothing as they desperately sought the nearest refuge. Stones were hurled in their direction. Abandoned police guns were emptied toward the sky. Car windows were busted, and fires lit up the street. The major general and his friends hurriedly took off their bulky *agbadas* and crouched down and away from the stands in their singlets and white trousers, and I trailed them, peeping out the corners of my eyes at the baptism of the revolution. The blood of the enemy splattered on the faces of their assailants as the twitching corpses purged themselves of all life. The people we had gathered and aggravated had spiraled out of control. A few minutes ago, we were the cock of the walk, but in the face of a revolution, the revolutionaries had become the feather duster.

"It's always darkest before the dawn," they said. Bastard poets always knit together pretty words that hold hardly any truth. The truth is: When it's darkest, it stays dark for a long while after. I could not understand why it all had happened at the same time, but things went from bad to worse faster than food from the mouth to the anus during a bout of diarrhea.

Effy might have grown a lot in the last few years in mind and body, but she managed to still be as mischievous as always. Boardinghouse peers were not loving family members who repaid mischief with reprimand and candor; rather, they repaid with chiding and vengeance. So, when the senior prefect ordered Effy to fetch a bucket of water from the borehole a thousand galaxies away, and Effy eased her bladder's burden of a little urine into the bucket of water as recompense, she hardly expected that when she was nabbed and reported to the senior prefect by the snollygoster of a friend who escorted her, she would be forced to drink from the very bucket. She gargled and swallowed while half the dormitory laughed and pointed. She went to bed drenched in water, urine, and tears.

It took just over seven hours, one yawn before dawn the next day, for her to start purging recklessly in the bushes on the path from the dormitory to the laundry where the girls bathed. The purging went on for two days, after which the school clinic deemed her sickness an unnecessary expense and contacted her guardian to take her home for any further treatment. For a double measure of certainty, they sent a letter to the address registered in her file, which was my mother's house in Omole, and placed a phone call to the number registered in her file, which was the phone line of her parents' house in Enugu, as my mother had stubbornly refused to install one. My mother responded with alarming urgency, and Effy was leaving the school premises just a few hours after the letter had been dispatched. Aunt Kosi had responded to the phone call with equal urgency, although not as efficient, and arrived in Lagos by bus just a bit under seven hours after the call had been placed.

Aunt Kosi arrived at the given address of Effy's school up in arms, embodying worry and overreaction in the true fashion of the typical Nigerian mother, and was livid when she heard her daughter had already been sent off with her guardian. She huffed and puffed but was completely ignored by her informant in the true fashion of the typically carefree Nigerian receptionist. Instead of returning to Enugu cradling her beloved daughter through a bumpy bus ride, she gathered all she had, which was really just her handbag and the address to my mother's house obtained from the receptionist, and stormed toward Omole. I never knew all of this had happened the day before, as I was dodging rioters at Obalende. I sneaked through the chaotic streets all the way to Berger and then the serene obscurity of the Omole suburb, looking to find refuge under my mother's roof, all the while having not the slightest clue that I was spiral-backflipping from the frying pan into the fire.

I banged on the gate four times, waited a few seconds, and then banged once more out of habit, the same way I had banged on the gate every evening for many years when I returned from playing football after school. Back then my mother would come to the gate with a sachet of water, so I would not have an excuse to hang around the kitchen pinching on the dinner being prepared instead of heading straight for a shower. This time she arrived at the gate as brisk as ever, and as she peeped through the pigeonhole, her forehead wrinkled. I straightened my jacket and pressed my palm on my trim hair, so the waves would rise; even though it had been true of my last few visits, I did not want her under the impression that I showed up only when something disastrous had happened.

But her mind was obviously on other things as the gate clanged open. "Is this how you people do in Enugu," she whispered, "showing up without invitation or even asking for permission?"

"Permission for what now?" I gave her a loose hug. "Since when do I need permission to come to my mother's house to hug her? *Abi*, does a baby ask for permission before jumping out from the womb into his mother's arms?"

"*Isi Aki.* Coconut head," she teased through a narrow smile. "How I wish you had asked for permission, it would have saved me all this your stress."

I poked at her pudgy belly and started singing. "Sweet mother, I no go forget you. For the suffer wey you suffer for me."

"Shhh! That's not what I'm talking about!" She slapped away my poky fingers as she returned to her whispers. "Your auntie from Enugu is here."

"Impossible! Aunt Kosi? She has never gone farther than Ogbete market. She doesn't know the road."

"She arrived yesterday evening and said someone told her that Effy was sick in school. I had only just picked up Effy from school. I had not even finished preparing her *agbo*. How did she know Effy was sick? Who told her? Is that how their Holy Spirit works? Or has she been monitoring us in the spirit world?"

I would have confirmed that this was exactly how the Holy Spirit worked and immediately offered her a chance to switch allegiances and give her life to the Jesus Christ who monitored all concerning the spirit world, but I was much too stupefied by the news. "And you let her sleep here under your Yoruba roof and eat your Yoruba soup? She did not wail about the civil war?"

"Was I meant to allow her to carry that poor girl back to Enugu on a night bus in that condition? And she had to eat, as long as she was staying, before she goes back and says I'm the witch who starves her in-laws the same way I starved their brother till he ran away from me."

"She never needed any excuse to call you a witch since she found out I never set foot in church all through my childhood. Does she know you have converted Effy to—you know?"

"Converted Effy to what? Say 'witch,' let me slap you."

"You know what I'm talking about. Ifá."

"Ihechi! Is that you?" Aunt Kosi bellowed from within the compound. My mother's face turned skyward, and she fiddled with her wrapper as if she had no right to have a conversation with her son. It was obvious she had not done any proper gossiping in a long time. Aunt Kosi went on, "I know I put some meat on your bones when you were in Enugu, but with everything I've seen your mother show Effy, I feel like I owe you so much more."

I knew my mother's affection for Effy was a desperate striving to fill up the trenches of loneliness in her heart that had been excavated by my and my father's departures, trenches that had been eroded to gullies by the attrition of neighbors' wicked words and silent snobs who stigmatized her devotion to Ifá. If Effy had not come along, my mother would have found someone else to fawn over—maybe the little children brave enough to defy their parents' instructions by coming to play in front of the "witch's house." I was bemused by how my mother could hate me for choices I made in my own life when she had first-class experience on how entrenching it felt to be hated for personal choices. But maybe it was because we have only what we receive and can give only what we have. And so if she spent her life receiving intolerance, then that was all she could give. I laughed at Aunt Kosi and swore that heaven could not have treated me better than she did.

"Speaking of heaven," Aunt Kosi replied. "I wonder how you expect to make heaven after hiding the gospel of *amala* and *ewedu* from me all these years. When your mother served it yesterday, I had to use broom and dustpan to gather my senses back."

"I tried my best with that one," my mother chipped in as if I were not standing in the room, "a toilet brush is more useful than he is in the kitchen. Like father, like son."

"I still wonder every night, my sister. You saw all the rich

Igbo families in Lagos, the Mbadiwes, the Orizus, and the rest, but somehow you decided to marry into these ones whose elbow cannot stretch out to give a helping hand."

"The gist that time was that Igbo people like money pass anything, that they have this tree they grow in their backyard where they can pluck a few notes every morning. To be honest, that's the only reason I got stuck in this palaver. You grew up knowing well that some Igbo men are destined to be church rats. What is your own excuse?"

"My head was washed, I have to be honest with you," Aunt Kosi said. "I fell for a chewing gum boy, his mouth always moving but never talking about money."

"Those are the worst! Invictus boys, instead of them to join oil companies and banks, they want to be the master of their own fate and captain of their own ship. When their ship full of containers gets seized at the port, they would now say it is the witches in their village."

They both laughed a bit too closely for my comfort. My mother dreaded the word "witch"; I never would have imagined her using it twice in the same day. But slander was the universal adhesive among women, as alcohol was among men. She continued, "That's where these younger girls are wiser. We spent our entire youth waiting virtuously in our fathers' houses for wonderful young men. But in every hunt, the hunter always has the upper hand, and the prey is handicapped by default because it never knows it's playing a game till the end."

"That's the thing, you have to adapt fast fast! I learned quickly to ask my husband for money as easily as he asked me for sex and refused him sex as easily as he refused me money. After all, marriage is about giving and receiving. My eyes are too open to stand by and get sexually defrauded." They laughed even louder, till eventually, Effy stirred up from sleep and the budding buddies retraced the dance steps of their youth to the music countdown show that aired just before the nine o'clock news.

My mother broke the tradition of watching the news that night; all the tricks up her sleeve were being rolled out for her guest, who was now as august as she had been unwanted a few hours before. Effy wanted to watch a movie as she ate her dinner, and both my mother and my aunt acquiesced. I didn't usually lose head or heart over television, but as the title came on, both my head and heart were submersed in a deluge of nostalgia.

A Mercury Production by Orson Welles
CITIZEN KANE

Blood rushed to my face, and my skin tingled all the way from my neck via the left side of my chest to my groin. And I remembered. It was the very text that had flickered on the television screen in the dark living room that afternoon when Zeenat and I shared our first kiss; the ominous score that introduced the cast was the very music that had paced the rhythm of our converged hips as we proceeded to making love. But the only memories I had of the images were as several shades of white light bouncing off Zeenat's skin in the darkness, outlining her silhouette and highlighting the contours on her flesh when my fingers pressed against it. I wept; silent throes of salient woes crushed my valiant soul.

Zeenat was always very deliberate with the videos she selected to watch with me. She skimmed through the lot in her idle hours, and we watched her favorites together as she explained how the different characters were all so similar to me. Only she could ever justify how one person could be akin to Thomas O'Malley the alley cat, Rick Blaine the soft-spoken nightclub owner, and Manny Ray the suave gangster, all at the same time. And if she had wanted me to see *Citizen Kane* with her, there must have been a character somewhere in the movie that mirrored me in her eyes. My curiosity indulged her buried intentions. I did not need a soothsayer to know that the character she had in mind was Charles Foster Kane, but I definitely needed one to understand how she would have known all of this. Kane was sent by his mother to live with faraway strangers when he was just a boy, and he grew up to become the publisher of the *New York Inquirer*, one among many in a newspaper empire and many other industrial empires that he controlled. And in his Declaration of Principles, printed on the front page of the *Inquirer*, after he took to the helm of affairs: "I will provide the people with a fighting and tireless champion of their rights as citizens and as human beings."

One of the first proofs of this point was his newspaper's campaign against the money-mad Public Transit Company that was robbing the people poor, regardless of the fact that Mr. Kane himself was the largest individual shareholder in the company. Ultimately, he died alone in a tomb of amassed treasures, and of his two divorced wives, few friends, and many workers who once admired his principles—some having lent helping hands—none of them were with him at the end; they realized that of all his declared principles and generous opinions and revolutionary gimmicks, the only conviction that Charles Foster Kane ever really had was in his megalomaniac self.

As the final credits ran, I wondered: If I'd died that night, would my final words and thoughts, scenes of the most memorable parts of my life that clung on to my fading consciousness, be allusions to my childhood and the years before I was corrupted by selfish ambition? Would Mendaus attend my burial after all the petty disagreements that had come between us? Would Pastor's son make prayers by my grave to a God I had so often pushed away? Would Maradona make libations to a friendship I had turned my back on with his backyard brew that I had spat out of my mouth? The major general and his cronies, too, would their world stop spinning or their monies stop minting even for a second? It was then, knowing that I would probably die as lonely and regretful as Charles Foster Kane, that I realized Zeenat's warning had arrived too late.

Well before the final credits but not long after my tears had dried, my mother and aunt had dozed off in their chairs, stumbling to their beds later on. Effy had fallen asleep on the couch, which was nothing unusual, so I spread a cover cloth atop her and let her be. When the noisy drain of the bathroom by my old room woke me up the next morning, the sun was just rising. Effy nudged me to affirm if I was awake or asleep, and upon concluding the former, she asked me to turn around and face the wall while she dried herself and put on her clothes. I obliged. She updated me on the events of the morning as I stared at the browned wall, my childhood bed-time companion.

"Don't be in a hurry to get out of bed," she said. "We are having half-caste ọkpa for breakfast."

"How do you know if ọkpa is purebreed or half-caste? To be honest, I always thought ọkpa was albino."

"Not the color of it, oh." She laughed and threw something soft at the back of my head. "It's the . . . ethnicity of the ọkpa. Food can have ethnicity, *abi*? Because my teacher always talks about how she never appreciated palm oil till she tasted Igbo soups, because her ethnic soups never needed palm oil."

"Well, I think people say ethnic food, but the same food cannot have originated from two different places, you know, so it can't be half-caste. The same way you can have ethnic languages but not half-caste languages."

"Okay, that makes sense." There was a slight pause, as if she was not thoroughly convinced. "Anyway, your mother somehow convinced mine to teach her how to make ọkpa before leaving this morning. The only issue was that your mother didn't have any breadfruit, so they improvised with regular beans. You have to clap for them because the experiment ended up looking like ọkpa. It's just that it tastes like *moi moi*."

"That must have been a terrible anticlimax, expecting ọkpa and tasting *moi moi*. Where is my mother leaving to, by the way?"

"It's not your mother who has to leave early, it's mine," Effy said. "She's heading back to Enugu. Yours would be taking me back to school by noon, and my mother does not want to wait till then, because that would mean she would have to wait half the day to travel by the night bus." She heaved in a deep breath. "See, it's a long story. You can turn around now." Effy twirled around in a circle and came to a stop with a curtsy, as she would all those years ago in Enugu when we prepared for church on Sundays. Then she returned to the mirror to set her blue beret, the crowning glory of the blue pinafore and checkered shirt that was the Queen's College uniform.

"I thought you were not leaving till noon?" I asked.

"I'm not. But my mother really wanted to see me in my school uniform." She was done with the mirror and was tugging on my arm now. "You should come out and say goodbye before she leaves."

Half-awake and half-dressed, I complied nonetheless. Aunt Kosi's big box was already by the door, surrounded by little black nylon bags of who knows what, and the scent of *moi moi* pervaded the room.

"I've gotten someone to drop you off at the motor park," my mother said, walking through the front door. "I've sorted him out already, so you don't need to give him a kobo."

They hugged tightly. "Thank you, my sister," Aunt Kosi said. "*Oya*, Effy, come let us pray so I can start going." Everyone in the room froze except Aunt Kosi, who was rummaging through her handbag, oblivious to any oddity. Aunt Kosi finally pulled a handkerchief out of her handbag and spread it atop her head. "In Jesus' name!" she declared. I looked at my mother and caught her staring back at me. "In Jesus' name!" Aunt Kosi declared again. My mother and I shifted our gazes simultaneously to Effy. There was a long pause with no more declarations. And then Aunt Kosi opened her eyes. "Ephesians! What sort of nonsense is this? Have you gone deaf or what?"

"I'm sorry," Effy responded. I could hear a parched throat in her voice. If she had stopped at that point, it would have been fine. My mother and I would have offered her cold water as soon as her mother left and teased her about it for a week. But she was a blossoming young Nigerian and, as such, had a natural instinct that forbade her from spurning the slightest opportunity for a confrontation. She continued, "I was planning to tell you. I did not know how to put it. I do not believe in God." Another pause. "Okay, I do believe in God but not your idea of it. I mean, I have been learning the ways of Ifá, and it has brought me more peace than all my time in church. And it feels so natural. I don't have to force anything . . ."

My mind zoned out and started processing things to say or do, ways of damage control. Aunt Kosi was a step ahead of me. She let her handbag drop to the floor and, in one swift and single motion, lifted her big box off the ground, hurling it into the air and across the room. Effy met the vertices of the box with her forehead, and the weight of her mother's clothes and personal effects pushed her back into the armchair. Old and frail as the chair was, it tilted backward, rocked perilously, and then tumbled over, carrying Effy and the big box along with it.

I rushed to the floor where Effy lay. My mother yelled. My aunt was undeterred, picking up one of her heeled slippers and taking aim, but my mother intervened, wrenching her arm and forcing the slipper away from her grasp. I searched Effy's face and limbs for a cut or bruise and then listened for her breath. Instead, I heard more yells and groans, then a chorus of slaps. Looking up, I saw Aunt Kosi's arms around my mother's thigh while she braved a rain of slaps on her back. As if overburdened by the added weight of my gaze, my mother's thigh buckled and her heel slipped. In a second, she was being raised toward the ceiling. She held on to the ceiling fan just before Aunt Kosi tried slamming her to the floor. I raced toward the circus show at the center of the room, getting there as my aunt yanked at my mother for a second time. Grains of cement fell to my face as I lifted my eyes, and then the ceiling fan gave way on my mother's head; she swayed in Aunt Kosi's arms for a second, then crashed down. I tried to break their fall but collapsed under the weight of the twosome, shattering the wooden center table beneath us all.

I never spoke again about the early-morning living room incident. Not with Effy, even when she regained her senses and tried to figure out why the center table was destroyed. Not with my mother, even when the doctor had asked how she had broken her arm. Not with Aunt Kosi, even when Uncle Adol tried to find out why she refused to talk about her trip to Lagos. And not with Tessy, who desperately tried to calm my brooding by cooking all sorts of soups for me weekend after weekend.

I was angry at everyone involved in the squabble, but more than that, I was confused by them. And it was the confusion that stomped me, because I had seen it rear its head time and time again as people all around me, who were bound within the borders of Nigeria by intertwined ancestral origins, continuously stretched the limits of their wits and brawn in search of a reason not to get along with a neighbor. Aunt Kosi justified her fruits of discord with religious differences, although sometimes she preferred to incite chaos from the infallible wings of intertribal grievances. My mother did the same; she was stuck in her traditionalist ways of doing things. Mendaus despised the traditionalists and looked to Western cultures and theologies for answers. Maradona did not care about the traditionalists or Western ideals; all he knew was that the rich were the scourge of the earth. They all sought after a reason to hate.

This whole nation-building affair I was tensioning my nuts for was just a pointless charade, and I decided to put it behind me. I just needed to find the right time to make my intentions known to all involved, including the major general and his friends. As with all other things—except the early-morning living room incident, of course—I talked to Tessy about it, but she was hearing nothing of it.

"Stop?" she screamed. We were at the Stray Dog, the large room with the great dome in Madame Messalina's house, and her voice echoed above the classical music playing from the invisible stereo system. "You know why you can't stop? You can't because you're almost there, Ihechi. And it's not even the chance of your success that should keep you going. It's the fear of failure, failing the ones who tried before you and the ones who would try after you." She giggled uncontrollably, as if privy to a joke I had missed. "Okay, let's say you're a ninety percent success so far. That means you're also a ten percent failure, right? You're a ten percent failure because some half-genius and half-junkie of a revolutionary who was so close to greatness failed somewhere along the line and quit. You can't stop because this race might not be yours to finish, and if you stop, the next guy you hand the baton to will never be able to win. You can't be the next half-genius and half-junkie of a revolutionary who failed his cause. You cannot afford to have the blood of an aborted dream on your hands. You get?"

I smiled at the thought of being considered a half-junkie; it had been years since I'd dropped the habit of lighting smokes. It was still not as ridiculous as being considered a genius. I had not contributed anything to the world to deserve such a title. Geniuses were Mozart or Beethoven or whoever composed the classical music that was playing, and as far as I knew, geniuses were defined by the spirits that possessed them. And not the sacred spirits of creation that guided their hands, but the spirits of deception that worked to direct their wandering minds. Despite my efforts to build a world worth living in, my own world kept crumbling, and I had begun dreading the road ahead, the very path I was paving, because it seemed like this road to nirvana was also the road to my personal perdition. I was coming to terms with knowing that, whether possessed by Beethoven's or Mozart's spirits, whether damned from within or without, geniuses were born to suffer. In that context, maybe I was a genius.

"My nerves are as fried as potato chips," I said finally. I poured myself some whiskey at the bar and sipped, cringing before it even touched my tongue.

"In that case, I should give you some ketchup to go with that." Tessy smacked her bloodred lips and stained my cheek with a kiss.

"Thank you, thank you, and thank you. But I'm a true Igbo man, so I'd rather have hot pepper over ketchup, because I'm never scared of the heat. And I'm not scared of the major general; I'll talk to him today."

"He's hotter than most," Madame Messalina said. I had not noticed her enter the room. Alhaji had also come in, beside a skinny young man with ultra-fitted clothes doting on him, along with the major general's other friend—a large, quiet man with a dark face marked like the Ife bronze heads. "You know the major general is a Yoruba man, and all his hard-guy-ness aside, he is a very . . . strong-handed man."

"My mother is Yoruba as well," I retorted. "Trust me, they aren't the spawn of the devil, as you all like to think they are."

"True enough, but he is more traditional than most. And among the Yoruba people in the olden days, when an insolvent debtor leaves a household or dies in more unfortunate circumstances, the *Baale* of the household was required by law to pay the debtor's debts. And whenever an insolvent debtor was sick, he would be taken away from the household by his own family members and abandoned in the bushes—a gesture of disownment. Ihechi, my dear, you are as insolvent a debtor to the major general as debtors come. Do you really want to end up in the bushes of this political community?"

"Who is throwing whom into the bushes? Why does anyone have to go into the bushes?" Alhaji inquired with a large grin betraying his faux rage. "What's going on? The only time I can stand talk about bushes is if it's going to end up with bush meat."

"I believe your *aburo* is fed up with politics," Madame Messalina replied. "I was explaining that if he wanted to throw away all we've given him and become a street rat again, he would have to return to where—"

"It's not even like that!" I interrupted.

"So how is it like? Explain yourself to us!"

"What's going on?"

We all turned toward the voice that had conveyed the question, and the major general stared back at us all, looking unusually disheveled: hair unbrushed, shirt unstarched, and composure unavailable.

"Well, speak up!" Madame Messalina urged me.

I swallowed a few balls of saliva and exchanged the sweat on my palms several times over. "I don't think I can run for president anymore."

"Oh, that's absolutely perfect," the major general said. I was not sure if he was being sarcastic. I was not sure anyone else in the room was sure, either; their eyes all looked as bloodshot as mine. "I'm just coming in from Abuja. Those soldiers have some big balls."

"You didn't say you had to be in Abuja," Alhaji said. "Why weren't we in on this?"

"There's nothing to get your *punani* wet about. I just got the phone call this morning to show up as quickly as possible."

"Why are you always harassing me?" Alhaji exploded from his seat, shooting the skinny young man on his lap into the air. "What is wrong with being a homosexual? Can I not fuck whomever I want to fuck? Does it make me less of a man?"

"Of course you can't fuck whomever you want to fuck," the major general replied coolly. "If it was okay for everyone to fuck whomever they pleased, then pedophiles wouldn't be in prison. They feel a natural urge to fuck children, right? It's the way they are. They can't fight their nature. Just because you can't be imprisoned for it because you have brother faggots making laws doesn't make it right. Who knows? Maybe someday we'll have pedophiles in power, too, and fucking children will be okay."

"Oh, behave, we're not here to fool around," the major general's other friend said. "What was the emergency in Abuja?"

"Well, the good news is, there is going to be a presidential election announcement next week. The bad news is, the head of state himself will be running."

"That's not possible," Madame Messalina muttered.

"I wasn't going to be the one to argue that with him," the major general replied as he came close to me and collected the whiskey from my hand, taking a swig straight from the bottle. "Each political party is going to declare unanimous support for his bid and then find a way to scramble into all the other positions of his new government that his cronies don't take for themselves." He took another swig and allowed the news to simmer into our senses. "You won't be president after all," he continued, talking in my direction. "Maybe you'll have to settle for a senator or honorable or something, a position with less pressure. But you'll be fine. I believe in you."

"But I don't want to be a senator or honorable or anything at all," I reiterated. "I just want to be done with all of this."

He slapped my face lightly and almost choked on his whiskey while struggling to contain his laughter. "What happened to your balls, young man? Did Alhaji take them? Did he touch them at all? And you had better be joking, because if you aren't, I'll have to really cut them off for you."

"Don't scare *aburo*," Alhaji said. He was seated again, and the skinny young man was atop his lap with a palm hidden in Alhaji's *buba*. "It's like this, *ehn*, we spent about a hundred million naira alone canvassing for support for you, and your campaign has not even started, they have not even announced the elections yet. And over half of this money went to the people in the military regime. Will we get it back from the Federal Reserve with a withdrawal slip over the counter at the Central Bank? You have to get into power and reward us with contracts now! What's all this talk about changing your mind?"

"This doesn't even make any sense," I said. It was hard to put a lid on my confusion, which was quickly turning into rage. "First, how do we just wake up one morning and decide to take sides with the military regime we've been fighting for years?"

"Major General, you've stuffed his brain with too much money," Madame Messalina chided. "The young man thinks he's attained a position to question us."

"Oh, yes, we've been fighting them for years," said the major general. "Do you expect us to go stark raving mad now that they've given us what we all really wanted?"

"Having the head of state leading a democracy isn't the democracy we all really wanted," I said.

"Democracy?" Major General's friend cried. "The last time there was a democracy, I was a civil servant, and I still managed to send all my children to the top schools in England. And I've had five acres of land in Equatorial Guinea for the last ten years, but a democracy wouldn't build and roof my mansion. It's not a democracy or the lack of a democracy that gives you anything in this bloody country. It's a seat at the table, and that's all we've really been fighting for."

I looked all around the room—the marble walls and glass chandeliers, the Persian rugs and Italian furniture, the testament of one person's wealth and a hundred persons' poverty—and I wept. "Someone has to stand up to all this madness."

"You want to stand up for the people? You want to stand up for the people, *abi?*" Madame Messalina echoed.

I noticed her stand up slowly, I watched her move toward me every step of the way, even when she collected the bottle of whiskey from the major general's hand, but I had no idea what was going on till she tilted the bottom of the bottle to take a swig for herself before bashing my head with the hardened glass. I felt the blood seeping out slowly from my skull as I raised both hands to deliver my head from the repeated blows smashing against my wrists.

"Stand up now, you bastard!" she screamed as I crouched slowly and fell to the floor. I could hear Tessy screaming; it drowned out the other words in the background as my vision went black. In the darkness, my body moved. I was dragged by my wrists till someone picked up my legs. The voices in the background resumed when my body stopped again. Tessy was still screaming. But when I felt a sharp pang on my right elbow, my eyes jolted open and everything became clear again.

"I'll cut off your hands before you can think of cutting off the hand that fed you," Madame Messalina screamed, butcher knife in hand and arm in the air. The knife came down again on my elbow, and another sharp pang of pain shot through my body. "This would take the whole day," she complained as she tossed aside the knife and stormed out of the room.

Alhaji and the major general's other friend pinned me down on the hard wooden surface; the cabinets and sink were on the other side of the kitchen, where the major general had his hand placed over Tessy's mouth. "Please, please, calm down," Major General was mumbling to her. "He fucked up already. There's nothing I can do. If you don't shut up, you'll probably join him, and I can't afford to see you go like this, baby. I'd beg her if it would solve anything, but you know how she is when she gets—"

Madame Messalina returned wielding a cylinder of cooking gas, leaning it against her leg as she dragged it, and both the major general and Tessy froze silent. She slammed the cylinder on the kitchen counter, just beside where my arm was, and pressed the head of the valve with the sharp edge of her knife, letting out a rush of gas. The pain this time was freezing cold, and it tingled as the room clouded with white propane. I pulled and kicked, struggling with every bit of life left in me till the pain stopped, but the gas kept on choking.

The mist cleared and the voices returned. Tessy was screaming again, and unbelievably, somehow, my right arm was still pinned down, covered in a white flaky cast. Madame Messalina slammed the cylinder on my whitened arm, but I felt nothing. I looked around the room, begging for someone, anyone, to come to my rescue. But each and every one was filled with as much dread as I was.

Madame Messalina slammed, and slammed, and slammed again, and did not stop until I started feeling pain again. This time the sharp pang did not go away. And when I looked at my arm, I saw nothing past my elbow. The white flaky cast faded into a ring of blood, and the other half of my arm lay unmoving a few meters away. The whole room, even Tessy, was silent save the chorus of woe that bellowed from my throat.

"Get this corpse out of here," Madame Messalina muttered as the metal cylinder dropped on the floor with a loud empty echo. "In fact, you know what? Drop it off with Yisa Adejo. Tell him it's a gift. And get a haircut before you come back here. I'll need someone for the meetings this week, and I can't have you representing me looking like a gorilla."

"Ah," the major general's friend pleaded with a forced smile, "but my wife says I should stay away from the barber for some time, so my hairline can grow out again. She says I'm becoming bald."

Madame Messalina asked, "And what does a haircut have to do with a receding hairline?"

"It's like that deforestation thing they're always talking about on the Tuesday-morning show on NTA. They say if you stop cutting down the trees, they'll keep growing and growing and one day the forest will be full again. And it will be good for the environment and all of us."

"*Ode.* Trees are not like hair. How many times do you see hair falling off the scalp like unripe guava? Every bloody day!

And how many times do you see trees falling off the face of the earth like unripe guava? Exactly. You can't outsmart a receding hairline, you idiot. In fact, you know what? Remain with Yisa Adejo when you get there. Tell him you're a gift, too."

When Madame Messalina walked out of the room, Tessy made to run toward me, but the major general held her back and clasped her head between his palms. "You know you can't mention this to anyone. Not your father or mother or even your bathroom mirror." His hands began shaking furiously and he broke down crying, kissing her cheeks and mixing his tears with hers. All the while, Tessy's eyes remained fixed on my amputated arm.

Epilogue

Still 1998

O f all the troubled misadventures of my Nigerian existence, the affair I reflect upon with least enthusiasm is my going to a prison cell. Not my first venture, which was at the age of eight, when I followed the prison-support team of my friend's church to evangelize to inmates back in 1983, even though that particular venture was quite uneventful. Not my second venture, which was about nine years later, the same night I spoke to Anikulapo. It was my very last venture that was my soul's greatest gloom, the same night I caught a little glimpse of Yisa Adejo.

I could not remember leaving Madame Messalina's kitchen, but by the time I awoke, I was out of her house altogether. My head bobbled around in the darkness, and it continued even as my eyes opened and struggled to focus. I was seated in the back of a moving pickup truck on a road that had a thick canopy of vegetation on both sides and a cloud of upset dust trailing the vehicle. Someone was with me in the back of the truck, and when I lifted my gaze toward the person, I saw her face, barely visible in the waking sun—Zeenat. It had been years since her face appeared to me last, and still the confidence in her smile fueled me with hope. The world we had shared was thoroughly different from the world I lived in now. Maybe it was for the best that death, the fleet-footed messenger of God, had couriered her innocent soul from this world of ambition, greed, and the wrath of men. She smiled at me. I tried to reciprocate, but a flood of pain gushed from the corner of my lips to my whole face, and my eyes fluttered shut again.

I woke again, still seated, but there was no bouncing around. I was in a huge room, an office complete with a few bookshelves and portraits cramped side by side along the wall, a wooden desk and two chairs, one on either side. A few men in matching khaki outfits took turns washing their hands in a bowl of water on the desk and proceeded to munch on roasted maize piled up just beside the bowl of water.

"*Ehen!* Oga Yisa," one of the men forced out midchew. "Your wife called as you deh *wele* the freshman, I think she wanted to know what you wanted for dinner."

"What's there to think about? It's either she wanted to know or she didn't." They stared at each other inconclusively for a while. "It doesn't matter. I won't be home for dinner. But today is Tuesday, so be sure you don't forget to take Jaja to teach the children math. And have a guard stay with him if you don't want to be there. I can't have a criminal alone with my children."

I felt like a fly on the wall, listening in on break-time banter between civil servants in a government office. What seemed out of place was the naked man floating upside down in the middle of the room, bound at the feet with a steel chain, hanging from the ceiling fan. He moaned as he tilted from side to side, and with each oscillation, a drop of blood dripped off his forehead into a stainless-steel bowl on the floor. I could feel bile rising through my throat at the sordid sight, but before it could reach the back of my tongue, my eyes fluttered shut again.

The next time I awoke, I was lying naked on the floor of a

small room opposite another naked body, under the keen scrutiny of a dim yellow lightbulb. I heard metal clanging against metal, and a door in one of the walls slid open. A man strode in whistling a tune—it took me a second to recognize Lagbaja's "Konko Below" even in my state—and he hauled the naked body opposite me out of the room, leaving behind a dark red liquid trail. He left the door open and returned a few seconds later and emptied a bucket of whitish something on the floor where the naked body had been. I recognized the something instantly from the scent alone—concentrated antiseptic disinfectant—from my boardinghouse days when I would sneak into the bathroom during afternoon siesta, right after the cleaners had finished washing the place with disinfectant and before the other boys rushed in to shower before afternoon prep, and I would masturbate to months-old thoughts of Zeenat like a caveman who'd just discovered fire.

"You don wake, *abi?*" The whistling man had returned. "E be like say you don ready to join your people. Oya stand up, *halele!*"

He forced me to my feet and dragged me out of the room. We went past a few shut doors, all the way to the end of the corridor, where an old man sat cross-legged behind a desk.

"Where the uniform?" the whistling man asked, and the older guy pointed to a black polythene bag leaning against his desk on the floor.

"Oya wear cloth quick quick before Oga Yisa change e mind," the whistling man continued. "We suppose don *wele* you as you enter, but Oga Yisa talk say one army man dey come tomorrow to pay for your sins. But if tomorrow come and nothing enter my pocket, I go still *wele* you my own. I no care if the army man wan marry your sister, if e like make e marry you join sef, I go still *wele* you and nothing go happen."

Though I had not finished dressing by the time his rant was over, he had started walking away, so I had to follow him as I tried to lace my oversize trousers. We went past a few more shut doors, an open yard littered with a few trees and benches. Two scruffy dogs retreated from our path, scurrying behind a little zinc shed and causing the loud eruptive flight of about half a dozen blackbirds. The noise had all fizzled out when we reached the other end of the yard, the gateway to the boulevard of prison cells. We went unnoticed through the chatter and odor booming from both sides of the dividing corridor to the second-to-last gate on the right.

"I suppose don give you food make you chop before you enter cell." I drew nearer to hear the whistling man under all of the noise. "But Oga Yisa talk say dem cut your hand comot because you deh bite the hands wey deh feed you." His head recoiled in laughter as the iron gates swung open. "Oya enter quick quick, *halele!*"

All the inmates remained quiet and unmoving as long as the warden was in view, but the moment he was out of sight, their eyes pried at the new prey. A few inmates circled cautiously and whispered to each other. Only one of them closed in. He was not much bigger than I was, but his uniform was much more fitted; his overgrown beard did little to hide a few scars on his face and seemed to taper down his chest like a necktie. My imagination wandered in search of what crimes he must have committed to bring him here.

"Welcome, Ihechi," he whispered, placing one hand on my shoulder and lifting my half-arm with the other. "The wardens had told me someone new was coming. When they mentioned your name, I thought it was impossible, but I told them to bring you to my cell nonetheless."

I looked into his eyes and surveyed his face to no end, but it was the voice replaying over and over in my head that found the answer. "Mara...dona?" I stammered. "Bee Money...Capone?"

"Inside here, it's Okunrinmeta." He smiled. "Don't ask me why or how. Even though I'm in charge here, I'm not the one who chooses the names."

He put his arms around me in a warm embrace, and I sobbed into his uniform, "I didn't do anything."

"You think it's only hardened criminals in Kirikiri?" he whispered into my ear. "Accountants are here, executive directors, and journalists, too. Many are in our age grade. It doesn't take much to get in here under this regime."

I tried to force out words through the tears and spittle. "This is injustice."

"Injustice is only injustice when it happened in the past. This is the present. There's no judge to decide justice in the present, just witnesses who are as powerless as victims." He lifted my head up and pointed a path through the crowd. "Come, let me show you something."

We walked through the maze of inmates—each of the many faces a labyrinth on its own of different stories, all manners of fortune and misfortune encrypted into their smiles, frowns, laughter, scars, and wounds—to the far corner of the room, and right there on the floor I saw Mendaus and Pastor's son folded knees in arms on the floor. Mendaus flinched as he saw me and tried to hide his face away, but there was no hiding place.

"I came in here not too long after the last time we saw each other," Maradona continued. "One of my boys tried jacking one NDA boy off his government-issued ride. The young soldier put three bullets in him before he could realize what was happening. Somehow my boy didn't die, so the soldier hospitalized him and beat the whereabouts of his crew out of his mouth as soon as he became well enough to take a beating. The rest of his crew never came back, so the soldiers took whomever they could see. I knew it was going to happen someday. It was just a matter of time.

"These two," Maradona added, pointing at Mendaus and Pastor's son, "have been here barely a week. Someone had been talking too much shit on the radio. It took them so long to get here, I'm beginning to wish I had their luck."

I heard weeping from the floor, rising slowly to accompany mine, but I could not tell whom exactly it emanated from, if not both of them. It was the first time since our innocent childhood that I had looked at my friends without seeing any shadow aspect to their personalities, without any likes or dislikes, without any catalysts or inhibitions to accepting them. And it felt sweeter and purer than childhood, when shadows could not exist because we were hidden in the blinding light of innocence, because now we were in the pitch darkness of our predicaments and it was easy to lose touch with reality, to hallucinate things that did not exist—Nigeria, in its entirety, a wonder of this world.

Acknowledgments

Shout out to my family. I became an avid reader off the bookshelves in the room previously inhabited by my Mummy and my Aunties—Ayo and Aunty Funke—in my grandparents' home in Surulere, Lagos. And I grew into borrowing the books from the bookshelves of their own homes. They've told all their friends about this book so I hope it meets their expectations and doesn't bring the family name to shame, even though I'm sure they're proud of me regardless. And my cousins—I could never ask for a more ride-or-die squad. To Daddy, Uche, Nneka, and Chika—you'll get yours in the groupchat.

Shout out to friends. Isioma, Ugo, Dosa, and Tobi—the initial Afrika Shrine crew. And then the Omole Coalition—Kunle, Femo, Bobby, Jide, Jeffrey, Ole, and Tobi. No words. All love. To Chisom, Bimbo, and Ibukun, who stress and spoil me beyond measure. To the boys at the back of Oghene's class, the folks who failed Ede and Olukanni's classes, and the incredible J2 family—this book is a compilation of my thoughts and lessons, of which you are all coauthors.

Shout out to my peers. I was and am still deeply motivated and inspired by Abimbola, Chinenye, Phids, Edwin, Fope, Ope, Tolu, TJ, Ayodeji, Zainab, Ifeoluwa, Aisha, Oke, Oluchukwu, Moji, Ona. Those who struggle to finish their stories, struggle to publish or struggle to overcome imposter syndrome #TalkIsCheap.

Also, shout out to the mailing list—Chihurumanya, Abimbola, Oluwatobi, Yemi, Rachael, Kiits, Dams, Nkem, Oke. My very first readers and editors. You pushed me to write, pushed me to finish and pushed me to publish. If this was an album, you would all have Executive Producer credits. I'll be sending you the first drafts of the next project in a minute.

Special mention to Femi Apata. He was the first person to call this back when I was still writing English class essays for tuckshop. And to Mensah Demary and the good people at Counterpoint, for making dreams come true.

© Adedunmola Olanrewaju

NNAMDI EHIRIM is a twenty-six-year-old Nigerian writer based in Lagos and Madrid. His writing has appeared in *Afreada*, *Brittle Paper*, *Catapult*, *Kalahari Review*, and *The Republic*. He cofounded a clean-energy start-up in Nigeria and is currently pursuing an MBA focused on entrepreneurship in the renewable energy sector. *Prince of Monkeys* is his first novel.